BHOOT, BHAVISH, BARTAMAN

Advance Praise For The Book

Indian thrillers in English are still at a nascent stage, so Mehool Parekh's novel is a welcome addition to the list. When the hobby detective trying to solve a murder is called Batty and has a sidekick called Robin, what's not to like? It is a twisty-turny and very enjoyable read.

Deepa Gahlot
Celebrated author, scriptwriter and film and theatre critic

***

Why Mehool Parekh a private equity investor will invest his time into becoming an investigative, whodunit author is a bigger suspense than the plot of the novel itself. Having said that,in his maiden attempt as a writer, he has been able to intricately and effectively weave a story which will keep you spell bound,taking you through a world of love betrayal,deceit and evil machinations.His narrative is fluid and gripping making him a master story teller.Do read this suspense novel as it unravels into a mysterious and intriguing tale of murder leading to a shocking denoument.One word-Unputdownable!

Shekhar Suman
Indian film actor, anchor, producer, director, and singer

***

Who doesn't love a great whodunnit? Sound gory though it may, there's nothing more compelling than a beautiful corpse on the very first page!

Mehool Parekh's novel seizes you by the throat and never lets you exhale until its last full stop.

A storyteller par excellence, its impossible to believe this riveting mastery over complexity & craft is Mehool Parekh's debut novel!

Absolutely loved it! –

Nina Arora
National award winning scriptwriter

***

A commendable debut novel by Mehool Parekh. He brings into play his close knowledge of the entertainment and financial worlds to weave an intriguing yarn full of colorful characters, surprising plot twists and language flourish to propel a compelling muder mystery

Ketan Mehta

Award winning Director and Producer

BHOOT, BHAVISH, BARTAMAN

BY

MEHOOL PAREKH

Leadstart
INKSTATE

ISBN 978-93-52019-83-0

First published in India 2019 by Inkstate Books
An imprint of Leadstart Publishing Pvt Ltd

Sales Office:
Unit No.25/26, Building No.A/1,
Near Wadala RTO,
Wadala (East), Mumbai – 400037 India
Phone: +91 9699933000
Email: info@leadstartcorp.com
www.leadstartcorp.com

Editor: Shayoni Mitra
Cover: Swayam Parekh
Layouts: Ashwini Jadhav

Dedication

My family, my friends and all those who encouraged me

Contents

Acknowledgements

Chapter 1 17

Chapter 2 35

Chapter 3 51

Chapter 4 75

Chapter 5 87

Chapter 6 105

Chapter 7 118

Chapter 8 125

Chapter 9 137

Chapter 10 154

Chapter 11 177

Chapter 12 194

Chapter 13 217

Chapter 14 229

Chapter 15 257

Chapter 16 271

Chapter 17 304

Chapter 18 315

About the Author

A finance professional, Mehool has, over time, worked as a management consultant, equity research head and a fund manager. He ran a successful venture capital fund and is currently a private equity investor in growth companies. In between these, he has dabbled in film finance and production and owns a well-known media company. He lives in Mumbai with his family.

ACKNOWLEDGEMENTS

The person who first put the thought in my head, that I can write a story, was my friend Aanand Mahendroo, the celebrated director of hit television programmes in the 1980s and 90s. He not only put it in my head, but kept insisting that I should indeed write. At the time, I was very reluctant to do something like this, as all I had written (and got published) previously were about 12-15 articles for business magazines on corporate strategy and product success and failures. But his urging and his great confidence in me, kept the thought alive at the back of my mind.

The next person that deserves to be thanked is my brother-in-law Sameer Mody, owner of Pocket Films, India's largest short films channel on Youtube. Sameer was discussing with me the idea of pitching a web series to a well-known consumer brand and I suggested that he do a crime series with memorable and repeatable characters that can lend themselves to various seasons for the series. I then, out of the blue, offered to create these characters and a plot outline for him which he happily agreed to. To my own surprise, I did that in less than three hours. The characters came to me almost instantly; the plot outline took a little longer. That web series never happened, but the characters and the plot outline just sat there, sort of staring at me. One fine day, on an impulse, I decided to write the book. Without Sameer's requirement, these characters and indeed this book would never have seen the light of the day.

My wife Gunjan, daughter Swayam, my sister Shwetal, my sisters-in-law Amruta and Tejal, my friends Praveen, Jayesh, Jayesh (yes, there are two), Nirav and Devang all deserve thanks. Gunjan read my first draft and being my worst critic, her endorsement that the draft had some merit, egged me on. My sister and sisters-in-law were very supportive and gave me the confidence that I could tell a story and I should keep bettering it. My friends gave me encouragement and several constructive inputs which bettered the drafts as time went by. My daughter was initially skeptical, then tried reading the almost final draft and gave up saying it was too detailed and slow for her. Being a first-class artist, she offered to do the cover design but since she couldn't do that until she had read the book, she finally finished the book and then designed this fabulous cover.

My parents were a little perplexed initially and then incredulous and finally delighted when I mentioned that I have written a book. I have not shared any drafts of this book with them since I wanted to give them the first published copy of my book in its final form.

My partner and mentor who prefers not to be named and whose astonishing life story deserves a separate book (which I may someday write) deserves special credit for encouraging me to absolutely write and publish the book. Satyameet "Sattu" who I met at the Himalayan Writers' Workshop and Chetan Mahajan, himself a published author who conducted the workshop, deserve credits for their valuable inputs. My first editor, Roona Ballachanda, did a fabulous job of pointing out several areas in the book that needed attention and tweaking.

A special thanks and deep gratitude are due to all those not named here, whose stories have been source material for me for writing this book and without these, the instances in the book would not have had a base in reality. Most of the anecdotes and episodic narratives in this book have happened in real life to real people who I know, some intimately so. I know that some passages from this book will bring both smiles of remembrances and painful memories to those not named. If something I have written here causes more pain than happiness to them, I apologize sincerely.

The superb team at Leadstart Publishing deserves full credit for taking a risk on an unpublished, first-time author. Swarup Nanda, Malini, Naina, Shayoni and the entire team deserves my wholehearted gratitude.

I may have inadvertently left out some names for which I apologize but that does not mean I am not grateful to them.

And thank you, dear reader, for picking up this book and trying out a new author. Your feedback would be welcome and eagerly looked forward to by me. Anything that you have to say will only help make my writing better.

Prologue

The Police party reached the apartment in half an hour. Considering this was Pune and it was Pune Police, it was remarkably fast. Of course, the police station was no more than ten minutes away from the crime scene. The husband was visibly distraught and had made the call on finding the body.

The murder scene was straight out of some crime novel. The woman, possibly in her early thirties, was lying in a pool of blood on her bed. The party was struck by how attractive she was even in her death. Her countenance was entirely at peace as if she was content to have died. It was the brutality of the act that was striking. It was as if the murderer had gone berserk and not stopped even after the life had been stabbed out of the victim.

The head of the police party instructed his team to seal the apartment and note the position of various personal effects in the room and the other rooms. They would come later for the panchnama. He issued instructions to arrange for the body to be sent to the morgue for post-mortem. Having ascertained that everyone else was busy with their tasks, he pulled out his phone and made a call.

There was an immediate response from the other end. He could barely contain his excitement, *"Madam, aapke liye kuchh special aaya hai..."*

Chapter 1

The loud, angry meow of the trampled upon cat made him jump. Cats were not his favourite pets. This was the third cat he had stepped upon in the last fifteen days. He was mildly ailurophobic and cats really bothered him. While he didn't have a full-fledged phobia, the horrible, unexpected, often blood-curdling whine that those creatures emitted when stepped upon made his hair stand on edge. While a dog just whimpered, a cat's whine made his blood curdle. He tried to give them the widest berth possible and avoided looking them in the eye. He was incapable of shooing them away. When confronted by a cat, he simply froze.

A wiry muscular frame of 5ft 10 inches, a pleasant countenance highlighted with thick flat eyebrows, dark brown intelligent eyes set slightly apart, straight aquiline nose and an almost cruel mouth with a thick chevron moustache quite adequately described Major Bartaman Bhowmick of the 97 Artillery Brigade of the 41 Artillery Division Southern Command of the Indian Army headquartered at Pune Cantonment. Apart from cats, there wasn't much he was afraid of. His personality often came across as that of an analyst more than an army officer. His mates often wondered what he was doing in the army in the first place.

The Military area of Pune Cantonment or Camp, as it is popularly known, is spread over 11 sq km and is an oasis of beauty in a bustling town known for its unplanned and haphazard growth. Often providing a sharp contrast to the dirty cities in which these are housed, cantonments provide the citizens of the city a glimpse of what is possible if the municipalities do their jobs. The entire military area is beautifully maintained with wide tree lined roads and British era buildings housing the military establishment. A cursory tour of the military area provided a sharp contrast to the squalor of the Sadar Bazar and Civil Lines areas abutting it.

Things had been fairly dull of late and apart from the peacetime routine of the army, there was really nothing happening. He often buried his free time in books. Even Bartaman's favourite author Keigo Higashino seemed to have suddenly hit a writer's block and another favourite Steig Larsson had been dead a while. He had a voracious appetite for murder mysteries which he devoured in private and preferred reading those on his iPad as opposed to buying paperbacks. Books created a disposal problem once read and if kept around, invited others to borrow, which he was okay with as long as the books were returned in pristine condition. Having seen people read books carelessly while eating and drinking and even while on the pot, he had no desire to part with his assets for such mutilation.

Not sharing books and other personal information also worked for him in another way. It helped him avoid unnecessary contact and discussions with his mates, most of whom he considered to be less intellectually endowed than him and there was nothing in their lives that remotely interested him in any case. He generally kept to himself, buried his head in his iPad in his free time and sometimes talked to himself while walking. His love for liquor was one of his other oddities which didn't quite fit with the rest of his reticent persona. During his drinking sessions, he also managed to be uncharacteristically social and charming, much to the delight of his mates. It helped that he could warble a tune or two once sufficiently drunk. His mates called him "Batty" with scarcely hidden delight and much as he hated it, the name stuck.

He involuntarily straightened his uniform, ran a check with a quick frisk of his hands and quickly glanced at his gold national emblem on his shoulders to ensure that he was all prim and proper. He flicked an imaginary speck off the gold Ashoka lion on his left shoulder and headed off to the Officers' mess which was a short walk from his living quarters. Their junior-most and most recent recruit Lieutenant Vivek Bhonsale was celebrating his birthday that night and he was looking forward to being a part of it.

Birthday celebrations at the Officers' mess meant a license to drink all one could, until midnight. The deadline was 11 PM but the Pune Camp was a little less strict about Officers extending the deadline on special occasions and it was often a contest of who could out-drink whom. Batty almost always won habitually, downing more than a full bottle of the Army Standard Issue XXX Rum on several occasions. Even after so much drinking, he was much less hammered than the others who were almost always too smashed to even walk unaided. On the contrary, Batty, after having consumed his party quota would calmly walk back to his living quarters all by himself, undress and change for bed in an orderly manner without creating any mess, quietly slide under his thin Jaipur duvet and in a matter of minutes, drift into a dreamy state of calm.

The celebrations were on in full swing when the loud jangle of his phone made him jump. It was Robin. Robin Chowdhury, crime beat reporter at Pune City Times, was a long-time friend and an accomplice on their various adventures over the years. Together they had solved many a baffling case in Pune City. His crime solving skills, her reporter's access and penchant for ethical hacking had worked wonders much to the delight of his cousin Additional Commissioner of Police Jagdeep Kumar "Juggy" who had, despite limited achievements, risen well in the ranks of Maharashtra Police and was now in charge of Pune South Zone.

Over the last two years that Juggy had been posted in the city, Batty and Robin together had solved four baffling murder cases and it was almost two years ago that he had first laid his eyes on Robin. Sitting in Juggy's office in early March of two years ago, Batty was listening to Juggy's theories about a murder when Robin was ushered in to see Juggy on some crime case she was covering for her paper. One thing had let to another and in no time all three of them got into an animated conversation about the crime which actually ended up being the very first case on which Batty and Robin collaborated. Batty's investigating skills and his flashes of brilliance had made Juggy a fan. On his part Batty had also realised that he could not have solved these crimes without Robin's unique skills. It helped that they liked working together and looked forward to such occasions.

Since both Batty and Robin were single, Juggy assumed the existence of a romantic angle between them but surprisingly neither Batty nor Robin had shown any inclination towards anything remotely romantic. Batty considered Robin as one of the guys and this is what Robin was most comfortable with. To Batty's great annoyance, Juggy would not stop ribbing Batty endlessly and hinting often that Batty was having the time of his life, by having a go at Robin. Batty did not have the patience to explain to Juggy that there was no real angle between him and Robin. For Batty, solving crimes was an all-consuming passion which left no place for any romantic involvement even though Robin was attractive and at times, threw romantic hints at Batty which he chose to ignore.

"What's up, Batty?", Robin teased him when he answered, knowing full well that he hated that monicker.

"You tell me", Batty replied slowly not wanting Robin to know that he was already buzzed.

"Seems like, a big party, huh?" she said. Batty always marvelled at how accurately Robin could figure out from his voice and tone whether he was bored, upset, busy, drunk or just plain preoccupied even when he tried his utmost to sound the same at all times.

Got to work on this a little more, he thought to himself.

"What will you say if I make your day?", she asked with expectancy in her voice when Batty didn't respond to her party remark.

Batty was suddenly listening intently. He stepped out of the party, into the otherwise still night. This opening was a precursor of something very interesting she had scented. "Cut to the chase, Robin," Batty said, alcohol rendering him impatient for small talk.

"I think we have something interesting. Just got reported and have talked to the cops a bit and am on my way to the police station to get more dope. Need to sync up," Robin said.

Batty was now completely alert. Funny how an adrenalin pumping development can clear the fog of alcohol induced stupor so quickly.

"When?" he asked simply.

"I can tell you a bit on the phone later tonight but it is better to talk when we meet tomorrow," she said.

"Got a tip that the Deccan Gymkhana Police Station is investigating a case of murder and that idiot Lokhande is, as usual, spinning his theories," she elaborated.

"And why do you think this is anything more than a simple crime?" he asked completely aware of the fact that Robin was keeping something up her sleeve.

"My source called to say this one is special. I trust his instincts. More when we meet. Lunch tomorrow at Shizusan?" she asked nicely ensuring that Batty treated her to a sushi lunch.

"Sure. See you then…" he replied.

Senior Inspector Ravi Lokhande of the Deccan Gymkhana Police Station shifted uncomfortably in his seat. "Shouldn't have eaten those two vada pavs," he thought to himself making a mental note of taking better care of his diet. Rohini, his wife of 18 years, would kill him if she found out, he thought guiltily glancing at the tiffin filled with diet friendly tit bits that she had packed for him that day for snacking. Why does diet food have to taste like mud? How does a man who handles so much stress in a day be expected to survive on such tasteless drivel? Bloody Dieticians!! No regard for the kind of work a person is doing, he muttered under his breath. Glancing down, he noted the extreme strain on the two buttons of his khakhi shirt around his abdomen and cursed himself for being too lax in these matters. Couldn't you have eaten just one? he berated himself. Maybe he would go in for a larger shirt soon, he thought.

Unhappily he turned to the matter at hand. Constable Rajan Shinde was updating him on the murder that had been reported of the woman who was found stabbed in her bedroom. "Shinde it is very simple - Dharam will break in two-three hours. After all we nabbed him from his kholi and it seemed like he was packing to leave town. We also found 25,000 rupees and one gold chain from his bag. Clear it is – motive clear, crime clear. Case solved," he summed up for his constable in his trade-mark English.

Nothing made Lokhande more happy than simple crimes which didn't involve unnecessary running around. He was thankful for the modern trend of killing for cell phones, cars, jewellery and other baubles and it was an open and shut case most of the time. He shuddered inwardly when he remembered those murders where the ACP had asked him to work with that weird Army Officer and that bitch who acted as if her shit didn't stink.

That woman was trouble, oh yes sir she was.

God alone knew how that Army guy tolerated her and even worked with her and God alone knew what he saw in her. *"Pudhchya sapat, Magchya sapat, mulgi ahe ke Godrej cha kapat?"* he giggled inwardly remembering his boyhood days when as adolescent boys they used to tease girls who had just entered puberty but were yet to fill out in the upper department. This one was how old – 25-26? – and yet flat as a cupboard! No front, no back! Nothing to hold on to, by God! A lot of present day girls mirrored that and then wore provocative clothes with nothing in them that helped provoking, he mused. No wonder they all appeared completely sexless. He thanked his stars for Rohini who, even after two kids, was more than alright in that department.

And how much *natak* those two did – Bartaman and Robin and what did that bitch call the Army guy – Batty? – like Batman and Robin? Sure, those two had cracked some apparently difficult crimes but the ACP was unnecessarily hasty in getting them involved. After all there was nothing that he, Senior Inspector Ravi Lokhande, could not do himself with his simple formula of hosting the suspects at his police station and giving them a taste of the famed police hospitality. After all, hadn't Rakesh Maria gotten a breakthrough in the Mumbai blasts case by administering strong medicine in the lockup to one of the suspects? The Police know how to do get things done but some of these new fangled ACPs thought that some of the crimes were cerebral and needed proper detection methods.

And what did that Army guy do? Mostly talked to various people, did some thinking and kept discussing various scenarios with him until his head reeled with the complexity of the scenarios being presented. *Arre baba, murder is murder, no? Ugach dokyala kashala evdha tras?* Why rack your brain so much when you can round up the suspects and get them to confess to any theory you liked? And how did these two treat him? Like some flunky. His blood started to boil at the very thought of how condescending they were towards him during these investigations. His Maratha pride swelled up with the imagined slight. Just because he occasionally pronounced English words phonetically didn't mean that he didn't know much English. So what, if he said "fox pass" when – what was it – he should have said "fo pa"? Did that make him an imbecile? He had after all aced English in his Tilak Vidyamandir days even if it was as a second language. The conceit of the convent educated! And these Bangalis... As if they had the copyright on education and culture. After all Marathi literature, poetry and drama were second to none. Except that these hadn't really been translated to English extensively and hence were lesser known than Bengali works. High time we Marathis got the admiration we deserved. With great difficulty he kept the bile down and opened and chewed on a Digene. Bloody non-Maharashtrians in his Marathi Pune. The seat of the Peshwas and the glory of the state.

His reverie was rudely interrupted. "Hi Ravi", came the breezy greeting and in walked Robin to Lokhande's great consternation. Now why has this one surfaced at this time? He looked at his watch hastily– it was well after midnight. He was just thinking of winding up and then this. Let's see, he thought to himself, I should be able to shoo her off in 10 minutes. After all, there is nothing happening except the routine anyway. Maybe she just walked in to say hi, he thought hopefully, though silent alarms went off in his head.

"Heard you have a murder?" she said without preamble. "Nothing baba just routine. Some lady stabbed by her servant, nothing to it. Very routine like our daily work. Nothing for you." he said hoping that this would be the end of it.

"And what have you been doing all these days?" he asked trying to make small talk.

Ignoring the question, Robin said, "Heard that she has been stabbed 16 times? Doesn't look very simple, no?" Lokhande was now getting a little desperate. "Arre baba, stabbed once, twice, sixteen times what is the difference? The servant got the money and killed her since she must have objected. Also, some of these ladies ill-treat their servants, so he must have paid her back in the same coin for all the insults," he theorised.

"No signs of resistance or struggle I am told," Robin said matter-of-factly.

It suddenly dawned on Lokhande that Robin had definitely spoken to his constables. She might even have been tipped off by one of them. He glanced angrily at Shinde but he was studiously avoiding his eyes. The mole! He made a mental note of taking Shinde to task for the indiscretion.

"We can't discuss ongoing investigations with the media as you know madam," replied Lokhande in his best bureaucratic manner.

"Oh come on, Ravi," Robin said disarmingly. "You know this is not coming to you from a reporter. I am just curious that how come a man of your seasoned intellect and crime solving abilities did not think of that as odd?" she asked, laying it on a little too thick. Lokhande suddenly felt as if someone had pinched his bottom and kissed him at the same time. Was that an insult or a compliment? With Robin he could never tell. He decided to treat it as a compliment and replied, "*Arre* madam, you are reading too much into it. We are seeing a lot of these *aajkal*. All these servants who are migrants from North India are committing all these robberies, rapes and petty thefts everywhere. Usually it is the watchmen or the servants and even the car cleaners. All rogues these days..." he said displaying a sense of supreme confidence that comes with a lifetime of police work that mostly involves beating confessions out of people and arresting the usual suspects and secretly hoping that this would be the end of the conversation.

"I am leaving for the day, madam. Very tired. Long day. Wife also waiting for dinner - it is much past midnight already. Good night madam." he said with finality.

Robin did not push any further. As soon as Lokhande left, she cornered Shinde who was waiting for his senior to leave so that he could discuss his private thoughts with Robin. Unlike Lokhande who was a cynic and jaded with years of police work, Shinde was what Robin classified as bright eyed and bushy tailed having joined the force just five years ago after having passed the recruitment exam. He was from Latur, a place known for its murderous droughts and surprisingly, for its excellent educational institutions. He was a diploma holder from one of its polytechnics and a regular reader of "*Dakshata*" the Maharashtra Police magazine known for its excellent reporting of investigated and solved crimes. He was by nature curious and was not easily convinced about a crime situation at face value. Lokhande had no interest in Shinde's theories and most of the time, beating up the usual suspects yielded the desired confession so Shinde kept his counsel to himself.

Now warming up to Robin he said in his Latur accented English, "Madam, 16 times stabbing is too much. Why would someone who just wants to steal some money do murder? and that much of stabbing?".

He was clearly not buying Lokhande's hypothesis and sensing Robin's interest he was beginning to assert himself. All the past cases he had read about in police reports and crime magazines started zipping through his head with great speed.

"Madam, *aisa hi ek case tha 1983 mein mere khyal se jidhar ek bai ko 11 bar chaku mar ke uske lover ne khatam kiya tha,"*he added. *"Idhar bhi mere ku aisa hi kucch lafda lagta hai,"* he said referring to an old case which he had read about in the police files where a lover had stabbed a woman 11 times and he saw some parallels here.

"Iska thoda detail batao Shinde," Robin said.

Shinde explained that the call had come from the husband, Deep Kalra, who had discovered the body when he had come home at night. Shinde had been to the site with the police team and described him as a much older person, perhaps 50-55 and visibly distraught at discovering his wife dead. The sight was gruesome. There was a fair bit of blood as can be expected from such stabbing. The victim was, however, at peace and there were no signs of struggle or resistance almost as if the victim had been stabbed in her sleep which may well have been the case. There was a pillow placed on the nose and mouth of the victim but there was no apparent sign of choking or asphyxiation from the countenance of the victim. The victim was described as an attractive young woman possibly in her late twenties or early thirties. The body had been placed in the morgue and a request generated for autopsy to be conducted by Professor Vinay Shahastrabuddhe, the Head of Forensics at B J Govt Medical College.

Robin asked if the crime scene had been secured, but in her heart-of-hearts knew that nothing much would come out of it as the husband who had discovered the body would have messed up the crime scene inadvertently and God knows what all stuff had been moved or changed before the police party reached the spot. Shinde assured her that he had indeed sealed the bedroom and ensured that nothing was disturbed. In fact, Shinde had gone a step further and sealed the entire apartment for a proper *panchnama* and investigation. Hopefully, Batty's eyes would pick something of value or importance there, she thought.

This could be fun or not. If indeed the servant had done it, there would be nothing there but her reporter's instinct which told her that there was more to it than what it seemed. But somehow, this did not look like an open and shut case. Anyway, there was enough in Shinde's conjecture and her instincts to tease Batty's naturally suspicious grey cells.

Senior Inspector Ravi Lokhande was famished by the time he reached home. Home was a two-bedroom apartment on the 3rd floor of a relatively new building on Prabhat Road owned technically by his brother but for all intents and purposes it was Lokhande's. After all it was bought with Lokhande's side income. The building lift was temperamental and Lokhande had to climb three stories to get home. He was out of breath, sweating profusely and swearing under his breath by the time he rang the bell.

Rohini got up from her nap when she heard him ring the doorbell. Welcoming him with a smile that was more a grimace, she said, "Today also late? There are no *morchas,* no riots, no *bandobasts* and still you manage to waste time until midnight every day?"

Lokhande decided to ignore her comment and coming straight to the matter uppermost in his mind enquired, "so what's today's special for dinner?" half-dreading the answer.

He washed up in a tiny cubbyhole that passed for a shower and toilet in today's buildings. One couldn't take a shower without drenching the toilet bowl and the wash basin in these bathrooms.

"It's a surprise. I found this superb recipe for weight control and I bet you cannot tell the ingredients from the regular ones in what I have made today. It is a very delicious recipe – *Ragi appes* in low fat butter and oil free sambhar", she said with the flourish of a Michelin Starred Chef.

Lokhande stopped urinating midstream when he heard this and his heart sank. He could have sworn he had smelled fried fish when he entered. Had he known this was for dinner he would have stopped enroute and filled up on some good stuff. Ragi, known among the health freaks as a super food, looked and tasted like coloured mud to Lokhande. Low fat butter was nothing but margarine that tasted like industrial oil and oil free sambhar was just watery dal with some vegetables. And *appes* were just shallow fried doughballs. He noticed that she did not mention any coconut chutney.

"Kids had the same thing for dinner?", he asked innocently. His two children Uday and Vaishali were fast asleep in the other bedroom.

"No baba, they had their pomfret fry. Have to give them proper food. They are not out of shape like you and they don't have health issues like yours. They burn all those calories effortlessly with their day long activity as it is. I also want them to grow up craving their mother's cooking. You have had enough good food to last for a lifetime. First lose 10 kgs, reduce cholesterol and show me," she replied with finality.

Uthale re Devaa, he silently implored God to pick him up and relieve him from this world. He knew the dangers of ignoring her fatwa in dietary matters and gobbled down 6 *appes* with watery sambhar.

Briefly, he thought of watching some TV in his living room but instead just changed and decided to rest. Lying on his bed, his thoughts were still on food. Tomorrow was another day. Maybe I will start early and have a sumptuous breakfast of Bun Maska, Masala Omlette and Special Chai at Cafe Goodluck first thing tomorrow, he thought. The price one has to pay for marital peace! On top of this there was a sinking feeling in the pit of his stomach that this was not the last he was seeing of that reporter girl. Shinde! That two-timing extra smart villager from Latur! His own people were working against him. He made a mental note of ticking him off tomorrow when he saw him. He thought with glee how Shinde's confidential report was in his hand and if he did not fall in line, he could really mess it up for him, so that Shinde fell back a couple of promotions. The issue of retribution for Shinde's misdeeds now addressed, he fell into an exhausted sleep drowning out Rohini's comment on how one should never go to bed immediately after dinner and a late-night walk was ideal.

Chapter 2

1996-1997

The soft warm sun of the morning in Vasai was streaming through the one room that served as living room, bedroom and kitchen in the Jadhav household. The end of winter or what the city of Mumbai, rechristened just last year from the sexier sounding Bombay and its feeder towns that liked to call themselves 'extended suburbs' (in a weak attempt to attach themselves to the glamour and glory of the big city) called winter, was near. In a couple of weeks or so, the morning sun would no longer be welcome and Mumbai's cruel heat would hold sway over the city and its suburbs with this oppression ceasing in mid-June when the torrential rains begin. Unlike other cities like Chennai where the rain brought more misery, Mumbai rains were refreshing and brought the sizzling temperature down substantially. This surprised many a Mumbaikar who went to a place like Singapore on work or pleasure and discovered that rain made no difference to the heavy, hot climate and did, in fact, worsen it considerably. Just like Indians associate sunlight with warmth - something that many Indians discover to their detriment in the US and elsewhere in the northern hemisphere in winter - Mumbaikars associate rains with relief and a cooling sensation.

Rupali Jadhav got up the moment the first rays of the sun hit her face. She preferred to sleep near the window of their small ground floor room in which she and her parents Vitthal and Saraswati Jadhav lived. The fan in the center of the room circulated just enough air to the extremities of the room and nothing in the center. Rupali had ensured a nice breezy corner of the room for herself while her parents slept in the center of the room that got almost no breeze. At one end was the kitchen. The toilet was outside in the common area and was shared among three other rooms. This was the part Rupali hated the most - having to stand in queue for going to the toilet. The only good thing it did for her was that it taught her bladder and bowel control. She could now hold her insides for as much as 30 minutes if needed. While most of the others shouted and squirmed, she was the picture of calm in that short line.

Having turned 16 and blossoming into a very attractive girl with an oval face and curves already in the right places, she was now the reigning beauty queen of her locality. Rupali was not naive in any sense of the word and was aware of the male gaze particularly when she dressed up and went out to meet her friends during the day. She had noticed the neighbours' looks as well as the wolf-whistles and cat calls of the boys who hung around the area when she came back from school. She already knew what an asset her looks were since she had experienced first hand how perfect strangers went out of their way to make things easier for her. Rupali took after Saraswati in her looks and features and she had Vitthal's fair complexion. She had all the makings of an attractive young woman very much aware of her sexuality.

Vitthal used to work as an accountant with a local factory making iron implements - mostly shovels and 'ghamlas' - the shallow circular bowl-shaped containers that construction labourers used, to carry material and debris around building sites. Saraswati was confined to the house but managed to earn a bit on the side by doing odd jobs for neighbours like making puran polis, stitching long strips of colour matched cloth to one side of neighbours' sarees that ensured that the saree did not hitch up and retained that graceful 'fall' with the weight of the fabric that was stitched to the saree and tucking in the edge of the saree and taking short stitches after rolling the edge in to give it a finish which was called 'bidding'. Put together, both husband and wife managed to eke out a living that took care of their daily desperate needs and some niceties like an occasional dress for Rupali or a saree on Diwali for Saraswati.

Early that year, Vitthal had lost his job as the owner's young son brought in a PC that could do all the accounting in a flash. It only needed someone to feed the data and one of the younger accountants was only too pleased to take that on. Vitthal was one among a staff of five and his role was to enter the vouchers in the account books.

Since this job was now taken over by the PC, Vitthal was declared surplus and asked to leave. A lot of poor Indian families are often faced with such calamities that render their existence asunder. The same thing happened to the Jadhavs. Money, or rather a severe lack of it, became the heavy atmosphere that hung around their little house at all times.

Vitthal tried his hand at various temporary jobs but in India at that time, jobs were hard to come by and the economy was just about emerging from a severe recession that saw bank credit being compressed and money getting tight mostly for the small and medium sized businesses. Vitthal was barely earning half of what he was getting earlier and this put a severe strain on the family's meagre finances. Faced with an alarming situation that threatened their existence, Saraswati decided to pitch in.

It started slowly at first. Rupali would see "uncles" whom she had never seen before drop in at home and take Saraswati out for an evening for helping them with saree selection, party organising or occasionally wedding shopping. Somehow these outings produced some cash and Rupali was happy that her mom's talents were being appreciated. Soon it turned into a regular affair and there was no more explanation as to who these people were and what Saraswati was doing with them. Though Saraswati's outings brought in some much needed relief to the household, but increased stress between Vitthal (who did not approve of Saraswati's evening sorties) and Saraswati who was beginning to assert herself more and more. Vitthal also took to drinking in the evenings until Saraswati came home.

One night, Saraswati came home rather late and Vitthal was seriously drunk by that time. He tore into her.

"Where were you *randi?* Hope you had a good fuck. Was he really big, you bitch?" he bellowed as soon as Sarawati entered the house. She was in no mood for his nonsense. After all she was the one who was running the house. She clearly deserved some acknowledgement if not gratitude. Irritated, she shot back, "what else can I do? I have a *bhadva* for a husband who is completely impotent. First prove your manliness then talk to me. Go get the money first *madarchod.*"

This went on for some time and finally Vitthal was too drunk to even answer her. Sarawati went to sleep muttering how all men were *madarchod bhadvas* who couldn't face reality when they had to live on their wives' income.

Rupali woke up when her parents' voices reached a crescendo. Groggy with sleep, she heard snatches of their conversation and the word *randi* a few times. This is when it dawned on Rupali what her mother was really up to. In her impressionable age, Rupali was shocked when she first heard it and then, over the next few days, tried to come to terms with her mother's activities. She saw her through the lens of a raw need for money coupled with understanding and even compassion. For a 16-year-old, that was maturity beyond her years. Even though all this was for the family's survival, Vitthal could not come to terms with this new reality and took out his frustration on Saraswati often. Rupali could not understand Vitthal's attitude, his insensitivity and lack of gratitude. In her young mind, she understood this as a struggle for money being the root cause of all the problems. She swore to never let lack of money hinder her in future. No matter the cost, no matter the means. After all, she had something that could be easily converted into currency. And after all, assets need to be exploited.

The late nineties was a heady time for the Indian consumer. The market was flooded with imported consumer goods and the cell phone was a must-have device for the Indian consumer. The idea of a personal phone instead of the ugly heavy black bakelite box that worked on its own whims and for which people had to wait for years, soon took the country by storm. Vasai, Rupali's little piece of Mumbai, was no exception. Even though mobile phone rates were really high, the cell phone became the object of lust for the well-heeled Indian consumer who wanted to show that he or she had arrived.

Saraswati now had spare cash to indulge in

consumer niceties like a compact music system and a colour TV with a VCR player which Rupali made the most of. In Rupali's own mind, she had arrived and wanted to show her newly acquired status to all. What better way than a mobile phone which almost no one had in Vasai except the likes of Bhai Thakur, the underworld don and overlord of the Vasai-Virar belt. In Narendra she found her perfect opportunity.

Narendra was the only son of Bhanwarlal Jain, a wealthy shopkeeper in Vasai with several shops that dealt in everything from groceries to medicines to photography to garments under the name of "Matarani" or Mother Goddess. Most of his shops were manned by young sharp boys from his own native place in Jhunjhunu in Rajasthan. He had recently opened a shop selling electronics called "Matarani Electronics" where he also sold televisions, cassette players, VCRs and such other home gadgets. The piece-de-resistance in the shop was a compact Ericsson mobile phone which was kept on a special display which people came to gawk at. The shop was his pride and he gave this shop to his only son Narendra, who was just about 18, to run under his oversight.

Narendra was a cartoonist's delight - an obnoxious, fat and ugly Marwari boy who lustily eyed all women and girls passing by his shop and those who came in to browse. This not being a wealthy neighbourhood, few people actually bought anything on weekdays. Most sales happened on Sundays when the man of the house was free. Rupali knew Narendra from school. He was a year senior to her, having failed in the 9th standard once. In school, Rupali was lusted after by many boys and was easily the most attractive of her batch. Boys frequently tried rubbing against her or accidentally pressing her breasts during breaks when students went to the toilets that were in an outhouse in the school premises accessible through a narrow passage. Rupali ignored these attempts but was very aware of the effect she had on the boys who were literally on their best behaviour when she was around trying to impress her. She was the queen and they were her subjects. Rupali received several love letters from the boys in her class and even from those of other batches. She had no interest in most of them but she had preserved Narendra's love letter. Written in English more suited for a 6-year-old, the note that passed off as a love letter went something like this:

Roses are red

Violets are blue

You are the girl I love

Only that is true

The handwriting was like a doctor's prescription and even at the tender age of 16 Rupali thought this was beyond ridiculous but having come from Narendra who was a rich man's son, she decided to preserve it.

Bhanwarlal had kept a satyanarayan puja at his shop for good luck. Narendra had come to Rupali's house to invite her for the puja. Rupali was not at home at that time so he left the invitation card with Saraswati and insisted that they all should come. Rupali did not go for the puja but went the next day. Narendra was at the counter looking at some of the bills and records. Everything was computerised in this shop which Narendra was particularly proud of and never missed a chance to inform all customers that there could be no mistakes in their bills as the computer printed it and not humans. She entered the shop and as soon as Narendra saw her, he came running to talk to her. Rupali gave some excuse about not being able to come for the puja and then gave him a chit of paper to read saying that this was her reply to his love letter that he had written to her six months back in school. Narendra was elated and could not wait to open the chit. His heart leapt when he read what she had written on it:

Roses are red

Violets are blue

I know that you love me

I love you too.

This was Rupali's first attempt at cashing in on her assets. Narendra could not believe that a girl that the whole area lusted after had accepted his proposal. Very soon, Rupali and Narendra started meeting clandestinely and away from the prying eyes of the world. Their most preferred place was the ruins of Vasai Fort which provided them enough privacy to meet. Instinctively aware that value lay in not easily letting people get what they want, Rupali ensured that it took four meetings at Vasai Fort for Narendra to be able to kiss her on the cheek. By the time Narendra could progress to feeling her, she had already wrangled a branded and highly coveted cell phone out of him. The Ericsson from the store's display was gone.

"You did what?", exploded Bhanwarlal when he was told that his only son, now rapidly turning out to be a liability, had dropped the sleek Ericsson phone from the Vasai Fort, presumably smashed to pieces and never to be found again. It cost 33,000 and would have sold for 40,000 in Vasai albeit to not more than two or three customers. But it was a matter of prestige for his Matarani shop to keep such an expensive phone in the first place. The bulk of the customers came to gawk at it and bought some cheap electronic music player anyway. But it gave his shop a uniqueness which was now gone as his only show piece was now lost thanks to his worthless tub of lard.

Rupali kept the phone well-hidden and took it out late at night after everyone was asleep to admire its classy lines and smooth feel. It felt like something she had never seen before. Mobile connectivity was out of question for her as the calls were 32 rupees per minute and the network at Vasai was really patchy. The phone felt good to hold and look at though and she wanted to experience what people with money felt when they acquired possessions that few could afford.

The next morning, there was a loud banging on their door and both Vitthal and Saraswati were surprised to see Bhanwarlal and Narendra standing on their doorstep. "Where is that whore?" Bhanwarlal shouted at the top of his voice. "Not only a whore, a thief also," added Narendra helpfully, not entirely sure what a whore was. That earned him a sharp slap on the back of his head from Bhanwarlal. *"Tu toh rehne hi de chutiye – teri wajah se yeh hua hai,"* rebuked Bhanwarlal. He was fuming inside thinking of how some girl was able to fool a pure Marwari bred boy into parting with something so valuable for practically nothing. The girl was a fraud and a criminal. Vitthal and Saraswati had no idea of what was going on and they looked at the father and son duo with expressionless eyes. "Call your *vishkanya,*" said Bhanwarlal referring to Rupali as a mythical poison-woman whose mere kiss could kill people. Saraswati was livid and could not stomach Bhanwarlal's continuous insults. "How dare you abuse my daughter? What has she done? If you don't stop right away, it won't be good for you I am telling you," said Saraswati in a tone that had the certainty of backing from some very powerful people which certainly did not include her diffident husband. Vitthal did not say a word. He went inside and woke up Rupali.

Half-asleep, Rupali came to the door and in a flash understood what had transpired. Bhanwarlal had not bought Narendra's story. She cursed him under her breath. She had asked him four times what explanation Narendra would give his father for the missing phone but each time he had brushed aside her questions saying with supreme confidence that he was good at making up stories and boasted having fooled his father a few times. Rupali did not really believe him but he did not want to talk about anything and get distracted while he was feeling her inside her pinafore. Now the idiot had confessed. Rupali, displaying the quick-witted intellect that was to become her hallmark later in her life, pulled a sad face and addressed Narendra, "I told you to ask your father before gifting such an expensive thing to me. No problem, I will get it for you," she offered helpfully. "What gift? You demanded the phone from my son if he wished to spend time with you, didn't you, you whore?", thundered Bhanwarlal. "Enough! One more word of abuse coming from your mouth and I will not stop then, you mother fucker," Saraswati finally lost it. *"Randi ki beti randi nahin hogi to kya hogi? Achcha training de rahi ho. Aur main kisi se nahin darta - jis yaar ko bulana ho, bula lo,"* countered Bhanwarlal. Internally he regretted sounding so confident. He had heard that Saraswati was the favourite of Bhai Thakur and the thought of getting a visit from Bhai's henchmen other than for collecting hafta made him nervous. Nothing a little money can't solve, he thought hopefully.

Rupali had brought the phone and the charger from inside and calmly handed over everything to Narendra. "You clearly don't have the balls for having me as your friend, don't show me your face again, you fat fuck," she flatly told Narendra. Never once did she even look at Bhanwarlal during this entire time. As far as she was concerned, this was between her and Narendra. Bhanwarlal was a nobody. The father and son left with the goods. Narendra did turn around twice to see if Rupali was watching but the door had been shut. He got hit twice on the head for looking back. *My son is really a dickhead. Where are his Marwari genes? How can a Marwari trade money for a girl's affections? Should send him to Jhunjhunu to spend a few years at my father's shop. Will do him a lot of good.* Bhanwarlal decided to do just that.

Saraswati was livid. She picked up the closest thing that she could use to vent her anger. It did not matter that it was a heavy metal spatula made of iron and which was hot from making parathas that morning. The first blow caught Rupali unawares. Smarting from the heat of the spatula more than the impact on her bare arm, Rupali ducked the next couple of blows. *"Dosti ki gift thi? Achha? Yedi samajhti hai kya mereko? Teri chaal main bahut dinon se dekh rahi hoon Rupali. Sudhar ja nahin to aage bahut musibat aayegi,"* thundered Saraswati. Even in her anger, her outburst was more based on fear that her daughter may choose to lead her life based on what she experienced around her instead of being a normal girl with regular dreams of marriage, home and kids.

Rupali bore her mother's anger and outburst with a stoic silence. Mentally, she made a note of not trying such stunts with weak men. Next time, she had to go for a sure thing. After all, her youth wouldn't last forever. Given that she was going on 17, she had about 10 more years to make her break from wants and needs. And the time to start was now. All she needed was a plan.

Dipu Dikle was the only son of Saroj Dikle, a widow who paid her bills by doing odd cooking jobs in the neighbourhood where Rupali lived. Dipu had dreams of breaking into Bollywood someday and in the process had caused Saroj untold misery. All because someone once told him he looked like Govinda. Saroj would often take out her frustration over Dipu in front of Saraswati, who she considered to be a good friend. That day Saroj found Saraswati in a terrible mood.

"What is the matter with you today Saraswati? I heard all about that *bhadva* Bhanwarlal and his *chutiya* son. I don't think you should blame Rupali. She is so beautiful, just like a film heroine," said Saroj.

Saraswati kept quiet but made a face. Rupali was lying on the bed reading *Manohar Kahaniyan,* a Hindi crime and thriller magazine supposedly based on true stories.

"My useless son is still trying to get a break. He thinks he looks like Govinda but honestly I think he doesn't even look like a B grade duplicate of him. I just hope he gets better sense and takes up a job somewhere," continued Saroj.

"But I am telling you, your Rupali has a future. She is perfect for the film business. She has the beauty, height and people will lust after her I tell you. She will be a big hit, you mark my words. And Saraswati, let me tell you something," added Saroj, now lowering her voice to a whisper for what was to follow, "it is really easy for beautiful women to make it big in films. After all, a beautiful girl has everything that the film industry needs to give them a break."

Rupali had heard every word. Saraswati's protests to Saroj did not even register in her mind. Now she had a plan and Dipu was her vehicle of choice.

Movies, or Films for Indians, are as popular in India as cricket. All popular music since the last 75 years in India has been, simply, film music. In this peculiarity, India stands alone in the world. Nowhere else do films have music to the extent Indian films do and nowhere does film music inspire such following and passion. In fact, Indian film music has composers, artists and the whole attached ecosystem almost exclusively to itself. Very few private albums have been made by singers or composers and of the very few, hardly any have clicked and if they did at the time of release, were soon forgotten. In contrast, even today, film music of 1940s to 1970s is avidly followed and enjoyed by a very large base of music aficionados who swear by their favourite singers, composers and lyricists. In fact, the deader the singer or composer, the greater and more passionate the fan following.

Films permeate the consciousness of every Indian from the way they seek to dress to their talk, their anecdotes, their way of looking at the opposite sex, their mental image of themselves in various situations, their interaction with their spouses or romantic interests, their dancing and all their celebrations. In fact, every pore of the being of an average urban Indian is fully populated with characters from films, the actors, the dialogues, the situations, everything. At various points of highs or lows in their lives, a very large population of urban Indians recall and attach themselves mentally to situations and music from their favourite films. Rupali was no different. The fact that several leading ladies had come from ordinary or disadvantaged backgrounds left an impression in her mind. Since almost all the leading ladies were objects of lust and she too saw herself in the same vein, it stood to reason that she could have a shot at being the leading lady someday soon. But for that she first had to get her foot in the door.

Chapter 3

Present Day

Robin checked her cell phone for the time. It was already 1.15 pm and she was still five minutes away from Shizusan. She knew Batty would have been there at 1.00 pm sharp and mentally cursed herself for being late. On entering Shizusan, she spotted him right away sitting at a corner table for two out of earshot of most of the customers there. Closest to his table were two college girls, a pretty, well-dressed one with green streaked hair and a nose ring and another who looked like she hadn't eaten in days demolishing a large platter of sushi. She could overhear them discussing the details of their college fest. Pune was a student city in many ways as there were a lot of colleges in Pune and students came from all over India to study in these colleges. She wondered how college students could afford to spend that kind of money on exotic food. Remembering her student days when money was really tight and a treat was when someone got food from home after returning from a weekend break, she marvelled at today's parents who spared no effort and money to ensure that their children dressed well, ate well and were comfortable. Academics be damned. "Wish my parents had a similar approach to my growing up," she mused wistfully.

Batty broke into a grin on seeing her.

"I see that you have maintained your usual punctual schedule," he teased her.

"Let's quickly order so that we can get into the matter at hand," she said.

Batty ordered a bowl of Thai Chicken Red Curry and Rice and he knew Robin would order a platter of sushi. He too loved sushi but was still practicing his chopsticks skills and was almost there but did not feel confident enough to use them in Robin's presence.

"So tell me, what has bitten you?" he asked.

"No, first tell me what you have been up to? It has been what - almost two months since we last met? No call, no message, no hello, how are you? C'mon, I don't think the Army keeps you that busy," she said.

"I could tell you but then I would have to kill you," he said lamely.

Robin rolled her eyes and said, "Too lame dude, which year are you living in,1980? Need to bring you into the present buddy."

Just then the waiter served up their order and before he could place Batty's bowl of Thai Curry and Rice, one piece of Sushi had already vanished inside Robin's oral cavity.

"Don't they feed you at the newspaper?" asked Batty. "They do but nothing this good," she said with her mouth full.

Batty noticed her chipped nail polish, her forearms that would soon need waxing and her general appearance. Her dark brown-auburn hair was hastily tied into a knot with what looked like a chopstick holding it together. As usual, she wore almost no makeup and her sharp features and her high cheekbones were the highlights of her oval face. Her soft angled eyebrows and large, intelligent eyes the shade of wild honey added significantly to her appearance. She had a straight almost snub nose that gave her an appearance of being a snob. Her generous lower lip sat underneath her thinner upper lip which gave an appearance of a permanent pout. She was attractive, no doubt about that.

There was also something else in her face which Batty couldn't put his finger on but which added to her mystique considerably. Maybe it was her permanent bemused expression which the lips contributed to. Or maybe it was the conflict between the lips and the eyes. While the eyes were bright and shiny, the lips hinted at a more good-time girl kind of countenance. She wore a simple military green singlet made of cotton and skinny jeans with her feet thrust carelessly into a pair of converse sneakers. She wore a thin gold chain around her shapely neck with a tiny peace pendant and no earrings. Her wrists were bare except for a charm bracelet. The only thing, that she accessorised her get up with, were her omnipresent white iPhone earbuds that were hanging around her neck.

Batty offered a sharp contrast to Robin. He

wore a crisp white shirt and a pair of khakhi chinos accented with a brown belt and brown oxford shoes with brown plaid socks. His shirt was unbuttoned at the top which gave a glimpse of his muscular chest. On his right wrist was a silver bracelet which looked like the Sikh kada and on the left wrist he wore his only item of value - an old Omega Seamaster watch which his dad used to wear. He wore his jet black hair short, military cropped. His appearance and ramrod straight bearing screamed military from a mile away.

Digging into his bowl, Batty remarked, "so what is so unusual about this murder?"

Robin was chewing furiously on her sushi and wolfed it down quickly to answer.

"For starters, someone stabbed this woman 16 times. That's just a lot. There is apparently no sign of struggle or resistance as if she was asleep when she was stabbed. There was a pillow placed on her face but there's no apparent sign of asphyxiation or suffocation either. Once the autopsy is done we will know more. But doesn't look like the servant did it." she said.

"Hmmm...who are the guys investigating it? Lokhande and Co.?" he enquired.

"Yes the very same. Since the last time I saw him, Lokhande has developed an even bigger paunch and Shinde has his own wild theories about a lover's spat," she said.

Batty whipped out his immaculately preserved iPhone 6 and dialed Juggy.

"You are still working with this dinosaur?" she joked showing him her shiny new iPhone X. He wondered how she managed such an expensive phone on the pittance the newspaper paid her. He, however, ignored her barb and spoke into his phone.

"Juggy, what's up? Look, there has been a murder reported in Deccan Gymkhana police station area which I think needs a little more digging into. What? Can't hear you well. Yes, Lokhande. Ok great. Will catch up with you soon. Bye." he ended.

"He will have a word with Lokhande. Let's finish lunch and pay him a visit," he said.

Lokhande stifled a yawn and buried a silent fart in the cushion of his chair. The post lunch period was always the most challenging. It was really hard to keep awake. Today had been a great day so far. He had started his morning with a massive breakfast of three-egg cheese omlette with bun maska and masala chai at Cafe Goodluck before reaching office. His routine morning breakfast at home was a cup of tea with very little milk and a piece of whole wheat toast without butter. How can a man function with this meagre nourishment? Don't they say that eating well is important for the human brain to function? He reflected on his lunch with great satisfaction. Only Maasoli made that pomfret thali to die for. His constables were subjected to Rohini's diet lunch this afternoon. Now, the next crucial thing was his late evening snack. After that he would be ready for whatever Rohini was dishing out for dinner that evening. Everybody was happy that way.

"Hello Lokhandeji, how are you?" Batty asked breezily and Lokhande looked up to find both Batty and Robin sauntering in and making themselves comfortable in the visitor's chairs in front of his desk. Just then his cell phone rang. Batty found it mildly amusing that Lokhande's ringtone was the tune from *Mission Impossible.* Seriously? thought Batty. There was nothing remotely impossible about the things Lokhande did. If anything, he was a complete anti-thesis of it.

It was ACP Jagdeep Kumar.

"Jai Hind Sir," he said snapping to attention. Batty had a feeling that he would probably get up and salute any moment now.

"Sir? Sir, Sir. Sir? Ok Sir. Done Sir." he hastily replied.

Batty noticed how Lokhande's demeanour had changed from being slightly annoyed to an expression of courtesy and co-operation after the call.

"Yes Bhowmick Sir, what can I do for you?" he enquired with false courtesy.

"Wanted to discuss an interesting case you

seem to be having on your hands at this time Lokhandeji," Batty said.

"Nothing interesting Sir but if you wish, I can tell you everything we know so far Sir," he offered.

"The woman's name is Rupali Kalra, wife of Deep Kalra. She has brutally murdered by her servant Dharam who is a Bihari and we have already taken him into custody. What is becoming of this society Sir - people are killing people for a mere 25,000 Rupees Sir," he elaborated.

During the course of the conversation, Batty and Robin discovered that Rupali seemed to have been murdered in her sleep and apparently the first two or three stabs were enough not to wake her up at all. The murder weapon was not found, but Lokhande was sure that Dharam would have disposed it off in some water body such that it would never be found. Her poor distraught husband had found the body and called the police station. The police had reached the crime scene in less than 20 minutes and sealed the apartment. From the wounds, it looked like a sharp instrument which could have been a kitchen knife - something the servant would be able to access easily. But an autopsy was awaited and once Vinay Shahastrabuddhe found some time, that report would also be in. Which in itself was another task since Vinay was known to be temperamental and extremely irritable.

"Can we visit the crime scene Lokhandeji?

And can we also see the body in the morgue?" asked Batty solicitously. "Yes, yes. I myself will come with you. As I already told you Sir, this is routine matter but since you wish to see it, I will be most happy to show you," Lokhande offered. "No Lokhandeji, please don't take the trouble. Any constable will do," countered Batty wanting to have a private word with Shinde without his boss. Shinde would shut up if Lokhande was around.

He looked around and caught Shinde's eye.

"Can we take Shinde with us? He is familiar and will help in getting us a few details," asked Batty.

"Sure Sir, no problem. Shinde will come with you. Would you like to go right away?" Lokhande asked.

Batty and Robin indicated that they would indeed like to do so.

"Shinde - please go with them and come back soon. After all, we don't want to waste Sir's time in routine matters and we have enough work to do here, don't we?" said Lokhande in his best reprimanding tone trying to convey to Shinde, that he should keep his wild theories to himself. Preparing to leave, Batty warily eyed a stray cat that was lurking around outside the police station. Nothing further happened between him and the cat to his great relief. With Shinde in tow, Batty and Robin set out for the residence of Rupali Kalra.

Vinayak Apartments on Apte Road was typical of the modern-day apartment constructions that were mushrooming all over Pune. Designed with a nice big lobby, high speed modern lifts and three apartments to a floor, the 11 storey building was almost ready. Batty noted that the construction work was still going on in the lobby. The lifts were covered in plastic on the outside and padded material inside indicating the continuous movement of men and material for the ongoing construction. A lone security guard was busy interacting with construction workers and checking the material deliveries and movement. Batty asked Shinde to inquire with the security guard about the occupancy status of the building.

Apparently, Vinayak Apartments was embroiled in litigation for the past four years and the builder had recently received a court order to resume work on the building. It was almost ready with the last 10% of the finishing work pending and once done was expected to receive an occupation certificate from the municipal corporation soon. Meanwhile, tired of waiting and having paid full value of the property, eight owners had moved in and another 8-10 had begun interior work for their apartments as the builder had given possession to all those who had asked for it. The rest of the building was unoccupied; the power connection was through a construction meter and the water supply was through tankers.

The security guard had been on the site

since the last five months and had reported that the Kalras and some of the other occupants had moved in much before he had joined. He claimed to know most of the residents by face but added that a number of interior designers, contractors and workers were continuously going in and out of the building. Also, some of the owners not yet living there came in at various times to check on the progress of work and some of the residents threw parties in partially done up apartments from time to time. The parking for the building was in the basement and while there was ample space for over 60 cars, at any point in time there were about 10-15 cars parked in the basement of the building. The elevators could be accessed from the basement of the building and the entrance to the parking lot was on the left before turning right on the driveway towards the lobby. The plan was to provide automated parking access cards to all residents and the basic outline of the parking system was in place without the barrier which would come once the system was fully operational. The building did not have a security system but there were plans to install CCTV cameras on every floor as well as in the lobby and the parking areas soon. The security guard lived on the premises, retired to his make-shift accommodation after 9 PM and resumed his duties at 7 AM.

The 9th floor of the building had three apartments of which two were not yet occupied and a naked bulb hung from the ceiling of the floor lobby. Deep's apartment looked no different from the other two on the outside except for a fancy name plate which proclaimed that the apartment belonged to "Kalra's", the poor grammar of which made Batty wince inwardly. Why people converted their Surnames into possessive nouns was a mystery he never understood. Would it be too much to ask to only see a simple "Kalras" to let people know that more than one Kalra stayed there? He shook his head and asked Shinde to unlock the apartment.

The two-bedroom apartment was laid out in a vestibule kind of manner. The front door led to the living room followed by the kitchen and then a common toilet, a smaller bedroom and finally in the end the master bedroom with the attached toilet all linked by a passage that started from the living room and ended at the master bedroom. The living room and the master bedroom were rectangular, roughly the same size and the entire apartment was no more than 800-850 sq ft of area. Inspired by tight Mumbai spaces, this compact apartment layout was now omnipresent in most of India's upcoming cities. The Builders just made that much more money by offering less for a higher price.

The living room and the master bedroom both had large windows overlooking the road below and had a waist high aluminium railing on top of the quarter wall to prevent an accidental fall. The living room had two sofas with floral upholstery facing each other, a centre table and two side tables on either side. In the corner towards the window was a television mounted on a standard TV rack with a cable set-top box and a DVD player underneath. There was a wireless internet router next to the television set. The other end of the living room in the corner opposite the main door was a round dining table with two chairs and a glass table top.

"Most of the furniture looks off-the-shelf," Robin remarked after having observed everything silently. "That's what people are doing more and more as they no longer have the time or the money to custom build furniture after having paid a fortune to buy a house," she added. "Or if people need to move in quickly," Batty said quietly.

The master bedroom was dominated by a king-size bed with a huge headrest and some shelves above the headrest housing a couple of yoga books and a copy of Satish Alekar's play Begum Barve in Marathi. Opposite the bed was the attached bathroom cum toilet. Between the bed and the window was a recliner chair and between the bedroom door and the bathroom was a large wardrobe with two sections - one each for husband and wife. Next to the bed was a dresser with a large mirror, a side table underneath the mirror with drawers and a table lamp on top of the side table with an unopened bottle of water next to it. Opposite to the recliner was an identical TV rack with a television set, a set top box and a DVD player in the corner.

The bed had two pillows placed one on top of the other and a third pillow on the side. The bed sheet covering the bed - red with dark blue print - was a shade of maroon in several places where the blood had trickled on to the bed from the body.

"What was the position of the body"' asked Batty.

"Sir the body was on its back with the head resting on the two pillows with the third pillow on its face. The rest of the body was supine and relaxed. The legs were slightly apart and the hands were on the sides with palm facing upwards. The eyes were closed and the mouth slightly open. Shavasan pose Sir," summarised Shinde. "Where were the stab wounds?" asked Batty.

"A total of 16 Sir. Two on the chest on the left side, three on the right, two on the abdomen on the right side, one on the abdomen on the left side, two each on the lower abdomen on the right and left, and two each on both the upper thighs. Almost like...," Shinde said trailing off.

"Like what?" asked Robin.

Suddenly unsure and remembering his boss's veiled warning, he said,

"Nothing sir, just was thinking that it looked like a love killing to me but of course this is just my theory and we will know more when the autopsy report is out. Until then, it won't be wise to say or even think anything otherwise Sir. It could also be revenge by the servant trying to ensure that she did not get up or report him Sir," he added trying to weave-in his boss's conclusion of the murder.

Batty did not reply and silenced Robin with a look as she was about to pursue Shinde further.

Batty slipped on a surgical glove that he produced from his front pocket and methodically opened each drawer next to the bed. The top drawer had the remote for the air-conditioner, a remote for the TV, the set top box and the DVD player. The second drawer had some medicine strips, some lozenges, some papers, a few face and skin creams and a bottle of expensive women's perfume and a couple of deodorant sprays. There was also a wallet which Batty opened. Inside were a few currency notes of small denominations, two credit cards, a partly used strip of contraceptive pills and a driving license in the name of Rupali Jadhav issued in 2010. That explained the Marathi book on the shelf. Rupali was apparently a Maharashtrian married to a Punjabi. It would be interesting to know how these guys met, thought Batty. The last drawer had some costume jewellery, the kind women wore these days which was more silver and stones and of not much value. With gold and diamond prices being what they were and the modern trend of dressing that was accessorised with chunky jewellery, a lot of young women had switched to casual costume baubles instead of the gold that their mothers favoured. Batty asked Shinde if he was able to go through the wardrobe and found that the police team had gone through both the closets and found nothing of any importance except for clothes, cosmetics, some property and banking papers and routine personal items.

Batty quickly ran through the other bedroom and the kitchen and did not find anything out of the ordinary except for a chef's knife set which seemed largely unused. There were other daily use knives and an assortment of steel cutlery. The apartment was a common middle class house with all the required appliances and gadgets and the contents of the refrigerator or any of the drawers in the kitchen offered nothing of value. The spare bedroom looked largely unused and was sparsely furnished with a made up bed with two pillows and a wardrobe. Apparently there's nothing of any interest in the rest of the apartment, thought Batty. Shinde proceeded to take all the contents of the drawers of the master bedroom for deposit with the evidence section, did a panchnama and issued instructions to keep the bedroom sealed while allowing supervised access to Deep's wardrobe section and opened the rest of the apartment for Deep for his use. He could shift to the spare bedroom once he collected his things from this room.

With nothing further to do, they decided to visit the morgue. Before entering the morgue, he quickly glanced around for stray cats to avoid, his recent experience at the Camp having set his teeth on edge and he did not want to take any further chances. The Sassoon General Hospital attached to the B J Medical College was where all medico-legal case bodies were kept. Shinde made a couple of quick enquiries and was told that the body was taken in a couple of hours ago by Professor Vinay Shahastrabuddhe, the head of Forensics. The professor was a grizzled temperamental old bird who had no patience for questions or explanations. His word was final and that was that. He didn't think any of the station heads in and around his area had much gumption and for the most part, the cops had no interest except to quickly close the case.

Professor Shahastrabuddhe was interrupted in the midst of his autopsy by a ward boy who announced that a certain Major accompanied by a constable and a reporter were there to see him. At first, irritated with the interruption, he almost told the visitors to bugger off but then suddenly recalled the bright Army guy and the sharp reporter whom he had interacted with a couple of times earlier. These guys were good and on more than one occasion in the past, they had probed his autopsy with observations and queries that had led him to a completely different line of thinking and conclusion. Those were fun times. Now, warming up to his visitors, he asked the ward boy to show them in.

On the autopsy table was Rupali's dead body and apparently the professor had almost finished with the evaluation of the wounds.

"Hello Professor, how are you? " Batty greeted him with utmost politeness aware of his irascible nature.

"Hello Major, good to see you and you too young lady," he replied with barely concealed pleasure.

"I presume you are here for this one. Let me be quick and thorough as I have reached my preliminary conclusion." Methodically, he took them through his observations. The 16 stab wounds were made by a mid-sized sharp object with high quality steel most probably a chef or a combat knife. The cuts were clean and deep and had severed major blood vessels cleanly. Death seemed to have occurred almost immediately after the first couple of chest stabs as some of the later wounds had bled less. Batty recalled seeing the knife set in the kitchen but unless there was another spare knife of similar caliber in the kitchen that was now missing, the weapon seemed to be from an external source. Maybe Deep could throw some light here. The Professor was going on about how these wounds were made with a lot of force and had instantly created the impact desired. He also theorised that this seemed to be some kind of vendetta or extreme provocation.

When told by Shinde that their prime suspect was the domestic help, the professor held back the rest of his observations.

"Seems fairly straightforward - death due

to multiple stabbings. We do come across a lot of these. In this case, the killer seems to have lost control over himself or herself as the persistence with stabbing all over after the initial two or three stabs is the work of someone having vented serious anger or having lost control of himself or herself in the process but then again, I am no psychiatrist," he concluded.

Having said this, he hesitated for the briefest of moments which Robin caught as Batty was preoccupied with looking at the body.

"Is there something else Professor?" Robin quizzed.

"No, not really but something about this is bothering me slightly. I am not sure what it is but I still have an hour or two of work left which I intend to take up day after once I dispose of another case that will take most of my day tomorrow. Once I finish, if I come across anything else, I will let you know," he said.

Batty wondered if he still had his cell number and if the Professor's number had changed.

"Hasn't changed since 1999," the professor said with some pride. "I have yours but I sometimes forget your name but I must say I remember this lady here very well. She and I interact even when you are not around. But call me at my office as I hardly ever answer my cell phone and it is permanently on silent mode."

Outside the hospital, Batty turned to Robin and

said, "Good catch there. I missed his hesitation." Robin beamed at this acknowledgement. If only he was a little more attentive towards her as well, she thought. She was momentarily lost in her reverie about what things could be between them.

Batty first cast a glance around to check for any stray cats and turned to Shinde to enquire about Deep.

"When can we meet him?"

"I will call him to Police station sir and then you can interrogate him," replied Shinde.

"No not the station - lets meet him at his apartment now that he is free to move in again. Set it up for tomorrow a little after lunch time ideally," he said. Just then Batty's cell rang.

"Hi Juggy," he answered.

"Sure, no problem. 6 it is then," he said.

"He's called us to the Poona Club for a sundowner," he informed Robin.

"I can't - need to file my report for the day. My editor has already sent me three texts and the last one is a stinker" said Robin.

"Call me once you are done and we will sync up on the phone," she said.

Poona Club was a sanctuary for the city's brown sahibs who still clung to quaint British era customs and mores. Quite a bit of Pune's geriatric Parsi population hung around the club all day playing cards, chatting and indulging in an occasional swim or walk around the grounds. The men's changing rooms were huge and it was common to see old men walk out naked from the shower and stand with their arms apart while an attendant from the club's staff dressed them.

Apart from the older lot, there were a lot of middle aged professionals and businessmen who had got club memberships in the 80s or earlier. Memberships were now closed for new members for more than 20 years unless one happened to be a son or a daughter of an existing member. Some corporate CEO types also came in on temporary corporate memberships that were renewed every five years for eye watering sums of money. These were what kept the club afloat and facilitated subsidised food and beverage for the members. Apart from corporate members, the Club also gave out service memberships to the top IAS and IPS officers in Pune. The corporate types and the service members were the ones that came to play golf on the Club's superb 18-hole golf course apart from an odd old timer and one or two travellers who used the Club on reciprocity basis. The Club also had an excellent housekeeping department that was proficient in keeping stray cats away from the Club's expansive lawns and common areas, much to Batty's relief.

Batty spotted Additional Commissioner of Police Jagdeep Kumar "Juggy" sitting in the lawns with his sundowner already in his hand. His table was to one side in the smoking area of the lawns where he could puff to his heart's content. Related to him on his Punjabi mother's side, Juggy was Batty's cousin as Batty's mom and Juggy's mom were sisters. While Batty's mom had married a Bengali, Juggy was a pure-bred Punjabi. Whether it was Batty's Punjabi genes that made him join the army or a quest for a structured, orderly and carefully curated life he couldn't tell but Juggy anyway thought of Batty having had the best of both the worlds - a sharp Bengali brain with the physicality of a Punjabi. He was very fond of Batty and treated him as his younger brother. He was in awe of his sharp intellect that had helped him a few times in the last couple of years and earned him much fame in the department as an extremely capable police officer.

Juggy's core competence was not police work, it was sensing shifting political winds and endearing himself to the top political king makers which had ensured his steady rise at a relatively young age. He was up for his next promotion as a Jt. Commissioner of Police in the next two years. He would be one of the youngest and if his career kept the same pace, he would be a Commissioner of Police of a major city by age 51 or 52 which would be great. Once that happened, with 7-8 years to go for retirement, he could even eye the top post of CBI or IB and if not, certainly retire as a DG. Life was all set for Juggy.

"Hi Juggy," said Batty easily.

"Bartaman, *ki bolchish,*" Juggy greeted him with the only phrase of Bengali that he knew. Unlike the others, Juggy insisted on calling him Bartaman. After all Bengali pet names were hardly like the typical ones that Punjabis had, but rather, these unrelated and ridiculous sounding words could result in extreme embarrassment when pronounced loudly in public. Besides, Juggy thought it was almost a sacrilege to spoil those beautiful Bengali names by giving them doggy sobriquets. "All good, man. How's *masi*", Batty inquired after Juggy's mother.

"She's good as always. Loves her evening walks and gossip with the women of the club," he said pointing in the distance where Batty could make out a frail old lady walking with two other elderly ladies around the track. Juggy ordered a scotch on the rocks and Batty's favourite Old Fashioned with Jim Beam and got into the matter at hand.

Batty briefly told him how Robin had alerted him to the murder and his own suspicions seemed to point towards a crime of passion rather than a robbery.

"That's not all that is there to it, right? I know you well. You smell something more," said Juggy.

Batty admitted that he had this feeling at the back of his mind that this was a special case and a proper investigation would be needed though he couldn't be sure of why he felt that way. It was just a finger of doubt right now in his mind. Maybe it was reinforced as Shahastrabuddhe had also echoed it.

"I will leave you to your devices but keep me in the loop. I am also tracking it and have told Lokhande to extend all support to you and Robin," said Juggy.

"And how's your paramour?" Juggy asked suddenly without any preamble, knowing full well that this irritated Batty no end.

"Dude, I have told you a hundred times there is nothing between me and Robin. It is just a friendly relationship cemented by a common objective," defended Batty.

"A friendly relationship can have a common objective which could semen-t it," laughed Juggy, not letting go and thoroughly enjoying Batty's apparent discomfort at his pun.

"C'mon you must have thought of it more than once for sure," he said.

"You cops have a one-track mind - always looking for a sexual angle when women are around and a great interest in who's doing whom. Some people are different you know," said Batty now getting annoyed.

"If you don't want to tell me I am fine with that. But I think you can definitely do better than that one. There are women everywhere and you are a handsome guy. Take your pick and play the field before it shrivels up. Just saying," said Juggy gesturing with his hands with his palms open.

"He just called you for a meeting to say that he should be kept in the loop? " asked an incredulous Robin.

It was after 9 PM and they were seated at one of the city's many lounge bars that was closer to her place of work. Batty shrugged but did not say anything. He could hardly tell her what Juggy thought they ought to be doing. But then again, Robin was sharp so he would have to come up with something to keep her satisfied. To his great relief, Robin changed the subject.

"Tomorrow should be interesting since Lokhande will have Rupali's call records from the phone company. Hopefully, our investigation will start from there on," she said. "That and our interrogation of Dharam and Deep tomorrow should provide some answers that we are looking for," said Batty.

Winding up a little after 1030 PM, Batty was back in his quarters by 11. As he drifted off to sleep he had this feeling that somehow this was not going to be a simple one.

Chapter 4

Early 1997

Kaka stretched and slowly looked up from his charpoy in his verandah. He was aware that his blue checked lungi was open from one side and his one hairy leg was jutting out almost to his thigh. He made a feeble attempt to adjust it but looking at the vision before him, he was worried that he would have to adjust a lot more very soon. Kaka, whose real name no one knew any more and who was nicknamed after his passing resemblance in his youth to the raging matinee idol of the day, was Hindi filmdom's dominant junior artist supplier and he had a virtual monopoly with several film production banners.

The Hindi film world called the unnamed actors who made up the crowds, bystanders, background dancers, goons and several such ancillary nameless characters whose faces were used to fill up the celluloid frames but were given no dialogue and weren't required to have any acting skills "junior artists" thereby infusing hope into hundreds of young and old boys, men, girls and women of a future mainstream role. The truth was, no junior artist had ever made it to the mainstream but there was plenty of folklore where film industry insiders spoke about how a certain leading lady was once a "junior artist" and was spotted by a known director who then gave her a break or how a certain young man who was today a matinee idol actually started life as part of a crowd scene and was then "discovered". Such legends, unsubstantiated for the most part, kept hope alive for these "junior artists" and gave them the fortitude required to bear poor working conditions, sexual exploitation, insult, insecurity and generally extremely depressing conditions under which most ordinary humans would collapse.

Kaka stared at Rupali for as long as he could. Everything about her that made him feel warm in the right places but at the same time wary of displaying his warmth, something about her not being easy. Her eyes practically forbade anyone from trying unless she wanted them to. There was no welcome there. Just cold reasoning. Dipu Dikle, who had featured in a few crowd scenes in mostly B grade films, said perfunctorily, "Kaka, Rupali is Saraswati kaki's daughter. You know Saraswati kaki. She has "friends" everywhere. Rupali wants to act in films. Take her under your tutelage Kaka. Make her life. She deserves it. She has a lot of talent and you can see how attractive she is. Definitely heroine material Kaka. The first one to become a heroine from your camp."

Kaka was not really paying attention to Dipu. He was just a body as far as Kaka was concerned. Earned him 250 rupees a day after deducting what was due to him as and when he got placed. Peanuts but enough peanuts like him and you could run your kitchen. Unremarkable face in the crowd. The girl was different though. Not meant to be a face in the crowd this one. He would start her as a background dancer. Those made him almost 1,000 rupees per day net. And then who knew? If some producer took a fancy to her, he would sign a contract with her for 25% of all earnings. Ah, that would be good. And she can always be given opportunities to express her gratitude in kind. That would be what they call *sone pe suhaga.* Controlling the spreading warmth in his lungi he asked, *"Dance aata hai?"* Dipu intervened. *"Arre Kaka, kya dance karti hai,"* he said. Rupali nodded. *"Chalo phir theek hai, kal aa jao. Mein kuchh jugaad karta hoon."* Kaka said flatly deliberately not wanting to show much enthusiasm. *Better to keep them guessing. They appreciate the effort that much more.*

Rupali had a hard time falling asleep that night. This seemed quite easy - where was the struggle they spoke about? If she can get into a major song as a background dancer, it would only be a matter of time before she was noticed. Saraswati was now trying to make up for being harsh with her by making small talk but Rupali was in no mood to even attempt normal conversation. Even though the cell phone incident was now quite old, she had mentally distanced herself from Saraswati and Vitthal both of whom noticed the change but put it down to something temporary due to that incident. Neither of them knew that this change was now permanent and a part of her rapidly evolving personality.

Priyavardhan, an acclaimed director from the Malayalam and Tamil Cinema, was trying his hand at a Hindi remake of his super-hit Tamil Film. The film was titled "Viraat" in Hindi. This was his first experience in Bollywood and it had frustrated him no end. Bloody Naarth Indiens. How the fuck does one function here? It is 12 noon, the set is ready since 8 am, the first full dress rehearsal was to start at 9 am and there was still no sign of the heroine. "What are you telling me man?" he turned in exasperation to his AD. "What do you mean we are one background dancer short *thaii olee mavane?*" Priyavardhan screamed. These mother fuckers, forever disorganised. His temples began to throb visibly and one large blood vessel in his neck looked like it may rupture anytime. "Get me that *thevaiya mavan,* that junior artist supplier", he fumed. Son of a bitch. Couldn't do one job straight.

The song being shot that day was the last remaining part of the film. The heroine had just shown up on the set three hours late and from her puffed up eyes, Priyavardhan could see that she had been up all night. *Sigh. What was wrong with these people?* He longed to be back in Kollywood and Mollywood. The actors and actresses were so disciplined. Some even touched his feet when they came on the sets. Even if the heroine had slept with him the night before, she still came and touched his feet before the shoot. Such wonderful work culture! Here, the heroine did not even bother with him since he was a South Indian and trying his hand at Bollywood for the first time. The hero, a *Naarth Indien,* had been balling this small-time heroine whenever he got a chance including while the shot was being set up. All these things happened in Kollywood and Mollywood as well but ah, the respect and the work culture. He didn't care if the actors slept with the entire unit or drank 24 hours. They had to report for the shoot on time and be prepared. God alone knew how Hindi films ever got completed. *Kena Punda all of them.* Stupid cunts.

The trembling AD, a Tamilian import called Ganesan, brought a nonchalant Kaka to Priyavardhan. "Sir, no worries. I have the best other girl. What a girl sir. Super dancer. You will make her heroine if you see her Sir. Shall I call her Sir? Just see her Sir," Kaka put on his best charming manner. These *Madrasis* were crazy. So what was the big deal if one dancer did not show up? This was the second day of the song shoot and who notices background dancers anyway? Replace one with the other and no one really cares. Priyavardhan was now very much used to the Bollywood exaggeration of everything. He gestured to Ganesan to check the new girl out and get her familiar with the steps. "You have 20 minutes to prepare her. Get on with it." he fumed.

Rupali was given the village belle clothes to wear. The hair and the makeup was a quick affair. The dance master, a fat ugly woman who was known as the raging queen of Bollywood dances by the name of Shehnaz Khan, was lining up all the background dancers and explaining the steps to them. Rupali was familiar with most of the steps and except for little twist that was like a hook step for the song, there was nothing special really. She could have done this in her sleep. Shehnaz started to dance and show the dancers the steps in all their style and flow. For a fat woman, she had amazing grace and could do dance movements that seemed impossible for her bulk. She was the force behind the knockout dancing skills of the reigning queen of Bollywood, Madhu Pandey. It was said that she could also make Dharmendra dance like he was a pro. Not that it ever happened.

Shehnaz noticed the new girl almost immediately. She reminded her of her protege Madhu. The same grace and what a wonderful smile. This girl was perhaps special. She called her out. "Hey you! New girl. Come here." Rupali panicked. What had she done wrong? "Yes sir," she blurted. All the other girls burst out laughing.

"Sorry madam," she corrected, horrified at her stupidity. Shehnaz was all smiles though.

"Why don't you move forward, in the front line?" she said.

"Second after the heroine. Kamal, you move

to her place in the back row," she ordered the one placed there. Kamal, a regular and a good dancer, was taken aback. God knows whose face she had seen first thing in the morning. Must be that of her drunkard husband.

Priyavardhan was horrified.

"Shehnaz Madam, how can you replace the frontline girl? She was in the camera frame yesterday. That would break the continuity," he argued.

"Arre Priyanji, no one notices these faces. Only the movements are important. This one is younger and a better dancer than Kamal. Leave my job to me Sir," she said. Priyan muttered another Tamil obscenity under his breath and sauntered over to the cameraman to see the frame. Shehnaz was right. The new girl did add that little extra to the dance. He was suddenly worried about the heroine. A poor dancer, Tanu was the heroine just because one of the producer duo Munir-Rehan was really sweet on her. It was also rumoured that Tanu was the squeeze of the narcotics smuggler Baba and the film was being financed by him. Whatever the truth, the fact that she was quite besotted with the hero Akhil Kapoor could not possibly end up well for her given that Munir and Baba were both in the fray as well. Shehnaz had solved the poor dancing skills of Tanu by having her stand and gyrate in the foreground while the background dancers did all the complicated steps. Tanu had nothing much to do in the song except move to the rhythm and the other dancers brought out the energy in the song. The extra movement was provided by the camera cutting in and out in sync with the music on Tanu.

The shot was soon canned - all of 30 seconds and after 13 re-takes, the unit called it a day around 6 PM. Shehnaz got hold of Kaka and told him to ensure that the new girl was there the next day as well. It was a six-minute song and would take at least 5-6 more days to complete. Kaka walked over to Rupali who had now changed back to her jeans and t-shirt. "*Arre baby, tu toh hit ho gayee re,*" he said in his best Rajesh Khanna mannerism. Rupali was delighted at being promoted and favoured on her very first day. She got paid 6,000 rupees for one day's work which wasn't bad at all for beginners. Kaka was pleased that he got to keep a full 20% of that. The additional bonus was for being bumped up to the first row of the dancers.

It was the last day of the shoot. Rupali had ignored all of Kaka's advances during the last three days of the shoot. He had offered to have an evening "chat" with her over a few drinks to plan her career.

"*Heroine bana doonga baby. Mere saath baith,*" was his frequently repeated line.

Rupali by now knew that Kaka was a spent force and no junior artist supplier could dream of breaking into the big leagues. She had met all the junior artists on the film's sets and many of them had been doing the same bit roles for years. These things just didn't happen. She was trying to catch "Priyansir"'s eye throughout these three days. While Shehnaz was chatty with her throughout, Priyavardhan was preoccupied with the shoot and the plan for the wrap. Unknown to Rupali, he had taken a good look at her through the cameraman's lens as well as on the monitor while observing the shoot. With the shoot about to wrap up and him itching to go back to Madras, he didn't give her too much thought. During the lunch break, Priyavardhan suddenly looked up to see Kaka and Rupali sauntering towards him. Rupali gestured Kaka to fall behind her and approached Priyavardhan with a smile. "Sir, a big fan Sir. Grateful for this chance Sir. Would like to offer my gratitude in person Sir," she said in one breath hoping it would stick. Actually, the words were said in Hindi and thus were mostly lost on Priyavardhan but he caught on to the personal thanks bit. In the film business, you don't get to be a 'Priyansir' and not know what that means.

"After 6, in the hero make up room," he said smoothly while pretending to look into the monitor for the shot.

The sex was hurried and messy. Priyavardhan was blowing off steam and finishing his Bollywood tryst. He had seen no action for the last several weeks while on this set as he was too proud to ask for it. In Tollywood and Kollywood, the girls simply offered themselves to him without him having to even seek them out. Ah, the respect and the work culture. Not here though. Madrasis were always going to be outsiders here. Rupali did not let on that this was actually her first time and Priyavardhan did not even notice. It was over in less than five minutes and Priyavardhan grunted his satisfaction to her. "Sir, maybe I can work in your next film," Rupali gathered the courage to ask now that she had expressed her gratitude.

"Yes, yes. Call me after three months," he said without really looking at her.

Rupali came out of the makeup room and felt everyone's eyes on her.

Kamal, the girl who was moved to the back row, commented as she passed her, "so this is the price of the front row." Rupali felt her skin burning. As soon as she came out of the makeup room, she knew that she had made another mistake. It was dumb of her to throw herself at the Madrasi director as he was not coming back to Bollywood anytime soon and least likely to remember her three days later let alone three months from today. Another of life's lessons learnt. Free samples always end up in the gutter.

The next few months went by with nothing happening. On Kaka's advice, she got a portfolio shoot done. The photographer was not very professional but he did a decent job. He offered to do the shoot for free if only they could compromise.

Rupali just stared at him and handed him the cash. Kaka made the rounds of several production houses and studios and other than an odd background dancing or crowd gig could not come up with anything else to Rupali's great disappointment. To make matters worse, word had gotten around that she was an easy lay. This made life difficult for her on the sets as some of the dancers would whisper that with her all one had to do was to ask and she would be willing. Rupali's troubles only worsened with tight money and not much work coming her way. She was soon getting less and less enamoured of this Bollywood dream.

One day, while she was sitting and chatting with Kaka, Dipu, her neighbour who had introduced her to Kaka dropped by. *"Arre Dipu, where have you been bhai? Eid ka chand ho gaya hai re",* Kaka drawled with no particular affection. Dipu was all puffed up with importance. Rupali noticed that he was wearing a clean shirt and a tie as well with nice shoes and a dark trouser. *"Kakaji* I have gotten out of this cesspool. I am now working with Metro Bank in sales. The pay is small but the commissions are very good. My Govinda looks didn't work in films but in the Bank, it is getting me a lot of customers. I am on my way to buy a bike. My boss drives a Honda car and he was in my position just two years ago," said Dipu. Rupali had also noticed that Saroj aunty seemed to be quite pleased with his new activities. Dipu was like her, just 12th pass. Not bad at all. Kaka made a sound to express his disapproval. *"Clerky hi karni thi toh filmi duniya mein kya kar rahe the?"* he asked Dipu wondering aloud how one can switch from performing arts to being a minion just like that.

"Rupali, why don't you meet my boss Arvind? The one with the Honda car? I am telling you Metro Bank needs people like you who are smart and good looking and the sky is the limit," Dipu said ignoring Kaka. When Rupali protested that she knew nothing about banking and didn't have a good head for numbers, Dipu pointed out that neither did he. In fact, as Dipu explained, all it needed was for one to be presentable and persistent. The bank did the rest.

That night Rupali couldn't sleep.

Chapter 5

Present day.

The morning hadn't started well for Batty. He had this disturbing dream where he discovered that it was Juggy who had had an affair with Rupali who was a cabaret dancer and Lokhande had actually carried out the murder at his boss's instance. On top of it, for some weird reason the track of the Hindi cabaret song "*Aa jaane jaan*" kept playing in his head all night with Rupali dancing to it bathed in red light. He got up feeling like he had hardly slept. Shaking his head to clear his thoughts, Batty quickly showered and dressed and after his morning camp routine and a quick breakfast, left the camp.

He had thought of putting in a short leave application to his CO but then he had to be sure that he would need the next few days for investigation. Today's events would determine that. He also thought of talking to Juggy about staying with him during his leave. That would be very convenient and save him from having to spend on a hotel. But then he would have to tolerate Juggy and his endless ribbing every evening. That didn't seem like an enjoyable prospect. He sighed inwardly.

Shinde was at his desk going over some photographs. Lokhande was yet to show up at work and when Batty and Robin entered, Shinde looked up and smiled,

"This Rupali was something, huh? I can bet that she could have been in the movies had she tried."

Batty and Robin looked at the photographs of Rupali that Shinde had collected from her wardrobe. A slim, attractive woman very aware of her sexuality stared back at them from the pictures.

"This is Deep," said Shinde pointing to a middle aged man old enough to be Rupali's father or at least uncle in one of the pictures.

He had his arm around her waist in one of the photographs and looked quite like the cat who got the cream.

There were around 100 odd pictures some of them from her school days with her friends, some from the time when she was apparently working early in her career, a couple of pictures in front of a sign that said Metro Bank and one on a film set with the actor Anil Kapoor. Looked like she may have visited a film shoot. There were some pictures of a business party with Deep and a few other people who could not be identified. Batty and Robin could see her transformation from an unsure teenager to a poised and self-assured woman in the pictures. Nothing out of the ordinary, nothing even remotely incriminating. Just the evolution of a woman from a young girl.

Shinde had unlocked her phone with the help of Deep who knew her password. There were more recent pictures of her and Deep and some of her alone but nothing much else. The analysis of WhatsApp chats showed just a couple of chat groups of her school friends from St Joseph school at Vasai, a distant suburb of Mumbai and another group called "JA Group". Most of the chats were birthday wishes, occasional photos of pets, nature, motivational sayings and forwards of jokes and videos. Each group had more than 20 members and these were those mind numbing groups where 15 people posted "good morning" messages and at least 10 people "good night" messages with all kinds of forwards in between. She had last accessed the groups in the morning before her death. Shinde said that her phone had low battery when they got possession of it and was lying next to her body near the pillow. She was apparently one of those who kept the phone next to them when they slept.

Her caller list followed the same prosaic pattern and most of her calls were to or from Deep, Raghu Stores, Living Liquids, Gayatri Medical, someone called Sudesh, someone called Abbas, someone called Devendra and some calls from and to someone just called Doctor. Her message list was full of promotions and stock market related sales pitches. This was too prosaic and it seemed to Robin that her calls and message lists may have been edited. That was hardly an issue since the call list and the message sender and recipient list could be easily obtained from the phone company. Plus, Robin's own considerable talents in this regard would come in very handy. She could retrieve files from even charred hard disks so getting back phone data would not be such a challenge.

Fortunately, this one was an Android - the darling of all the phone hackers everywhere in the world. The iPhones were a little problematic and first had to be jailbroken and then worked on but Androids were easier to hack and there were literally thousands of software apps written for Android hacking and data theft which could be used for recovery as well. Batty had no idea how she did it and Robin never offered any explanations and never revealed her secrets when it came to extracting data from phones, computers and tablets. Batty was clueless and often wondered. He even went to the extent of imagining that she had a network of criminals who seem to do favours for her for free. Batty didn't want to ask her. Better not ask those questions for which one was not ready to hear the answers.

"Hello, hello! Good to see you both first thing in the morning," came Lokhande's voice as he saw them when he entered the Police Station, his tone conveying the exact opposite of his real sentiments.

"What is happening Shinde? " he enquired of his deputy to get a sense of what was going on.

Shinde quickly updated him on the contents of her phone.

"Isn't it strange that she had no messages from anyone else except for stock market tips and other such stuff? People get messages from people all the time. Hers seems to be edited," said Robin to Lokhande. She was not letting go of her suspicion that Rupali's phone seemed to have been wiped clean.

"Arre Madam, simple people lead simple lives. You are trying to find something jabardasti where there is nothing. Look at my phone - except for Rohini, nobody sends me any messages of any importance," he said.

Robin almost blurted out that there was a big difference between leading a simple life and being simple minded but she held back deliberately.

"So basically, looks like stuff has been deleted which could lead us to something," muttered Robin, her suspicion now taking a firm shape.

Batty heard her muttering and was sure that it was only a matter of a few hours before Robin started digging into that phone.

Lokhande busied himself by picking up the file on top of the heap on his desk not wanting to go into this discussion. He briefly wondered if he should step out at lunch time and have the usual pomfret thali at Masoli or for a change try the Chicken Biryani at Good Luck. Maybe the latter. His *dabba* from home was carried in by a constable but he knew better than to think of it as real food.

His planning was interrupted by Batty.

"Lokhandeji, we would like to speak with Dharam right away."

Lokhande gestured to Shinde to grant them access.

Dharam looked the way someone who had been in Police custody for two days was expected to look - visibly distraught and bedraggled. He looked at Batty and Robin with expectant eyes when he narrated his tale of woe. Dharam was employed by Deep when they moved into this apartment a couple of years ago. At that time, they were the first ones to move into their home and it was quite scary as no other apartment was occupied in that building. He was a full time servant and came in early in the morning around 7.30 am and left around 7.30 pm each day. He had his meals in the house and would look after the day to day chores and groceries and consumables in the house.

He had a key to the apartment's outer door with which he let himself in each morning. Often, when he left in the evening, there would be no one at home as both Deep and Rupali were out a lot. He described Rupali as a difficult woman to work for who was hard hearted and tough. In his opinion Deep was more decent of the two. He had no real opinion on how the relationship between the two was as whenever he saw them together, each was doing their own thing. Deep would be reading newspapers and magazines while Rupali would be watching television. Rupali was also more confined to the bedroom as she got up around noon each day and would slowly go about her daily routine and would get ready around 5 PM to go out on most days. There wasn't too much cooking in the house. Deep ate breakfast which was made by Dharam and at most times would go out around 11 am and returned only in the evening or later at the night. Rupali did not have any breakfast given that she surfaced only around noon and would have a basic lunch of dal and rice with an occasional vegetable or chicken or fish curry that Dharam made for her like she had taught him. In the evening, Deep would have the same for dinner. He was never around to see what Rupali did for dinner.

The husband and wife used to eat together earlier when Dharam had just started working for them but over the previous two years, they had begun to maintain separate schedules. They didn't speak much and whenever they did it would be behind closed doors so Dharam never had any real idea of anything. Dharam had been wanting leave for 10 days to visit his family in Munger in Bihar and had made repeated requests to Rupali and Deep for a loan of Rs. 50,000/-. Since his salary was 10,000, he had offered to payback 1,500 each month until his loan was repaid. Rupali had flat out refused and Deep had said that maybe he could think of 25,000/- but even that had not been forthcoming. He was thinking of leaving the job if the loan did not come through as he had to visit his family since he had not gone home for over two years.

With his travel date approaching, he was desperate for money. He was also owed some wages for the current month which he had hoped to get in advance in addition to the loan. Rupali had threatened him with dismissal if he left for Bihar and Dharam was in a really unhappy situation. That day, when he saw Rupali fast asleep when he entered the room after knocking around 7.00 pm, he spied a bundle of new notes in the half open drawer. Having planned to leave the next day for Munger, he helped himself to the cash and left the house. That was all that happened that day according to Dharam.

"Do you normally enter the bedroom without permission?" asked Robin, picking on the one thing that sounded odd in Dharam's story.

"No madam. Rupali madam had told me to knock first and if I do not receive a response, to gently open the door if it is unlocked and then enter. Since I used to do the evening cleaning and she would be sometimes lying down or watching TV on the recliner or be in the bathroom, she had told me the procedure."

"I rarely received any response when I knocked. Usually, when madam did not want me to enter, she would lock the door. At other times, I entered after a gentle knock and often found madam watching TV while on the recliner. Most days, madam wasn't even home. Of late though she had been spending more time at home in the evenings and would sometimes be resting in the evenings. She appeared to be weak and unwell."

Also, of late, Rupali had also started drinking fairly heavily according to Dharam. Earlier, she hardly drank at home. Lately, it had not been unusual for her to start drinking as early as 5 PM and continue until Dharam left and even beyond as he could tell from the alcohol levels in the bottle the next day.

Batty marvelled at how observant servants tend to be. The employers may not think so but servants and employees tend to know exactly what is going on in a home or in an organisation often far more than the employers suspect or think. Nothing escapes their attention.

Dharam admitted his crime of stealing Rupees 25,000 from the drawer but requested Batty and Robin to convince the Police that he had not committed any murder.

"After all, many servants have their grouses against their employers but do they all commit murder? She was not kind hearted, was tight-fisted but then she did not abuse me or harass me. She was a hard task master and would pull me up for sloppy work harshly, but I am not a murderer," he said.

Robin glanced at Batty and motioned for him to step out. "I am more or less convinced that he is speaking the truth, at least most of it. He might have a thing or two to add if quizzed in further detail but this is certainly a dead end," she said. Batty nodded in agreement.

"Lokhandeji, why do you think a servant would murder their employer for ill-treatment if the option to just quit the job is the easier one?" asked Robin.

Lokhande pretended to be engrossed in reading a file. Sighing visibly, he looked up at Batty and Robin.

"Then why don't you tell me Madam, who should I arrest in this case?" he asked his voice laced with sarcasm.

Robin was about to lash out at him for being so obviously stupid but thought better of it. Arguing with idiots had the same effect as spitting at the sky. Your projectile landed back on you sooner or later.

"That is what we are here to find out Lokhandeji and if we work together, we will find the real culprit soon," said Batty ignoring his undertone.

"Arre Shinde, chai lao sahabke liye," Lokhande ordered his underling.

"Shinde, did you call the other numbers of Sudesh and Abbas to see who they are?" asked

Robin while sipping the extra sweet police station staple tea served in chai glasses.

Batty did not touch his glass while Lokhande seemed to be enjoying his.

"Yes I did. Sudesh's phone was only ringing - I called 3-4 times. Abbas's phone is out of coverage area. I will try again tomorrow," he replied.

Lokhande reflected on his predicament briefly. That reporter was right. It was very unlikely that the servant would have committed the murder. But then, as chief investigating officer, he needed to have an alternate hypothesis quickly in place otherwise his boss would pull him up for not doing his job. He cursed his luck and then quickly took Shinde aside.

"Who do you think it is? " he asked Shinde.

Then without waiting for his response he ordered, "bring her husband in for questioning..." and Shinde rushed out to bring Deep.

Batty was bewildered at this sudden turn of events. Robin was fairly conversant with basic Marathi and she updated him on what Lokhande was trying to do.

"Wow - he is actually calling the husband now after all this time has passed!" Batty said.

"I guess it is morning when you wake up," joked Robin.

Lokhande overheard their conversation and

bristled.

"Sir, I am only doing my job. I have to grab the next suspect immediately otherwise he will flee. If not the servant, the husband must have done it." he said with an air of finality.

Batty and Robin looked at each other with an air of incredulity. Clearly Lokhande hadn't registered any of their sarcasm at all.

"Did Vinay call?", asked Robin referring to the professor.

"Not yet, but why don't you chase him," said Batty.

As the good professor had indicated, his cell phone just rang endlessly. Suddenly recalling their conversation, Robin then tried his office line. After a brief pause, Professor Shahastrabuddhe came on the line.

"Yes my dear, how can I help you?"

"Was wondering if you have something for me?" asked Robin.

"My apologies, but I have not forgotten. I have had a string of urgent cases. It seems the city is seeing a sudden spurt in unnatural deaths. Most are routine though. I think I will go back to our case in a couple of days. I will call you once I have some answers for you," he said.

Deep was brought in by Shinde just when Robin had finished a lengthy discussion with

Lokhande on the merits of Bengali cuisine versus Maharashtrian cuisine. Batty chose to check his messages on his phone rather than participate in the discussion. Lokhande believed he had successfully proven that Maharashtrian cuisine was far superior and had better flavours than Bengali cuisine. Robin tried in vain to convince him that the food of each region was a function of what was available in abundance and the composition of its population. It was a pointless discussion but Batty was thankful that Robin was humouring Lokhande as he did not want him to feel that just because he knew his boss, Lokhande was dispensable. Better not to make an enemy out of a fool. That would be most unwise.

Lokhande greeted Deep in his usual Police manner.

"Murder karke servant ko phasata hai kya re? Lockup mein dekhta hun tereko" he opened with a bang.

Deep was stunned with the full-frontal attack as he was now being taken in as a key suspect.

"Sahab bahut gusse mein hain," Shinde intoned.

Not knowing how to react, Deep just collapsed in the chair in front of Lokhande's desk.

"Lokhandeji, should I just chat with him for a while?" asked Batty hoping to put Deep at ease which would facilitate a proper conversation and investigation.

No point having a key person connected to the victim scared out of his wits. A lot of small details get obfuscated once fear takes over.

"Ok with me but once you are done, he is all mine. I will question him properly at night," said Lokhande.

Sensing a kinder approach, Deep turned towards Batty. He spoke at length about him and Rupali. Apparently, Rupali was a very good and caring person who had virtually no enemies. In fact, they were stressed about her not conceiving for the last two years. He also went into great detail about how he had recommended a very capable city gynaecologist, Dr. Mukesh Manohar for her and she used to consult him regularly. She was undergoing his treatment to help her conceive quickly. He had no knowledge of how anyone could have any motive to murder Rupali and why would anyone even consider doing that? According to Deep, their little world was idyllic and there were no bad elements anywhere. Batty patiently heard him out.

"How did you guys meet? She was much younger to you, yes? By what - about 20 years? Was it an arranged marriage?" asked Robin, always interested in human relationship dynamics.

"I had met Rupali when I was working with a stock broking firm as head of key client accounts. I met her quite by chance when my boss introduced me and over time, she started to consult me on her business matters. I was impressed with her business acumen and I think she was also equally impressed with my insights and experience," he said.

Robin noticed that it must have helped that Deep was the embodiment of a good looking, though older, financial markets professional with impeccable sense of dressing and highly finessed speech.

"She often teased me and called me Shashi Kapoor and I was head over heels smitten by her I confess," he said.

Pretty much inevitable, thought Robin. Throw in two highly combustible elements united by a catalyst and watch the chemistry.

"When Rupali found out that I was divorced, slowly our friendship turned into a relationship and I then proposed marriage and she acquiesced. We bought this apartment and moved in as the building was getting delayed but we were in a hurry to start our lives together. After marriage, Rupali sold her business and I also took an early retirement from work. We were comfortable and though money was not unlimited, we did not need to really earn a living and could live reasonably well," he completed.

"Your servant claims that of late Rupali was depressed and prone to drinking. He also claimed that she was unwell and weak," Batty said.

"Rupali was depressed as she was unable to conceive and being a touchy subject, we did not talk much of late as she had become very moody. I believed that this was due to the stress of not conceiving as well as the side effects of the medication she was on and not wanting to disturb or upset her, I more or less kept to myself and did not speak unless spoken to," Deep said.

"And pardon me for asking this but how was the intimacy in your marriage?" asked Robin.

Deep hesitated and looked at Batty as if to ask if he really needed to answer this. When he got no support from Batty and also noticed that Lokhande and Shinde were also keenly following his answers, he decided to be forthright about it. He turned to Batty and said,

"We had very good intimacy. After all we were trying to have a baby and I believed that with good frequency, conception would just be around the corner."

"Did you guys fight often?" asked Robin.

"No Madam. Apart from conception, there were no other issues between us and things were normal like any other couple. She had, of late, taken to drinking. And, I thought if alcohol gave Rupali relief... although it was not advised as it could interfere with conception, I understood that this was her way of coping with it and even when she would have 4-5 drinks every night before going to bed, I never objected. I wanted her to be happy. In the recent past, she was more and more withdrawn and sometimes when I came home a little late, she would be asleep or lying down on the bed trying to sleep," he said.

"Who could it possibly be Sir? Do you suspect anyone yet? I know that you have taken Dharam into custody and while I don't know him that well since he has been with us for just two years but it does not seem that he would do it, Sir. This seems to be someone with a revenge motive Sir," Deep said to Batty, changing track and trying to get some answers.

"We fully suspect you *harami,* just wait, let these good people go. In two hours you will confess," sputtered Lokhande.

"Why will I kill my wife Sir? We were trying to have a baby. I loved her. All we wanted was to start a family Sir," Deep pleaded with Batty not daring to look at Lokhande.

"That is why we have Police in this world *labadya,*" said Lokhande with supreme confidence. "They all come here saying they are innocent. We get the truth out of them eventually."

Leaving Lokhande to his devices, Batty and Robin left the Police Station and headed to a nearby bar to recap. Just as they were about to enter, Batty froze. Lurking near the entrance and threatening to cross his path was a black cat that was looking at him with a great deal of interest. Batty tried to determine the relative speed of the cat crossing his path and him entering the bar and in his head projected a course. He was unsure whether he could make it without encountering the cat. Robin, aware of his mild ailurophobia, came to his rescue and shooed the cat away.

Once they were seated inside, she said, "with no murder weapon, how are we ever going to get a breakthrough in this case Batty?"

Munching on popcorn, Batty said quietly, "But we already have our first piece of the puzzle that does not fit."

Robin looked at him quizzically and suddenly exclaimed as it struck her, "Oh yes! the birth control pills! Why would Rupali be taking birth control pills if they were trying to have a baby?"

The answer was clear to them both. *Because she did not want to conceive.*

"But then she did keep up the Doctor visits all the time though - was it just to please Deep? Or was there something else? But why was Rupali against having Deep's child? Her worsening health? What was she hiding?" asked Robin in a staccato.

"You have pretty much laid out what we need to know. That only Rupali can tell us; or her Doctor. Time to meet the Doctor," said Batty.

Chapter 6

The Doctor turned out to be Doctor Mukesh Manohar, the city's leading and most respected gynaecologist. Chatting with the receptionist, Mrs. Bharucha, a 60 year old Parsi lady, prior to Dr. Manohar's arrival, Robin found out that Dr. Manohar was single and had never married. He was also the only son of a successful businessman who refused to join his father's business and sought a career in medicine instead to his father's great chagrin. The business was sold after his father's untimely death and upon the death of his mother a few years ago, Dr. Manohar had inherited the entire wealth and all the properties as well as other assets. With properties in Pune, Alibaug and Mumbai, Dr. Manohar was among the Pune upper crust and counted among his patients the ladies of the industrial houses of Bajaj, Firodia and Kirloskar - the Pune business elite. Once more Batty marvelled at how Robin's journalistic talents could elicit information from normally reticent people.

Doctor Manohar ran his hand through his hair and tried to settle his appearance. He had just got into his clinic and was surprised to find two unusual patients sitting in the waiting area chatting up his receptionist. Dr. Manohar's clinic was in Koregaon Park, a tony area of Pune made famous by the Rajneesh Ashram and the stories of free love and freer drugs that did the rounds of Pune's society circles in the early 1980s. The Ashram was still there but after Osho's death, Puneites had all but forgotten about the place and there was nothing interesting about the politicking that went on among Osho's disciples. For Indians used to the daily shenanigans of their colourful politicians, Osho's Ashram and its goings-on were of not much interest any more. Dr. Manohar's clinic reflected his status. With original artworks on its walls and tastefully furnished, the clinic belonged to a man who was used to wealth and not afraid to demonstrate it in an old money way.

The morning papers that day were agog with the sensational murder of a beautiful woman and Rupali's picture was in each and every one. Pune Times had the best coverage thanks to Robin's reporting but Robin had been careful not to advance any theories lest it jeopardise their investigation. Since Rupali was Dr. Manohar's patient, Batty and Robin were keen to see his reaction and what information he would volunteer. They entered his consulting chamber and were struck with how different it looked from the usual doctors' consulting rooms. There was a beautiful oil painting depicting Krishna playing his flute and his cows grazing around him and a long side table. Batty's keen eyes identified the painting as a Manjit Bawa and he noticed that on the long side table was a veritable display of old surgical instruments in the open. The Doctor was clearly a collector of the tools of his trade.

Batty and Robin were struck by how much Dr. Manohar epitomised the "Good Doctor" sobriquet. In his late forties or early fifties with a full head of salt and pepper hair and distinguished old-money looks, the doctor inspired immediate confidence. Dr. Manohar was pleased to confirm that the painting was indeed a Manjit Bawa and those were indeed instruments used by Doctors and Surgeons in the yesteryears which could now be called implements due to their crude nature. Batty remarked that these seemed ready to use and the Doctor proudly told him how he maintained all the old tools to their maximum potential though clearly these were more than a 100 years old and would be laughed at today.

On the subject matter of the murder of Rupali, his first reaction was surprise and a slight hostility as he did not consider Batty and Robin officially empowered to meet him and ask him questions about his patients. In any case, unless it was a criminal investigation, he was not required to volunteer details of his patients. Since he dealt with the cream of the society, it was even less likely that he would be willing to speak about his patients. Apart from a few well-connected Doctors like Dr. Manohar, the principle of patient confidentiality was mostly unknown in India and most Doctors would happily chat about other patients' illnesses with sometimes friends of those patients or even unrelated people. It took a phone call to Juggy from Batty to get the Good Doctor to start talking about Rupali.

The Good Doctor then recalled clearly that Rupali had been coming to him for consultation as she was having difficulty in conceiving. She used to come often with her husband Deep and sometimes by herself. On her last visit just barely less than a week ago, she had come in with Deep. He was saddened by the murder of Rupali who he described as someone with incredible *joie-de-vivre* and a wonderful woman.

"She was so full of life. It's a pity. Any idea who would have done it? Multiple stabs seems to indicate motive, no? " he asked.

Batty informed him that the police were trying to pin it on the domestic help but it seemed improbable and hence they had stepped in on behalf of Juggy to lend a helping hand.

"Have you done something like this before Major? After all, being in the Army does not lend itself to sleuthing, does it?" asked Dr. Manohar.

Robin reminded him of couple of cases in the last two years that were sensational which had been solved by her and Batty.

"Ah, the Koregaon Park murder case...right in my backyard," mused the Good Doctor. "I had no idea it required your inputs. How very interesting. You two make a great team," he said. "Pardon my lack of investigating experience but doesn't look like the domestic help may have been responsible here," offered the Doctor.

The Good Doctor did not volunteer any other theory though.

"Thank you Doctor, we will see you again soon, once we have further updates," Batty said not wanting to reveal more at this stage until he was ready for him.

"You should have asked him about the contraceptive pills, why didn't you?" asked Robin once they were out of the clinic.

"He is not going anywhere and we still don't have enough information on this case. We should do it when we are prepared enough," said Batty.

"The Rupali this Doctor described does not seem to be the same Rupali that the servant was describing. Did the Doctor not notice the change? And I don't understand why would she take contraceptive pills while taking fertility treatment?" asked Robin.

"All in good time, Robin," he said. "There are still several things to look at. Let's park this for the time being."

A quick call to the Deccan Police Station told him that forensics had finished their job and nothing noteworthy had been found out of the ordinary. The blood was Rupali's and there were Rupali's, Deep's and Dharam's finger prints all over the house. There was no other print. Deep had been allowed to move back to the apartment now, since the examination was over and all the relevant material was in police possession.

Rajan Shinde informed them that Abbas's number featured in Rupali as well as Deep's caller list. While Rupali had received several calls and missed calls from Abbas's number, Deep's phone showed incoming as well as outgoing calls to Abbas. The most recent call from Abbas was to Deep on the evening of the murder. Deep had also called Abbas around the same time as the murder. There were no calls on either Rupali or Deep's phones after the murder. Shinde found this highly curious as the murder was now public knowledge and if Abbas was someone known to the couple, Deep should have got a call. On the other hand, Abbas's number was continuously not reachable so maybe it was out of range because Abbas may have been travelling. That would explain the lack of phone contact as per Shinde.

Meanwhile Sudesh's phone, after having rung quite a few times, was finally picked up by a woman who identified herself as his ex-wife and informed Shinde that Sudesh had died on the day of the murder in his sleep, possibly by way of a heart attack. Since Sudesh had no children and there being no hint of a foul play, the body was cremated and there was a prayer session held by his ex-wife which is why the phone went unanswered for a long time. Shinde had already asked her to come to the Police Station and bring Sudesh's phone as well. She was on her way to the Deccan Police Station.

Vimla was a self-assured, wealthy looking woman in her late 50s. They had had an arranged marriage. Sudesh owned Morningstar Securities, a city based stock brokerage and financial services company that had the city's top high net worth individuals as clients. Business was good and Sudesh was quite well known in the city and enjoyed a good reputation and loyal clientele. Sudesh and she had divorced seven years back after 20 years of marriage by mutual consent. The reason she gave for the divorce was irreconcilable differences. Sudesh had high blood pressure and was under some financial stress due to his business and the state of the financial markets. The domestic help had found Sudesh dead in his sleep late in the morning when she came in for cleaning and immediately called Vimla.

"Aey Madam, humko summary nahin chalega. We want to know everything ok? Murder case hai," Lokhande said in a raised voice.

Lokhande's raised voice had the desired effect. Vimla launched into her story immediately. Apparently, a few years ago, Sudesh had made some errors of judgement and got involved with a company which went bankrupt. There were allegations of fraud against the company owners and Sudesh, being a part of the company, suffered heavy losses as well as client desertion as the company's troubles started creating ripple effects in Pune's investor and financial circles. This lead to the closure of his business and also frequent fights between him and Vimla as she blamed him for being reckless. These arguments led to huge fights and she had left the house and shifted to her parents' apartment in the city. The following year, Sudesh filed for divorce and she did not contest it.

"What was your husband's connection with Rupali? We found records of calls between them and several text messages that seemed to have been deleted on Rupali's phone?" asked Shinde.

Vimla's face showed no emotion except for a little flaring up and reddening of her nostrils. Lokhande was looking bored but Robin caught the slight discomfiture. She replied that Sudesh, Deep and Rupali knew each other and were directors in one company that had gone bankrupt a few years ago. Deep was Sudesh's ex-employee and Sudesh was a Director of that company. Vimla was certain that ever since that company was formed, Sudesh's downfall had started.

On a whim, Batty asked, "Do you know Abbas?" Vimla nodded and said Abbas and Rupali were the original partners in that company and Deep had joined them later and Sudesh had supported the venture.

"Do you recall the name of the company

Madam?" asked Robin.

It was India Biofuels.

Robin let out a low whistle. Batty looked at her quizzically and said, "Does this ring a bell?"

"Alarm bells, actually," said Robin.

India Biofuels had been a hot topic a few years back. The company had raised money from a lot of city based wealthy investors for farming of the Jatropha Curcas plant which it claimed could be used to derive bio-diesel which being half the cost of diesel would enrich the company and its investors. Jatropha Curcas was a plant that grew in the wastelands and the President of India at that time, Dr. Abdul Kalam, was a big supporter of Jatropha cultivation and use for bio-diesel which lent the entire venture some legitimacy. The company claimed to have proprietary technology for bio-diesel extraction that promised better yields than all known competitors. The investors had been promised very high returns from the third year of the investment. Something went wrong at the company and the promised returns on investment failed to materialise. Some of the investors complained to the Economic Offences Wing of the Pune Police and one of the directors who was the main scientific brain was arrested on charges of fraud. The case made headlines every few days for a while and then media interest died down. Apparently, the EOW was still investigating the case evidence for fraud and the director who was arrested was released on bail but his passport was impounded.

A simple search and a company filings investigation by Robin listed all the directors of the company - Rupali, Deep, Sudesh and Abbas, the man who was arrested and released on bail.

"What is all this got to do with this case Sir?", Lokhande asked Batty.

"*Ugach complication kartait.* Rupali has died of stabbing - if you don't think it is the servant, I am telling you it is the husband. Are we now saying that some investor stabbed her seven years after he lost money in the company?" he said sarcastically.

"Maybe," said Robin.

He longed to get off this case which was practically solved by him at the first instance until these two had appeared and made it complicated. Now all these stories made his head spin. He was quite sure that this case will be unsolved in his lifetime.

"We are thinking as if Rupali was the kingpin of this entire money losing racket and someone killed her out of grudge. Even for you both Sir this seems really farfetched," he protested.

Must ask for a transfer outside Pune. At least I will get rid of these pests. This was the fourth time in the last two years these two had descended on him in a seemingly straight forward case and destroyed his entire theory. They finally nabbed the main culprit and while it was brilliant work which he grudgingly admitted to himself he was sure he would have got on the same trail of thought sooner or later anyway. And how much stress they had created? In the last case of the Koregaon Murders, they had given him sleepless nights and palpitations. Towards the end, he had even lost his appetite and for the first time in his life had decided to skip a meal! Lokhande mused unhappily.

Batty ignored him and was already dialling Juggy.

"Need to meet, Juggy. A new angle in the case has opened up," he said.

"Same place, same time? And bring your lady friend along. Haven't seen her for a long time," Juggy said.

While Shinde got busy investigating Sudesh's phone, Batty and Robin left for Poona Club to join Juggy for a sundowner. On the way, Robin said, "Vimla was not being forthright. She is not telling us something. At the mention of Rupali's relationship with her husband, her nostrils flared up a bit. If I know women, this is clearly a tell."

Batty appreciated Robin's keen observation, "Why don't we pay her another visit soon and then you can have the pleasure of getting it out of her yourself?"

Robin grinned at the thought and braced herself in anticipation.

"Hello Bartaman and Ms. Chaudhury," Juggy

said extending his hand.

"So what brings you both here? Ms. Chaudhury you seem to have put on a little weight since I last saw you and must say it suits you rather well," Juggy observed.

Batty mentally prepared himself for a long pantomime where at first pleasantries were exchanged, drinks were ordered, current state of affairs in the city, state and nation was discussed, and only once the drinks were served, the real business at hand was taken up.

Juggy took a long sip of his scotch and lit up a cigarette. Batty was holding his old-fashioned without drinking it and Robin gulped down a large part of her vodka-redbull-soda combination.

"I need you to find me the name of the officer who was investigating the Jatropha case of India Biofuels about 5-6 years back," Batty said without preamble.

Juggy lifted an eyebrow.

"It is a long story but all the people known to be connected to Rupali seem to be involved in a common situation a few years ago," Batty explained.

Juggy made a couple of calls.

"It was Prabhu More, DCP. I believe he is now with local arms," Juggy informed them.

Local arms, which was nothing but a store

of weapons, was mostly a punishment posting for officers that had a poor record or were involved in some scandal which remained unproved. Usually, a superior's assessment of their incompetence was enough to put their careers in cold storage for a couple of years.

"Could we know why he was assigned to local arms?" asked Batty.

"Let me check and come back to you on that. Should not be too difficult," said Juggy.

Batty lay down in his quarters and reflected on the events of the day. Sudesh's dying on the same day as Rupali's murder was decidedly odd; too much of a co-incidence here. Could also be a random occurrence but he was getting a strong feeling that somehow a break-through in the case would come from the India Biofuels mess. Was there something between Rupali and Sudesh? Now that he had all the players linked together, there would be insights that had to have some bearing on the case. Where the hell was Abbas?

Chapter 7

Bartaman Bhowmick woke himself up at 5.30 AM, showered and shaved for his routine drill and other army activities and joined his fellow officers for breakfast. He was getting more and more certain that he would need to take some time off his army duties if he were to pursue this investigation in all seriousness. He made an appointment to see Colonel Bipin Bakshi, the superior of his immediate superior, who was fond of his sleuthing skills. In his entire unit, he confided in and discussed his sleuthing work with only Col. Bakshi. The colonel's interest in Batty was more professional than personal.

Batty's sleuthing skills could be best utilised by the Army in the Signal Corps in cryptography. He had tried to motivate Batty to join the Signal Corps as a lateral move and had offered to recommend him for a short course in electronic warfare at the Military College of Telecommunication Engineering, at Mhow near Indore. Batty was also seriously interested in pursuing it but his inertia and the fact that Pune felt like a second home to him kept him from plunging headlong in that direction.

Col. Bakshi looked up as Batty entered his office and saluted smartly. Having encountered no cats on the way, Batty was already in great spirits. He greeted Batty with a bright sunny smile.

"Major Bhowmick, what a pleasant surprise!" he said. Col. Bakshi was almost certain that Batty had dropped in to seek a favour, which he had been doing once in a while in the last two years at the Southern Command in Pune. However, he hoped that this time, Batty was seeing him for professional reasons. Batty knew what the Colonel was hoping to hear and started with the topic that was uppermost in the Colonel's mind.

"I have decided to seriously think about joining the Signal Corps. Like you had mentioned the last time we talked, maybe a short course at the Mhow College would be the starting point after all," Batty said.

"But that is not what brings you here today, is it?" asked the Colonel appreciating Batty's tact and thoughtfulness.

"In fact Sir I would like to take a week or so of leave, so that I can read up some books on cryptography and electronic warfare and study some material as well, before I seek your intervention for admission to Mhow," Batty said. "Also, since an interesting murder case has come my way, it would be a fantastic opportunity to take some time off and do justice to both if I may Sir," he continued.

"Another murder case? This is your fourth in the last two years Major. And what is so special about it?" he asked.

"Sir, so far nothing special but just a strong feeling. There seems to be almost no known motive for this murder. The police are trying to close this case quickly by pinning it on the household help but the brutality and the peculiar manner in which this case is unfolding makes me think that I need to get in a little more deeply and ensure that the culprits do not get away Sir," he said.

"I appreciate your commitment to bring perpetrators to justice. Wish you would apply the same to your career in the Army Bartaman," intoned Col. Bakshi.

"Sir I promise you I will not take up another case until I have applied to Mhow and taken concrete steps in the direction of joining Signal Corps. I need a week or maybe 10 days on the outer side," said Batty.

"How much leave do you have in balance?" Col. Bakshi asked.

"Sir, I've only taken Casual leave in the last one year and I don't want to utilise my annual leave for this purpose. I can avail of furlough leave of which I have almost 50 days left in my three-year cycle. I would like to use 15 days out of that balance Sir," Batty said.

"You are of course aware that furlough leave is at half-pay, right?" asked Col. Bakshi.

Batty nodded in response.

"All right then. But you need to check-in with me every three or four days and update me on the progress of the case and your studies as well," said Col. Bakshi.

"Sir, I will report to you twice a week," agreed Batty. Col. Bakshi wished him "happy hunting" and sent him off.

In his quarters, Batty quickly packed his suitcase with all the essentials and left the cantonment area. He went straight to Juggy's house. Juggy's wife Sushma was pleased to see him and made him a cup of tea and offered him some hot parathas which Batty smilingly declined. This was the flip side of staying with Juggy. Sushma, a fantastic cook and a very keen host, made it her mission in life to feed all her guests four times a day until they could eat no more. Batty was not new to her hosting skills and knew how to avoid getting overfed without offending her.

"Arre Bhabhi, just had a huge Army breakfast after my morning drill. Nothing will budge in the stomach until lunch time. No point wasting your masterpieces on a full stomach. I am here for another 10 days at least and looking forward to having your delicious cooking," he flattered her.

Sushma was pleased and soon got busy instructing the cook for lunch. Batty dialled Juggy.

"In your house Juggy and staying until this is done," he declared.

Juggy teased him, "Arre on the one hand I give you something worthwhile to do and then I have to bear the cost of that as well?"

Batty laughed and said he would see him at dinner.

After a relaxed lunch, over which Sushma tried to interest Batty in several of the "perfect" matches for matrimony for him in her opinion, Batty set out to meet Deep along with Robin.

Deep Kalra looked like he hadn't slept in three days. He didn't seem to have shaved either. His eyes were bloodshot and there was a slight smell of alcohol in his breath. To Batty, it did not look like grief. It was something else entirely. Fear? He couldn't be sure. Batty came straight to the point.

"We know about India Biofuels and how you and Abbas swindled all these investors. You made your wife a partner in such an enterprise and gave her a bad name as well. When did you decide to silence her?" wagered Batty.

Deep's haggard face bore a shocked expression. Slowly, the shock on his face turned into indignation.

"How dare you accuse me of any wrongdoing? I am the victim here. It wasn't me who started this company. I was the distributor who brought in people's money into this company. I had to resign from the company because of this. I am the victim here I am telling you. You guys have got it completely backward," he screamed.

Robin persisted with Batty's gambit and said, "Sudesh's wife was very clear that it was you and Abbas who had set up this company. She did not even name Rupali. She said you and Abbas destroyed Sudesh's reputation and business."

"She is talking nonsense. How will she know? *Arre you didn't know Rupali.* I am telling you once again I am the victim here," said Deep.

As an afterthought, he added, "Poor Rupali was swindled. She had told me later that it was Abbas's idea and she had trusted Abbas blindly. Anyway, it is all in the past now and all I know is that the woman I loved is dead and I have lost everything. Everything."

Later, once Deep was calmer, he went over the entire chronology of events. He had first met Rupali when Sudesh had introduced Rupali and Abbas to him as budding entrepreneurs. Abbas was the scientist who had developed a more efficient process to extract bio-diesel from Jatropha plants. He had all these studies and test certificates. They needed to raise 100 crores and Deep was asked by Sudesh to help them. Sudesh was Deep's boss and he handled all the top client relationships for Morningstar.

"Abbas was so convincing and Rupali was so earnest that I got convinced. We couldn't raise all the money but I remember we raised more than 50 crores for them to get into business. They said this was enough and they would borrow the rest. Somehow, they made some bad land investments and the money was lost and the company had to be shut down," he said.

"There was this EOW case where Abbas was arrested and later released on bail? What was the nature of the fraud?" asked Robin.

"You know how investors are. Never like to lose money. All of these investors were wealthy and connected. Someone must have complained. We were all called for questioning numerous times. The company papers were scrutinised. Somewhere I think they found that Abbas had forged the test reports and the scientific papers on which basis the money was raised. Abbas got bail but the matter is still in courts. Abbas's lawyers are fighting it out in the courts. The EOW charge-sheeted Abbas and absolved all of us of any charges," Deep said.

"DCP Prabhu More was the investigating officer, yes?" asked Robin.

"I am not sure. Maybe as that name does ring a bell but it was so many years ago, like 7-8 years I think," said Deep.

Batty and Robin quickly converged at the nearest watering hole to discuss what they had so far witnessed. *Was there fear on Deep's face? Was Deep's shock an involuntary reaction to the accusation of murder? Where was Abbas? Exactly how complicit was Rupali? What the hell was going on here?*

Chapter 8

1997-98

Metro Bank was a new bank among a plethora of Indian Banks that had started in the late nineties when the Reserve Bank of India allowed the issuance of new banking licenses. Before this, the Indian Banking system was dominated by public sector Banks all of which had a few things in common - a firm belief that the customer was the most inconvenient and the least welcome person in a bank's premises, loans were a huge favour to be given only to those who had the ability to chase the bank officials endlessly even after greasing palms and anything that the customer wanted including updating their bank passbooks took several hours if not days. Over-invoicing of asset purchase and siphoning of funds after borrowing from the banks was rampant. In this environment, new professionally run banks like Metro Bank were a whiff of fresh air. They made customer service with a smile their motto and chased customers for business. It was an amazing new world indeed for the India in the late nineties.

Dipu took Rupali to meet his boss Arvind Nair, the Sales Head for Mumbai's Western suburbs. Arvind sat at Metro Bank's Kandivali Branch since the Bank had just opened its first suburban branch there. Kandivali was a prosperous suburb of Mumbai that is to say it was richer than Vasai but obviously not in the league of South Mumbai or even close to its suburban alter-ego Juhu. Mostly traders and professionals at the beginning of their career or whose careers were dwarfed stayed in Kandivali as also factory owners who could afford a better location but wanted to stay within decent commuting distance of their factory or office. M.G. Road, where the branch was located, was a broad winding road which saw heavy traffic in the mornings and evenings but was mostly quiet during the day time when all the men went to work.

This morning, Arvind Nair immediately wished he had worn his new white shirt and the new expensive Satya Paul tie that his wife had gifted him on his birthday. Thankfully, half of his hair was still on his head and he always carefully combed one side of his hair over to the opposite side to create an illusion of having a full head of hair from the front. A common trick among the balding men in India before bald became beautiful, this feat involved growing one's hair on one side of the head to an absurd length just so that it could be combed across to cover the bald patch in the front. Just like those who wear a cheap wig and expect the world not to notice, the wearer of this creation stepped out with great confidence totally ignorant of the sniggers of those who were subjected to this vision. Presently, Arvind Nair drew to his full height of 5 feet 3 inches, sucked in his abdomen and tried to look aloof and professional in front of Dipu and the stunning girl that was with him.

"Sir, this is my friend Rupali. She is very smart and talented. I have brought her to be a marketing agent for the Bank," said Dipu.

Arvind looked at Rupali with perfunctory interest outwardly, doing his best to suppress the stirrings within. After a few official questions, he asked her to attend a two-day training course conducted by the Bank for new recruits.

"Does this mean I am selected?" asked Rupali in genuine surprise.

"Selected to be on probation for three months. Don't raise your hopes. The Bank only hires the best and it is a tough job with targets. If you fail, your probation will not convert into a permanent job and you will be terminated," he said with as much sternness he could muster. *Better have her think that Nair Sir is a tough guy who is hard to please. Will of course give her enough options to please me later, he thought gleefully.*

"Don't worry Sir, I will not fail and you will be happy to promote me Sir I promise you," said Rupali with the confidence of someone who knew how to use her charm to its best effect.

Most of Rupali's work in the Bank involved prospecting for new customers to open bank accounts and deposit money into the Bank. Add-on offerings like debit/ATM and credit cards and safe deposit lockers were all the rage in the late 90s. India had just discovered consumerism and the Indian customer, now willing to spend, was fed up of the public sector banking system's indifference and ill-treatment. The new private banks stepped right into this void. Soon, Indians started getting calls to open bank accounts, avail of safe deposit lockers and so on - things which took several visits to the bank or waiting for several years started to happen from the comfort of their home as the bank representatives came home with all the paperwork to get a bank account opened.

Rupali quickly got into the groove. Initially, the work was fun. She was able to convert a lot of the client visits into business for the bank. Her attractive personality was now further embellished by a way with words that made people comfortable dealing with her and made them trust her implicitly. It was the Bollywood experience that had taught her the gift of the gab. *Bolbachan Amitabh Bachchan* was a common saying in the junior artist circles referring to those who could talk their way through to work and better opportunities than most of the others. Rupali had seen it work first hand when she smoothly told Priyavardhan that she could sleep with him if he wanted. Even though it did not translate into gains for her, she had figured out how to convey delicate things to her advantage. Over time, she had gotten better at it.

Six months into the job, Rupali had seen it all. She was even promoted to group leader for her area which now stretched from Malad West, an adjoining suburb on the northern side, to Kandivali West but left out rest of Kandivali. The Bank was doing its best to attract customers from neighbouring suburbs to increase the business. Rupali was easily one of the Bank's best performers for the Mumbai Western Suburbs region. But she also realised that her lack of a college degree meant that she had more or less reached where she could in such an environment. Money was alright but nothing great and work was intense with long hours. On top of that, Arvind Nair's constant advances were getting irritating even though she easily fobbed these off with charm and style.

Rupali had no qualms about trading sex for personal gain but she just couldn't, for the life of her, figure out what Arvind Nair could do for her that she couldn't anyway do for herself. Her performance forced him to promote her and her lack of education meant that he could do no more even if he wanted to. Arvind kept on propositioning her every time they were alone in his glass cabin. Even though everyone could see what was happening inside, they could not hear what was transpiring. Arvind was smart - he would not say things that she could complain about to anyone. He would often discuss his personal life with her and crib about how his wife ignored him and was forced upon him by his parents; how he was looking for a live wire soul mate; how he and Rupali were kindred souls and so on... in the same vein. He also offered to chart Rupali's career over a drink - one of the most obvious and off-putting of all passes a man can make to a woman and generally made by those who have never wooed a woman in their lives. When a woman hears an invitation to dinner or drink, it translates in her mind to "I want to sleep with you." Unless she shares that sentiment, such a crude invitation will only cement her desire to be as far away from the speaker of these words as possible. In this case though *Rupali had completely misunderstood Arvind.*

Arvind Nair, a commerce graduate from M L Dahanukar College of Malad, came into banking after diverse stints in Logistics, Consumer goods and Office Equipment. He was a salesman in each and every one of his jobs and was quite effective in bringing in new business. His last sale was a Xerox machine to Metro Bank's Central Office for the Vice President's chamber. The VP had taken a liking to him over the transaction, sold him the dream of building Metro Bank all over India and recruited him to head Sales for the Mumbai Western Suburbs which was basically just one branch between Bandra and Borivali - the two ends of Mumbai's western suburbs. It had now been more than three years and Metro Bank had not been able to expand their Mumbai footprint. They had chosen to grow in New Delhi instead and the Northern Operations were booming. In Mumbai, the Bank was facing competition from some of the newer arrivals like ICICI Bank and HDFC Bank which were very aggressive. However, Metro Bank excelled in customer service and its clientele was loyal since its service was one of the best. Lack of growth in his present job had frustrated Arvind but what had really angered him was that despite having done a great job for the Bank, he was sidelined for promotion twice. He should have been the first choice for heading the northern sales but someone put into his Punjabi boss's head that a South-Indian in the North was a liability.

Indians, to the outside world, are one population but the fact is that it is a deeply divided society. People from other regions, languages or cultures are seldom trusted. People from the South of India have a deep mistrust of North Indians and in the same vein Punjabis don't trust the South Indians whom they derogatively call Madrasis and look down upon what they consider as timid souls. Arvind was a Malayalee but that was a minor detail in this entire episode. Everybody south of Maharashtra was a Madrasi. The job had gone to the Sales Head of Mumbai City, a Punjabi whose performance record was not even half as good as Arvind's but his roots were Northern. Arvind's boss had promised him that he would be sent to the South as soon as they expanded there. The Bank was owned by Raja Kapoor and Arvind was sure he had no immediate plans to expand in a region he did not understand with customers whose language and customs he could not fathom. Arvind was in a no-win situation with Metro Bank. He had applied for jobs in newer banks but there had been no response. It was being rumoured that Metro Bank had made huge loans to an industrialist friend of Raja who was now having difficulty repaying the loan. Add to that, one of the Bank's customers turned out to be Sada Pawle, a known gangster who was gunned down that year by the Mumbai Police. He was operating an account with the city branch of the Bank using an alias and a forged identity but the news made headlines. Both these events happened within the space of four months and the Bank's image had taken a severe beating. When a Bank suffers from such reckless lending and careless banking practices, somehow the entire team gets tainted as if such an event was a cumulative fault. No one was thus hiring Arvind Nair.

Sada Pawle's case gave Arvind Nair the germ of an idea. He was good friends with the Bank Manager, Baba Bhosle who had seen his little fiefdom grow beyond his wildest dreams. He had implicit faith in Arvind and his team and the branch had become the entire Bank's largest deposits branch. In the late nineties, interest rates had hit record highs and in the private market, businessmen were borrowing at even 36% interest rates when Bank credit was not available. The Bank, of course, charged between 17 and 19% and the gap was massive. Baba Bhosle was a worried man. His lending activities were not taking off despite such a high demand for funds as his credit team was conservative and except for the incident relating to Raja Kapoor's industrialist friend, most of the Bank's lending was above board. In a masterstroke of manoeuvring, Arvind managed to convince Baba that he and a couple of his top performers be allowed to pitch for lending business to his deposit customers and their contacts which would increase Baba's own stock in the eyes of the Bank's management. Now all he needed was a couple of accomplices who could carry out his plan. Rupali was an obvious choice and he was desperately trying to build a relationship but somehow that idiotic woman did not seem to be interested in talking to him about how to advance her career.

Faheem Sheikh was another of Rupali's colleagues at the Bank. A tall, athletic and good looking Muslim boy from Mahim, Faheem came into banking much the same way Arvind did. A closet artist, Faheem's skill was perfect reproductions of the objects placed before him. His first job was with a printer who did all of the bank's printing and would liaise with the branch for all their stationery requirements. The Bank's printing, apart from letterheads, also pertained to deposit receipts and bank statements for customers. The new banks had done away with passbooks and introduced phone banking as well as relationship banking where a customer could simply call to know his account balance or for any other banking work. Cheques and Cash for deposit were collected by the Bank's agency from the customer's premises and visits to the Branch were discouraged. This allowed the Bank to operate a far larger branch by numbers in the limited physical space it had for its establishment. Faheem's company handled all the printing for the bank in Mumbai and Faheem was the printer's regional sales manager. Arvind had liked Faheem and had offered him a job at the Bank which the youngster immediately accepted.

Arvind and Faheem frequently hung out together after work and often grabbed a couple of beers at Kandivali's famed dance bar Daawat. There, ogling over the female waitresses and the trainee dancers, the two of them would spend a couple of hours before the big spenders hit the bars. The best and most attractive dancers came in after 9 pm. The trainees lorded the stage before that. The early hours in the evening - from 5.30 to 7.30 pm - was the time for the small guys to have a drink at "happy hours" prices and being the only customers at that time, be treated royally. Even the dancers would flirt with them at that time.

On that particular day, they were late. Arvind was already fretting that once the big spenders came in, small fry like them would be ignored. Soon their talk turned to how people made money and how the outside world was rolling in it while people like them were just toiling away for peanuts. Arvind's mood was getting worse as the discussions went on.

By this time, the big spenders had arrived and the top dancers had eyes only for the big spenders. The bar took an entirely different character now. The dancers were stunning, the music had changed to recent hits, money flowed freely and the place took on a life of its own. Suddenly, there was competition among two groups of big spenders over showering money on one of the dancers, a bar favourite who went by the name of Bobby. Clearly used to being a prima donna and all the attention, Bobby used her well filled out body to gyrate to *Saat Samundar Paar, Jumma Chumma de de* and a couple of other hits. The bar erupted with delight. Both Arvind and Faheem saw that the amount of money that was showered over the girls in one hour was more than their salaries for several months. This darkened their already sour mood. To add insult to injury, the bar manager came and requested them to finish their drinks and vacate the table as a group of high spenders were hanging around looking for a table and the bar was quite full. They had, after all, outlived their utility for the bar for the evening!

Just then, the bar announced their headline act for the evening - *a Choli ke peechhe kya hai* dance by their new hot dancer called Kashish. To Bollywood fans in the late nineties, *Choli ke peechhe* was the raunchiest number that would excite a lot of otherwise tame drinkers. Both Arvind and Faheem ordered another beer each to the manager's chagrin and settled down to watch. The dance started with a veiled dancer standing with her back to the audience. As the number gathered pace, Kashish turned and lifted her veil to groan provocatively to the beat of the song. The crowd erupted in response and both Arvind and Faheem choked on their beers in shock and disbelief. *It was Rupali!*

Chapter 9

Bartaman Bhowmick got up with a start. He had dozed off early after a nice dinner of Butter Chicken and Nan. Juggy hadn't come home until the time he had fallen asleep which was around 10 PM. Sushma was hell bent on making Batty's stay memorable. She knew what foods he liked and had laid out a gastronomic timetable for him for the next two weeks. Batty had meekly surrendered to her will.

It was 5 AM and he was wide awake. Lying in bed, he reflected on the various inputs he had received in the course of the last few days. He was now beginning to enjoy himself. Many angles had now opened up for investigation. It sure looked like his two weeks would be indeed be eventful.

After a hearty breakfast of parathas, eggs and tea with Juggy, Batty met Robin on the way and reached the local arms department at Camp at the Pune Police Headquarters. DCP Prabhu More was expecting them courtesy of Juggy's early morning phone call to him. Juggy had also dug up More's background and had found that he had been relegated to local arms division due to the India Biofuels mess. Some very influential people had lost money in the chaos and More was being blamed for a tardy investigation.

Over cups of extra sweet tea, Batty posed him the question.

"*Moreji,* you were in EOW some years ago and probing the India Biofuels case. Can you help us with some recollections of what had transpired then?" he asked.

"That poor woman Rupali was murdered, I saw the reports," he replied.

Prabhu More then got into the details of the case.

"One investor had complained that the company had swindled them of their funds and diverted these for personal gains of the directors. I investigated the entire affair and found that the broker and his employee were blameless as they had no knowledge of the actual working of the company. Some people were not convinced but I stuck to my guns. After all, my first allegiance is to the truth," he said.

If he saw Robin's smirk, he did not react to it. He continued, "As it transpired later, the broker lost his clients and business because of this episode so I was vindicated in my decision later. It was mostly then down to Rupali and Abbas, the scientist whose findings and research were the main attraction for the investors. I interrogated Rupali who then confessed that she had relied entirely on Abbas and she also produced evidence that the entire day to day management of the company was in the hands of Abbas. She also confessed that she had blindly trusted Abbas since he had the technical knowledge and had agreed to invest the company's funds in whatever land that Abbas had selected for the company," he said.

"Don't you think Rupali was involved?" asked Robin. "After all, she could have been the mastermind behind all this."

"That poor woman had no knowledge of business, did not know anything about the project and had been introduced to Abbas by a common friend, and since she knew the broker, had taken the deal to them. Abbas had offered her partnership and she had simply agreed. She also showed me documents of the company which clearly showed that all powers were vested with Abbas including all financial powers, and she was merely a co-signatory to the cheques that Abbas issued for expenses and land purchases. But, as she was a director, I had also included her in the charge sheet but without any serious charges," More said.

"On further enquiries and investigations, I found that the lab certificates had been forged and all the scientific data and research was bogus. Although, I must say, the forgery was artful, but unfortunately for Abbas, I am a very thorough investigator, so he got caught. I charge sheeted him and got him remanded to custody. His lawyers posted bail and the case is still in the courts where I am needed for proceedings every time the date comes up," he concluded.

"Where did the money go?" asked Batty.

"All their land purchases were grossly inflated and apparently Abbas had siphoned off the cash. The lands were useless, the Jatropha crop never yielded anything worthwhile and all the rest of the money was used up in expenses including high salaries to directors," he said.

"Where is this Abbas? We can't seem to reach him," asked Robin.

"Arre, today is his court date. He will be there; he is required to attend as per his bail conditions. The case will come up post lunch. It is before Judge P B Sirdeshmukh. Why don't you guys come to the court in the afternoon? You can get him there," said Prabhu.

Batty chewed on his jowar bhakri at Mathura on Jungli Maharaj road which was quite close to the Pune District and Sessions Court in Shivajinagar while Robin was sipping at her chocolate milk shake which also doubled up as her lunch. When does this woman eat? wondered Batty. He had, except for that day at Shizusan, never seen her eat a hearty meal. Maybe she is one of those who have selective hunger, thought Batty. He knew people from his family, particularly the younger generation, who could devour an entire pizza but if served with regular home fare, would eat a tiny bit with great difficulty. They were usually not hungry unless it was their favourite food. And then, you couldn't stop them.

"Rupali seems to evoke a lot of sympathy and goodwill from all," she said. "Even Prabhu was very sympathetic to her plight," she added.

"Either that or she was an excellent manipulator. Remember, an attractive woman finds eager believers and a good manipulator can always mould her story the way she wants to. We also make the mistake of assuming that the victim, since she has been murdered, was innocent," replied Batty. "It was clearly not a simple domestic help robbery as we know by now. So a lot of passion got aroused in someone that ended up with that person killing her," he said.

"But Prabhu is a seasoned investigator. Why would he not investigate her as well?" Robin objected.

"Is he? You only have his word for it," said Batty, "and remember he is so good that he got sidelined into a punishment posting from EOW to Local Arms."

"In any case, once we get Abbas today, we will know a lot more," said Robin.

"Something tells me Abbas is not going to show up today," Batty said quietly.

Sure enough, Abbas was a no show in the court. A surprised Prabhu More told Batty that this was the very first time Abbas had missed a date in court. His lawyers had cited ill-health, produced a doctor's certificate and sought a later date which was a month away. Batty groaned inwardly, whipped out his cell phone and called Juggy.

"I want a look out notice for Abbas to be sent all over India at the earliest with his picture. He may be absconding," said Batty. Juggy swung into action.

Batty and Robin headed to the Starbucks on Ferguson College Road which the locals referred to as FC Road. Robin wanted to use the free wifi there. The other attraction was the the Mocha Frapuccino which was her perennial favourite Starbucks beverage. She whipped out her MacBook Air and started to google furiously. Just then Batty's phone rang. It was Shinde.

"Sir, Lokhande Sir is on leave for 4 days. He has a family wedding for which he has gone to Kolhapur. In his absence, I am the station in-charge. I was thinking that I should send a police party to Mumbai to ask around Vasai area in Mumbai about Rupali's background and if someone who knew her could shed more light on her," he said.

"What an excellent idea Shinde!" said Batty.

"But sir you know Lokhande Sir - I can do this only if you ask me to as I have received instructions from Lokhandeji to help you as per ACP Sir's instructions. I will do what you ask me to Sir," he said.

Batty grinned at Shinde's chicanery and told him to go ahead and to let him have the search report once the team was back from Vasai.

Robin was getting excited. She had managed to recover a string of text messages from Rupali's phone that were deleted on the phone and a different picture started to emerge.

"I think we are on to something here," she said excitedly.

Batty, always curious about her methods, enquired how she did that.

"I mapped the sender numbers against Deep, Sudesh, Abbas and the Doctor's phone numbers and apart from these, there were several other numbers which I did not recognise. Bulk of the messages were fairly prosaic with nothing out of the ordinary. There were some that stood out. There were several messages to and from a number which were short and pertained only to rendezvous dates and times. This is where it got interesting. *The sender of these messages was Sudesh,"* she said with a hint of triumph in her voice.

"There were other messages that had an urgency in them for a meeting and what was vaguely referred to as settling past issues. *The sender of these was Abbas.*

The last message on her phone was the one she sent out which asked the receiver of the message to come over urgently as she was feeling very unwell and needed to see that person at once since it was an emergency. *This message was sent by Rupali to Doctor Mukesh Manohar,"* she finished with a flourish.

Batty stared at her. Slowly she nodded.

Rupali apparently met Sudesh often. Abbas had tried to reach out to her to settle something. And she had called Doctor Manohar urgently. Something the good doctor never mentioned.

Vimla Mittal was surprised to find Batty and Robin at her doorstep. She had since moved into Sudesh's now empty flat.

"I have told you everything I know," she said with more than a touch of mild irritation in her voice.

"You did not tell us Madam that your husband was having an affair with Rupali," said Robin plainly, deciding to call her bluff and relishing the moment, though not obviously.

The statement hit Vimla like a bolt of lightning and drove all the wind out of her sails. She was suddenly diffident and she physically deflated in front of their eyes. Her face contorted with a mixture of anger, resentment and sadness. Out came a flood of outpouring.

"She was the reason why Sudesh got separated from me. Ever since she came into our lives, she has brought us nothing but trouble. First she hooked my husband, got him involved in a scheme that cost him his business and reputation, destroyed our marriage and it finally killed him. My husband apparently died of a heart attack but I am telling you, he was killed by Rupali. That woman was no good. She used her charms to manipulate people. When she discovered that it was Deep that got her the money, she dumped my husband and got attached to Deep and ultimately married him. My husband must have been heartbroken. I have no sympathy for that lout but I lost everything because of her," she said breathlessly.

Vimla told them that Sudesh Mittal had set up Morningstar Brokerage in the late 1980s and in a span of less than 10 years, he had built it into one of Pune's top retail brokerage firms. Being from an old Marwari family, Pune's industrial and trading elite were his natural customers. That being the time when India's retail and high net worth investors discovered stock markets and aided by the economic liberalisation of the early 1990s, Morningstar was in the right place at the right time. Rupali had met Sudesh through a common acquaintance and pitched him the idea of a bio-fuel company. Sudesh was totally enamoured by Rupali and soon his fascination turned into an affair. Vimla soon realised something was amiss when he started having frequent late nights and phone calls late into the night. When she confronted him, Sudesh denied that he was doing anything other than business but when she threatened to go to her parents' house, he did not object or stop her. Sudesh was beyond caring. Vimla's absence, in fact, worked very well for him.

After she left Sudesh's house, Vimla kept tabs on him through the household maid who was a live-in at the household. Sudesh had not changed his behaviour even after she left. Then suddenly, one fine day Sudesh came home early from work and for the next few days did not venture out to the office at all. Once he had a fall in the bedroom from a bout of dizziness. Vimla had visited him and consulted their family doctor who told her that Sudesh was on anti-depressants for some time. Earlier, he had also been diagnosed with high blood pressure for which he was then being medicated for the last several years. Once again, since the last few months, his mood had improved despite his business having practically shut down due to the bio-diesel fiasco. He was off anti-depressants and his late nights had again started and though he didn't have much income, he had enough invested to provide for himself comfortably though not up to his past standard of living.

"May I see his medication madam?" Batty asked on a hunch.

Vimla brought Sudesh's pill box from his bedroom.

"This was the only tablet that he took twice a day - our maid used to take it out in the pillbox and keep it for him at his bedside," she said. The Prescription in Sudesh's medicine box described it as Amlodipine 2.5 mg, standard blood pressure drug. Batty saw that there were some loose pills in a pillbox. He almost put it back but something caught his eye. The pills were etched with the number 10 in the pill box. *Why would a 2.5mg pill be etched with 10?*

He asked Vimla if there were any full strips in the house as the pill box had all loose pills. Vimla found a strip of Amlodipine 2.5mg. Batty tore out one pill. *It had no etching on it. It was similar in size but clearly it was not the same pill as that in the pill box. Why was the number 10 etched on the pill? Was this a 10mg dose?*

"How much was his blood pressure?" he asked.

"Not sure but I think the Doctor said it was borderline" Vimla replied.

A vague feeling of unease stirred Batty and he decided to dial his army doctor friend Diljeet.

"For 145/95 which would be slightly above normal for a male in the mid to late fifties, I would prescribe Lisinopril 10 mg once a day," Diljeet said. "If it is Amlodipine, it would be 2.5 mg twice a day," he said.

"Amlodipine overdosing can cause arrhythima or irregular heartbeats and very fast heart beats or palpitations," said Diljeet when Batty queried him about an overdose.

This could cause a heart attack. If the etching on the pill was any indicator, Sudesh was taking a massive overdose!

Batty called Shinde and asked him to collect the pills and have them checked for their dosage with a chemist.

"This is too exciting. We are back in our old elements. My head is already spinning with all the possibilities. Let's recap what we have uncovered so far," said Robin, sipping on her favourite Frappucino. They had now gone to her favourite Starbucks.

"Rupali has been painted as a manipulator and gold digger by Vimla. She apparently had an affair with Sudesh and then once her work was done, dumped him for Deep who she married. This drove Sudesh to despair but apparently from the messages that we saw, Rupali had started meeting with Sudesh again recently. All this while Deep was encouraging her to start a family which she was avoiding by taking contraceptive pills on the sly," she completed.

"Rupali is turning out to be a multi-faceted personality. Deep paints a different picture of her while Vimla paints a totally different picture. What a woman!" Robin continued.

"But do you notice that somethings don't seem to make sense here. For example, if Rupali was indeed a manipulator and a gold-digger, why would she rekindle her affair with Sudesh? There is clearly nothing to gain for her with Sudesh any more. This does not fit the person being described," Batty said.

"We have also another problem before us, which there is no way to investigate since Sudesh has been cremated - *and if the etching is correct, why was Sudesh taking such a high dose of the drug? In other words, what made him take that dosage? Did he commit suicide or...?"* asked Robin.

"Was he murdered in cold blood? " finished Batty.

Robin let out a toneless whistle.

The Good Doctor was finishing up with the last of his patients when Robin and Batty entered the consultation chambers. Mrs. Bharucha was delighted to see Robin again. She enquired after how her work at the newspaper was progressing and if they managed to find out who had killed their lovely patient. Robin had confided in her the first time they met that they were investigating Rupali's death and in that connection, Doctor Manohar's description and insights into the patient would be a great help. Mrs. Bharucha was very excited about solving this crime and offered to help in whichever manner she could.

"Did she come often, this Mrs. Rupali?" Robin asked.

"She was a patient since the past one year and of late, the frequency of her visits had increased. Earlier she used to come with her husband once a month. In the last 3-4 months, she had been coming weekly and also sometimes twice a week and sometimes the husband accompanied her," she said helpfully.

"What is the average frequency of the visit for

the Doctor's patients?" Robin asked.

"Usually once a month, or at the most twice a month. But Mrs. Rupali would come and sit for a long time. Often hers was the last appointment and sometimes, the Doctor would ask me to leave if Rupali was going to take longer. Doctor spends a lot of time with his patients. Some of them have psychological issues relating to gynaecological problems and our Doctor is very good with people and believes in providing a helpful and patient ear in addition to a prescription. There was one case where the Doctor had treated one patient in the past where she would come and sit daily since she was depressed. The Doctor gave her ample time and soon she was cured and then stopped coming altogether," she said.

"How long did Rupali usually sit?" Robin asked.

"Sometimes she would wait in the other chamber which is a separate waiting room for VIP patients until the Doctor finished attending to others. Maybe an hour or more in total," she said.

If Doctor Manohar was surprised to see them, he did not show it.

"So tell me, what progress have you made?" asked the Doctor.

"Why didn't you tell us that Rupali had sent an urgent message to you to come over on the night she was murdered?" asked Batty.

"It must have slipped my mind. I saw the message fairly late and tried calling her but her phone kept ringing. I called her the next day as well but again no response. Then, of course, I read it all in the newspapers," he said.

"What was she consulting you for Doctor? " asked Robin.

"She was trying to conceive as I told you last time," he said.

"Did you know that Rupali was taking contraceptive pills?" Batty asked.

The Good Doctor was quiet for a long time. Batty just let the silence sit there. His face was inscrutable but Batty sensed a conflict brewing within the Doctor.

"She never wanted that guy's child," he said.

Batty let the silence sit there for some time. Robin was about to say something but Batty kicked her to keep quiet. Silence works wonders in creating pressure on the person who is talking. Most times, people keep talking just to avoid the discomfort of silence.

"She was in an abusive marriage. That man is an animal. He took advantage of her gullibility and her love. The stories she told me I cannot even talk about. She was forced to come to me since he wanted a child. She told me the first time she came to meet me that she had no intention of having a child which would then bind her to this man. I became more of a friend and a therapist than just her doctor. She was a wonderful woman full of life and deserved better! My only regret is that I could not save her," he said.

Doctor Manohar told them how she had blindly trusted Deep with her financial affairs as well as her wellbeing and he routinely performed unnatural acts of sexual intercourse on her. She may have still tolerated some of the abuse as quite a few Indian women tend to do in their effort to save their marriage but then she also realised that Deep had mortgaged all their assets and left her penniless. She also confided in me that in her previous company, Deep had convinced her to pin the blame for the fiasco on her friend Abbas and she had done it like a dutiful wife. She realised much later that Deep had married her only for her money and her assets. She was very unhappy with the situation and did not want to continue with her marriage. She had taken to drinking as well. There was no question of having Deep's baby in such a situation.

"Why did you not tell us this earlier Doctor?" Batty inquired.

"I was very upset over her murder. I was not thinking straight for a few days I guess," he said.

"If I were you, I would arrest that bastard. I am sure he did it".

"Everything seems to be pointing to Deep," said Robin excitedly on the way back from the

Doctor's consulting chambers.

"By when will you have a complete call list with names of the numbers that are unknowns?" Batty asked, ignoring her.

"Give me a couple of days, need to do a caller ID search on various apps for all the numbers as there are several," she replied.

"Just focus first on the ones that have been called frequently," he said.

"I think there is one more name," said Robin.

"Though not that frequent, there have been a few calls to and from that number. Some called *Devendra.*"

"Good catch Robin. Let's find out who he is."

Robin was wondering as to why Batty had ignored her earlier statement. Batty sensed it.

"As to your original statement of having got our guy, there is still something we don't know. What would Deep gain by killing her? If the Doctor is to be believed, why would he kill the one person who was supporting him financially? *Where is the motive?"* asked Batty.

Chapter 10

Between 1998 and 2000

Rupali did not notice Arvind and Faheem at Daawat. The lights were on her and it was difficult to see people at the back anyway. Her tryst with bar dancing had started quite by chance. One day, on her way back from meeting a client for the Metro Bank, she felt a tap on her shoulder. As she turned around, she saw a grinning Kaka blowing on a cigarette in his best filmi imitation. With mixed feelings, she gave him an awkward smile.

"Arre Rupali, where have you been? *Aur kya haal bana rakha hai? Clerky kar rahi ho kya?"* he said, commenting on her office attire of a grey pencil skirt and a white blouse with the deep disdain of those in artistic fields who looked down upon office workers as petty clerks even though Kaka was as close to being an artist as Rajesh Khanna was to being a businessman.

"Kaka, Metro Bank mein hoon aur meri badi tarakki bhi hui hain," said Rupali trying to convey a sense of self-importance and achievement.

"Chalo achcha hai, lekin glamour business ko miss nahin karti ho kya?" he asked putting his entire foot on Rupali's one sensitive spot.

"These days I have diversified. I organise

private dance shows for wealthy customers. There is a lot of money there. One or two days overnight and we are back. Good money. You can easily make 25-30 thousand in one night just by dancing. I have some very good girls but if you join me, we can set the stage on fire," he said.

"I can't take time off from my job Kaka," Rupali said, trying to avoid further conversation. Kaka was not giving up that easily.

"Arre weekend per thoda enjoy kar lo. You loved to dance, don't you miss it? Aur extra income bhi toh hai na?", he said, trying to lure her.

"Aur tum dono kar sakti ho – job bhi karo aur dance bhi. I will give you a new name and no one will know. *Itna toh is Kaka per bharosa karo.* I have always been your well-wisher", he said.

"I can call you when we do shows in Mumbai city for sure. There is also another idea. Just to get you back into practice. I know the owner of Daawat dance bar in Kandivali near the railway station. Why don't you practice there? The money is not as good as the shows but you can easily make 5-15 thousand per night, you get to keep 40% of the money that the customers shower on you. Navin Shetty, the owner, will guarantee you 5 thousand just to show up and dance. That I will get done for you. Shall I?" asked Kaka.

"But Kaka, so close to my bank? What if someone sees me there?" Rupali asked.

"Arre which clerk has 10-15 thousand to blow every day?" asked Kaka with a crooked smile.

And so it had started. Despite Rupali's better judgement, the lure of extra money and the chance to dance again did the trick. The day Arvind and Faheem saw her was her third month at work and she was already popular.

Arvind noticed Rupali come into the bank at her usual time and get busy with planning her visits. He threw a meaningful glance at Faheem who sat across his glass cabin and Faheem smiled in response. Arvind gestured to Faheem to come into his cabin.

"Let's meet her after office hours today, just the three of us. Say it's your birthday or something. And say that you are only inviting close friends in the evening. Just get her to say yes and I will do the talking when we meet," Arvind told Faheem.

Rupali was surprised to see only two of them seated at the table at Sarovar, the multi-cuisine restaurant at Kandivali Station. They were seated at the "Celebrity" - the Bar area of the massive three storey structure that housed a multi-cuisine restaurant, a pure vegetarian restaurant, a banquet hall and a bar. Faheem explained that he had invited more people but they did not seem to have turned up until then.

"Happy Birthday, Faheem. I got you something," said Rupali taking out a nicely gift wrapped slim package that looked like a pen set.

"Thank you, Rupali. Actually, it is good that only three of us are here as Arvind Sir wanted to talk about something that is best kept restricted to a small group that trusts each other" Faheem said. Rupali found Faheem's assumption about the existence of trust between them very odd but kept quiet as she wanted to know more about what was coming next.

"I am not sure how much you know about what is going on in the outside world these days Rupali," said Arvind.

"Interest rates have gone through the roof and most people are borrowing at interest rates between 30% and 36% per annum. Meanwhile, we at the Bank are lending at 18% and not finding enough takers due to our stringent norms," he continued.

"We have all been working at this Bank for a while now and it is apparent to me that the Bank only rewards those that are close to Mr. Kapoor so despite all three of us having done exceeding well, we are stuck in the same position since last 2 -3 years," he said.

"The Bank has also gotten into a couple of rotten deals -one large industrial group having a downswing in its fortunes and thus not being able to repay the bank and here our bank has a very significant exposure. Then there is also the matter of Sada Pawle and the bad publicity the Bank got in the bargain," he explained.

Rupali was wondering where this was leading. She was also hearing words like "exposure" for the first time which was typical banker talk for the amount of money the bank had at risk with a particular client. Anyway, it sounded very interesting to her and she was all ears.

"All this has meant that while Mr. Kapoor runs the bank like his personal fiefdom, it is our hard work that brings in all the customers who entrust the bank with their money for safekeeping. The rate at which this is going, I would not be too surprised if this Bank heads into trouble in the next 3-4 years or is taken over by a stronger bank. I am hearing rumours of ICICI Bank having shown an informal interest. Our goose is cooked from all sides - Mr. Kapoor's wanton disregard for sound banking practices is endangering the bank, the present negative image of the Bank makes it difficult for us to switch jobs, Mr. Kapoor anyway only promotes his own so there won't be any upward movement for us and in the event the Bank gets acquired, we will all get laid off as we will become surplus. So unless we do something to take care of ourselves, in less than 2-3 years, we will all be working in some of these night call centres that have started coming up in Mumbai, answering customer queries of dumb Americans and earning less than half of what we are making today with no future whatsoever," he concluded his grim prognosis.

Rupali was alarmed at these sudden turn of events. She had no idea about any of this and in her mind, she was comfortable with the idea of a bank day job and a dancing gig in the nights. She was earning serious money now that she had developed a small fan following at the bar. This only worked if she had the Bank job as a fall back at all times. Bar Dancing was hardly the route to big bucks. Although she was just three-month-old in the profession, she had made friends with some of the girls and had come across horror stories of alcoholic husbands, money-grabbing parents and siblings and a societal stigma which made it difficult for them to raise normal families. Rupali was certain that this was not what she wanted out of her life. The extra money did not hurt and came in really handy - she had got her Vasai home properly repaired, painted and well-furnished and even put an air-conditioner in the tiny apartment among other things - but this was not something she could bank on.

"Arvind Sir please guide us what to do. You are the master of this business and please protect us and show us how to take care of ourselves. We will follow what you say Sir," said Faheem laying the foundation for Arvind Nair to construct his edifice.

"I believe we can help ourselves by making

some money on the side without harming the interest of our customers and without endangering their money," Arvind said.

Rupali, her feminine intuition working overtime now, sensed this to be the true purpose of this little get together and the reason why no one else had showed up. *Because, no one else had been invited in the first place.* This was an apparent plan concocted by Arvind and Faheem to include her in their scheme. But why me, she thought. The answer came soon enough.

"We need to keep this tight and between the three of us. Rupali and Faheem - your clients are the ones with the largest amounts of deposits with the bank. Some of your clients have lakhs lying in savings accounts for months altogether. We need only the two of you to handle the clients. I will handle all the other details and transactions," Arvind said.

"The plan is very simple. I know Mangalmurti Finance Company - one of our customers that enjoys some loan limits from our Bank. They use this money to onward lend to a lot of small and medium sized businesses at very high rates of interest. The top executives are known to me and one of them was a class mate of mine in college. The Bank lends to the Finance company at 18% and the Finance company lends to the businessmen at 24-26% thereby making a nice margin. But here is where the cream is - the borrowers actually pay almost 36% and not 26%. The balance 10% is paid in cash, upfront and for the entire duration of the loan which is around one year to the executives of Mangalmurti Finance Company. For every Rs. 10 lakhs that Mangalmurti Finance lends, the executives make Rs. 1 lakh upfront and risk is entirely of the Finance Company," he explained.

Both Faheem and Rupali looked at each other. Between them, their clients had between Rs. 15-20 crores in the Bank as deposits and savings account balances. If they were to use all this money for onward lending, they could make 1.5 to 2 crores upfront! It was insanely lucrative. She could buy a 3 bedroom flat in Lokhandwala in Andheri for around Rs. 40 lakhs and still have money left over. A lifetime's achievement in one year!

"But Sir, how can we do this without the clients' consent?" asked Rupali.

"I have got that all worked out. That I will tell you once we all shake hands and drink to making this a success," said Arvind.

"But Sir, what are the chances of our getting caught?" asked Rupali.

"Almost zero and I will show you how once we all shake hands on this deal", said Arvind.

Rupali wasn't convinced. This looked like a straight fraud and embezzlement to her. Getting caught would mean a prison term. Not an exciting prospect even though the money seemed more than adequate for such a risk.

"I am in Sir, lets shake hands," said Faheem excitedly.

"I am thinking about this still Sir but what if I don't want to get involved? I will never disclose anything of this to anyone ever you have my word for it but what if I don't want to be a part of this?" asked Rupali.

"You are your own boss in these matters, Rupali. I cannot force you. But think of this as a capital accumulation opportunity that does not come often in life. If you don't want to be a part of this, it is fine with me but the next time my Boss comes for a Branch review, *I will bring him to Daawat for a drink and to watch our star employee in action."* said Arvind with a smirk.

Rupali's face was drained of all colour. Right then she knew the decision to include her was already made well before this evening. She had no choice but to join them.

Arvind's scheme was devious and something only an insider could execute with perfection. Faheem and Rupali were the key elements in this scheme. Faheem's artistic reproduction skills could be applied to customer signatures easily and Rupali was adept at handling customer relationships and queries. With Faheem's help, he had got the bank's printer on his side promising him a piece of the action. Thus were compiled his tools of the trade. When a customer made a cheque book request, Rupali and Faheem would order two chequebooks instead of one. And, they would start writing cheques - with Faheem's help in duplicating signatures - from the customer's account to Mangalmurti Finance Company in small denominations of 50,000 to 1 lakh making sure that the customer account retained at least half the funds as genuine balance. There was no internet or mobile banking then so the only way in which a customer checked his balance was by way of calling his relationship manager or checking his quarterly bank statements. The Bank only issued monthly statements to current account holders and all savings bank account holders got quarterly statements. They were careful to only tap savings accounts since these saw much less activity and balances remained dormant for long periods of time.

Mangalmurti Finance Company then made onward lending to its clients from these funds of the Bank's customers at 26% interest. The interest on the monies lent by the Bank's customers was paid out to Faheem, Rupali and Arvind in a 25:25:50 ratio at 18% per annum by way of bearer cheques. On top of this, they got 50% of the cash upfront which was split between the Mangalmurti executives and them. Between Faheem, Rupali and Arvind, they made 23 paise on every Rupee that they stole from their clients. Around 20% of this went to the printer. At the end of the loan period, the money was simply returned to the client's account by Mangalmurti Finance.

The Bank outsourced its printing to Faheem's previous employer by sending electronic files of transactions to be printed. These were text files and could be easily edited. Faheem, Rupali and Arvind would sit at the printer's office the night before the printing and edit out all the cheques that were issued from the second cheque book and money received back from the Finance Company and adjust the balances accordingly. This was back breaking work that took several hours but they kept detailed records on spreadsheets of the customer cheque leaves they used and the amounts so the work progressed pretty quick. The customers never sensed anything amiss, the phone calls from their customers were handled by Arvind, Rupali and Faheem and everything was executed smoothly. Part of the reason why despite having dipped into hundreds of accounts, the three of them were able to handle the balance queries with ease was a simple tool - each of them had, on their computers and buried into the plethora of excel sheets they used for various bank work, a detailed account-wise spreadsheet that had just one numerical value. Depending on how much had been taken out of the account which was again in multiples of Rs. 50,000, the spreadsheet mentioned against each account a numeral with a '+' sign. For example, if Rs. 1 lakh had been taken out, the account would have a notation of +1. That way if a customer called for his balance inquiry, all any of them had to do was to pull up his balance from the bank's system, open the spreadsheet, check the numeral to be added and simply give the customer the adjusted balance. Whenever the amounts were returned, the spreadsheet was updated immediately.

This incredible scheme ran for almost two years and in the process, the three partners deployed Rs. 30 crores on which they earned 20% average return or Rs. 6 crores. Of this, the Printer made around Rs. 1 crore, Rupali and Faheem each made Rs. 1.25 crores each and Arvind made Rs. 2.5 crores. *A lifetime of earning in two years indeed.*

As it happens in such cases, an innocuous query created a ripple effect that undid the entire scheme.

Ramesh Chaturvedi was a successful trader who had made it big in trading chemicals. He ran a mid-size firm and his business required excess liquidity to be kept available at all times. He was a client of Rupali's but being a very high value customer, Arvind used to service him directly. One day, his accountant, Ajay Agarwal, came to him with a puzzled visage.

"Saheb, the savings bank interest amounts are not tallying with the balances," he declared.

The banks in India credit the savings account holder with a low rate of interest between 2.5 and

4 percent per annum depending on the prevailing deposit rates and these amounts are credited every quarter. In the ordinary course of business, most people do not bother to check the accuracy of these amounts as they are calculated by way of a slightly cumbersome method called the product method which involves calculating the number of days for which a particular amount has been lying in the account without any addition or subtraction and is done for each and every transaction for the entire period. Most people don't even give a second glance to savings account interest credits as the amounts are not meaningful.

"Kya Munimji, looks like you have no other work. These are computerised statements, there cannot be a mistake by the Bank," Chaturvedi said.

"Nahi Saheb, I am telling you my calculations are correct. We should have got atleast double of what we have been credited as per my calculations. I am convinced I am right," said Agarwal.

"How much money are we talking about Agarwalji?" asked Chaturvedi.

"Saheb around Rs. 1 lakh differential at least as per my calculations. In all your five family accounts put together you have about 50 lakhs balance almost throughout the year. You should have got quarterly interest at 4 percent per annum of around Rs.50,000. I am seeing less than Rs. 25,000 in all accounts per quarter since the last one year," said Agarwal.

Agarwal explained that he suddenly realised that the Bank is crediting less interest when he noticed that there was hardly any movement in the account and yet the interest was low. He initially did not notice it, but when he sat down to prepare tax computations for the Chaturvedi family members, that is when it hit him.

"I am taking all these statements and going to the Bank tomorrow. I will check their computer and also tally the interest amount," he said.

Ramesh Chaturvedi smiled and said, "You must satisfy yourself fully Agarwalji. But I am sure the Bank will have an adequate explanation. They have been good to us - the amount of working capital limits they have provided us with has helped our business grow quite well in the last three years. Please do not rub them the wrong way. Be nice but also ensure that you come back happy. Let me call Arvind and tell him to expect you tomorrow so that they don't feel we are doubting them or anything."

Arvind sat up when he got the call. Ramesh told him that his accountant wanted to double check some queries he had on the calculation of savings bank interest and that he was sending his accountant to assuage his doubts. Ramesh was also apologetic and requested Arvind to humour his accountant. Arvind realised immediately that this was a fatal flaw which could unravel the entire scheme. Alarm bells started ringing loudly in his head. He did not inform Faheem or Rupali lest they panic and he decided to handle it himself.

Ajay Agarwal was positive that there some bug in the Bank's software that calculated savings bank interest to be credited to the customers. *I wouldn't be surprised if the Bank has deliberately done this. Imagine the savings running into crores of rupees. Bloody cheats!* he thought on the way to the Bank.

Arvind greeted him warmly, asked about his well-being and offered to resolve any doubts that he had. Ajay pulled out last four quarters of bank statements of one of the family accounts of Ramesh Chaturvedi and showed Arvind why, according to him, the savings interest amounts were lower than these should be. Arvind immediately offered to send an internal memo to the Head Office in this regard and asked Ajay to give him a couple of weeks' time to revert to him. He did not admit to an error, he merely said that he would convey this complaint to his bosses. After all, he was just a customer relationship guy. Ajay was happy and satisfied that the Bank had heard him out and was willing to do something about his problem.

The moment Ajay left, Arvind went over to Faheem and informed him that they needed to meet at their usual place. Celebrity, the Bar at Hotel Sarovar, had become their usual meeting place since this was where it had all started.

"We need to stop this immediately. We overlooked the savings interest calculations and one customer has come asking for an explanation about the discrepancy," he said with palpable tension in his voice the minute they were all seated and their drinks were served. For Arvind, it was Black Label on the rocks, for Faheem it was Old Monk and Thums Up and for Rupali it was Kingfisher Beer.

"I don't understand, what does the interest calculation mean?" asked Rupali.

"Arre, you leave it. Just take what I am telling you. Not for you to understand these technical things. This is not bar dancing you know," said Arvind bitterly.

Rupali was taken aback by the venom in Arvind's voice. It must be this new development. It could also be because Rupali had not given up bar dancing despite Arvind and Faheem's repeated suggestions that she do so. Arvind lived in fear that some bank customer may see Rupali in Daawat and it would create unnecessary headaches for them. Despite opposition Rupali had continued with it. She somehow always had this strong intuition that her bar dancing would come in handy one of these days in case things went south. *At that time, she had no idea how right she was.*

They disbanded their operation immediately. Arvind managed to convince Ajay Agarwal that it was a computer bug and would be set right soon. That kept Ajay at bay for some time but Arvind knew their time was up. He thought of trying to set the account right in the next quarter but he was struck by the fact that there were hundreds of accounts and others may not be far behind in their discovery. The game was truly up and the one flaw they had not foreseen was about to bring them down. Accepting the inevitable and not knowing what else to do, he resigned with one months' notice and skipped town along with his family hoping that there would be no proof of his involvement. They were anyway living on rented premises in Mumbai since his wife never got along with his parents. Faheem stayed on for another three months and he too put in his papers. Meanwhile, Ajay Agarwal started getting more and more upset since there was no response from the Bank even after Arvind's assurances. He visited the Bank one fine day only to discover that Arvind had quit his job and the new manager in his place had no idea of what Ajay was talking about. Irritated, Ajay decided to complain to the Bank Head Office along with detailed calculations and attached copies of the Chaturvedi family's Bank statements.

The complaint finally landed on the desk of Bhavesh Dalal, the head of internal audit for the Bank since this looked like a matter that required a detailed review. Bhavesh immediately asked for Bank records for the same period for which Ajay had submitted the Bank statements and was stunned to see that these were completely different. In fact, several cheques issued and received by the customer were not reflected in the copy that the customer had submitted as a part of his complaint. Sensing a fraud, Bhavesh immediately alerted the Bank's forensic audit team.

Big organisations move slowly and by the time the auditors started digging around, three months had passed by. They realised that the client's account had been systematically defrauded but they were foxed by the fact that monies seemed to have been returned as well. The matter went all the way upto to Raja Kapoor. He called up the CEO of the Finance Company and asked him to come over for a cup of tea to discuss future business.

"We have been defrauded by our own people," he told Bhupinder Singh, the CEO of Mangalmurti Finance giving details of how he had come across one such instance and he suspected that there would be multiple such instances. Singh had recently taken over from his predecessor and had discovered the massive cash payoff racket that was going on in his company.

Having sacked those responsible, he was still looking into the entire episode. What Raja Kapoor told him came as a shock. He promised to investigate the matter promptly. These small deposits taken from individuals were illegal and he wondered how these had gone unreported. But then he realised that in his predecessor's quest for growth, a lot of checks and balances were given a go-by and the swelling loan book was the only criteria that was focused on for a long time. This had damaged the company and his quality of loans had also suffered. He was facing a large amount of unrecoverable loans and what Kapoor told him further worsened his position. *This could make his company insolvent in one stroke if the amounts were large.*

Bhupinder provided Raja with a list of all individual deposits outstanding in his company's books within a week of their meeting. *There were a total of 738 accounts which belonged to the bank's customers. The amount outstanding in Mangalmurti's books was Rs. 12 crores.* Bhupinder, now relieved that the problem was manageable, promised to make good the entire amount to the Bank in three instalments over three months and Raja agreed as there was no other choice.

Meanwhile, since Arvind had left and the operation of their scheme had halted, customers started getting bank statements showing much lower balances in their savings account which did not tally with the previous statements. All hell broke loose but Raja had already provided his team with the answers. The Bank claimed that there was a massive software glitch due to which the recent statements were not reliable and assured the customers that their last statement which showed the different balance was correct. The Bank asked the customers to wait another quarter for the next statement and until then if anyone wanted to issue cheques or withdraw funds, they had to simply bring their previous statement showing the balance in their account along with their current statement showing the incorrect opening balance and they would be paid in full. This restored the customers' confidence and Bhupinder kept his word. During the quarter, the funds were credited back to the customers and normalcy returned to the Bank. It was assumed that the bank statements were forged as the final mailing was done by the Bank to the customer. No one thought of investigating the printer since the problem was seen as involving a few specific accounts.

Raja was furious. He made the Bank executives file an FIR with the Kandivali Police Station and named Arvind Nair as the primary suspect along with Faheem who had also quit earlier and Rupali. Arvind was picked up from his native place in Thrissur in Kerala where he was awaiting his work visa for an employment in a Bank in Bahrain. He confessed and the police recovered half the money from him. He also named Faheem as his forger and Rupali as his co-conspirator. The printer's name never came up as a co-conspirator. Perhaps because he was seen as the compliant labour component in the entire scheme.

Faheem Sheikh was never found. His home address proved to be a rented place which was vacated once he left the Bank. His bank account was cleaned out and there was simply no trace of Faheem. His previous employer, the printer, did not know his whereabouts but gave a glowing report of him as a worker.

Rupali was interrogated. She claimed that she was forced to do Arvind's bidding as he was threatening to expose her about some personal matter. She claimed not to have made any money from this episode and Arvind was the mastermind behind this all. API Sunil Thakre was the investigating officer who grilled Rupali for her involvement. Rupali broke down and confessed to Sunil that she was a bar dancer and did not want the world to know. Her parents needed supporting and Arvind was not promoting her despite her having done well. She was in financial difficulty and then one evening Arvind had seen her in the bar and started to blackmail her. She had no choice but to comply. Sunil was taken in by her apparent honesty and found the story quite plausible. She explained the source of cash and jewellery in her house as having earned it from her bar dancing and some of her "special" friends from Surat who were big diamond traders she could not name. Rupali implored Sunil to absolve her since her parents had no other support and she had done all this under extortion. In a throwback to her Bollywood days, she offered to show Sunil her gratitude in person and Sunil ended up getting thanked a few times in the process. Now full of gratitude, in his final investigation report and chargesheet, Sunil absolved Rupali and pinned the entire blame on Arvind and marked Faheem a wanted man. Arvind was remanded in police custody and a hunt was launched for Faheem. Days turned into months and months into years but Faheem was never found.

Rupali learnt another of life's lessons - the one which stayed with her throughout the rest of her life. This was the first positive lesson she had learnt in terms of something that worked for her. On the previous two occasions, it was about what not to do. *A beautiful woman can get away with anything. The trick lies in making men think through the lower part of their body. And that part provides all the right motivation for the woman to walk free.*

A couple of years later....

The harsh mid-day sun of Bilaspur in Madhya Pradesh in May was beating mercilessly down upon the hapless population of the small town. Faheem, now sporting a beard and wearing a skull cap with his hair dyed reddish brown, was taking a nap in his mamu's small house on Imlipara Road in the outskirts of the town. He had taken upon himself to be a religious scholar and was a favourite of Mullah Naseeruddin at his local mosque. He headed straight to his mamu's house after quitting the bank as he knew that once Arvind left, this scheme would unravel. Best place to lie low. Having spent a considerable time in his childhood with his mamu, it was an ideal place to hide for him. He told his mamu everything. Being his dead sister's only child and mamu being unmarried and childless, he was doted upon since childhood. His mamu told him not to worry. His *qaum* would never give up one of their own.

Just then, Mohammed Yusuf, his contact from Calcutta, arrived with the news that he was waiting for.

"Bhai, I got your documents. Look - perfect in all respects," Mohammed said excitedly.

Faheem saw the passport, the West Bengal driving license and his Calcutta voter registration card. A bespectacled, learned man in his early 30s looked back at him sporting close cropped black hair and a trimmed beard. He focused on the name on the passport and the other documents and smiled to himself. Mohammed was indeed a magician with identity documents. He also quite liked the name he had chosen for himself for his new identity. *Abbas Kadri had a nice, professional ring to it.*

Chapter 11

Robin noticed herself in the mirror. The double shift work - first at the newspaper and then for the investigation - was taking a toll on her. The general impression was that she didn't much care for her looks but in reality, her careless look and lack of obvious personal grooming to some extent was a carefully cultivated image designed to fit in with her male colleagues without appearing to look too feminine.

People didn't notice that while her nail polish might have been chipped sometimes, the rest of her wasn't un-groomed. She generally took care to remove excess unwanted body hair give or take a few days here and there and her mane was always well cut though tied in a careless bun most of the times. That way, she could simply touch up her nails, let her hair loose and alter her personality when needed. Not that those occasions were plentiful. Her casual, slightly dishevelled look helped people focus on her work, her words and not on her body parts. But what she now saw needed some serious fixing. Tonight, she expected to dress up a bit as Batty had suggested they get dinner at Baan Tao at the Hyatt in Kalyani Nagar - a little night out after several days of eating on the fly and rushing around to complete things. Now since Batty was on leave and nicely ensconced in Juggy's place, his evenings were free and he wanted to live it up a bit. Suited her just fine; the place wasn't far from her rented two-bedroom apartment, which she had entirely to herself thanks to a generous inheritance from a deceased aunt who doted on her during her lifetime.

She hastily applied some make-up to lighten the shadows under her eyes and accented her eyes with eyeliner. Opting to wear a push-up bra underneath a black top and her lone pair of DKNY designer jeans, she finally liked what she saw in the mirror. *Let's see what you have to say to this Mr. Bartaman Bhowmick.*

On the way to the Hotel, she ruminated on her feelings for Batty. At some level, she found him attractive but his personality was very one-dimensional and after two years, she wasn't sure if there was another side to him that was fun loving and romantic. She had no idea what a romantic Batty would be like since they had hardly socialised without a work agenda. The only time she had seen him let his hair down was when they went out to celebrate after they had solved the Koregaon Park murders at the Classic Rock Cafe which was not very far from the Hyatt where he had surprised her by singing a couple of Billy Joel songs. He was a decent singer but what she found really interesting was the total involvement with which he sang. He was practically oblivious to his surroundings and did not even need to look at the lyrics. She remembered that he had brought the house down with his rendering of *You may be right, I may be crazy* and the crowd had given him a big ovation for that number. She could only guess from that one instance that he just might make a very good lover. *Clearly this guy did everything with his whole heart, mind and soul.*

Apart from that one incident, she only knew some sketchy details of his past and childhood. Born to a Punjabi mother married to a Bengali college professor, he had been a drifter throughout his teenage years. Fed up of constant nagging and insults from his father, he had applied himself seriously to academics and joined the army just to snub his father who went on and on about the bright future that awaited his son in the corporate world. Batty hated the rat race and this was his way of demonstrating it. His father was aghast though his mother was secretly delighted at his choice having belonged to a family where some of her relatives were in the armed forces and a career in the army was a very Punjabi thing to do anyway. Batty's father had finally come around and gifted him his Omega Seamaster when we joined the Army as an officer. He had passed away shortly thereafter and his mother had moved in with her brother and father in their ancestral Delhi bungalow since she was all alone. Being a professor, Batty's father hadn't saved up much and had never owned a house. They had rented their last house in Jabalpur where Batty's father taught. His mother had simply given up the house and moved to Delhi.

She was waiting for Batty just outside the lobby of the hotel smoking her Marlboro Lights when Batty rolled up in a shiny, almost new-looking blue Yamaha FZ 25. Robin gave out a low whistle.

"Wow, the civilian life has certainly started growing on you... in just two days it seems!" she said.

Batty laughed and told her that he had borrowed it from Juggy. It belonged to Juggy's only son Amitesh who was away at Warwick University in the UK finishing his bachelors in business management.

"I can give you a ride home," he said.

"That does not mean you are getting invited for a nightcap, ok?" she said flirting with him.

Batty decided to let that one pass without comment. In the light of the hotel lobby Batty noticed a new Robin. It was his turn to let out a low whistle.

"Wow - look at you! Didn't know this could happen to you," he said.

"Meaning what? Must I always look like a low paid journalist who is just getting by?" she teased.

Batty looked really relaxed in his untucked fitted olive green shirt, black slacks and suede loafers. His shirt was open at the neck and the first button was undone showing his muscular chest.

His rolled up sleeves showed off his sinewy arms. For the first time in the two years that she knew him, she was happy to see him relaxed and though he always looked attractive to her, today he was actually looking dishy. *That nightcap may not be a bad idea at all, she thought.*

"I am famished," said Batty. "Shall we order?"

He gestured for the captain to take their order. Batty ordered his usual Old Fashioned with Jim Beam and looked quizzically at Robin.

"How about a bottle of Fratelli Bianco?" she asked.

"Excellent choice Madam," said the Captain. "May I also suggest that you also consider our excellent Santa Cristina, 2010?" he added, trying to upsell.

"No thank you Captain, I will stay with the Indian one, the Fratelli Bianco," she said politely but firmly.

"Also, please get us some prawn spring rolls, some tea smoked tender lamb and some bang bang chicken salad," she added. "Once we are done with these appetisers, we will let you know about the main course," she completed.

The Captain brought the drinks and kept a small portion of honey chilli cashew nuts between them. Batty and Robin drank to "many more such occasions together" and after taking a couple of sips of their drinks, neither of them seemed keen to start the conversation. There was an awkward silence and both of them were avoiding discussing the investigation. It was strange that without the investigation, there seemed to be almost nothing they could talk about. While they were struggling with this, the appetisers got served.

Batty broke the silence as soon as the server had left.

"You should dress up more often Robin. It suits you. I can see why you don't, but seeing you like this has actually made me aware of how striking you can look when you want to," he said.

"Batty, I am sure you never had girlfriends growing up. You just don't know how to compliment a woman. Striking? I am looking bloody gorgeous. You can say that if you want to be truthful. One thing is sure though," she said.

Batty looked at her with one eyebrow elevated.

"You will never talk a woman into sleeping with you. You are most likely to talk her into falling asleep," she teased him.

Batty let that one pass. He did not want to take the bait. He did not want to tell Robin that he had not always been this way. There was a time when he could easily talk girls into sleeping with him. But then after Shalini, things hadn't been the same. He hurriedly pushed Shalini out of his mind and said, "Let me see if I can talk you into keeping quiet first. That seems like the most difficult part. I am guessing sleeping with you may not be such a challenge seeing that you have almost made up your mind to give it a try."

As soon as he said it, he regretted it. He meant it as a joke and a jibe but it came out all wrong. *God help me, he inwardly pleaded for this not to get escalated.*

Robin's eyes narrowed and her face was livid with suppressed rage.

"Hadn't taken you for one of those who think that just because a girl has dressed sexily, she is looking to sleep with someone. You aren't very far from those who blame girls wearing short skirts or revealing dresses for their rape Mr. Bhowmick. Why is that underneath a civilised veneer, even the most liberal sounding men are actually Neanderthals? Where do you guys get these regressive ideas from? Movies?" she thundered.

"And now if you don't mind Mr. Bhowmick, I need to leave as I have an early morning editorial meeting that I must attend," she added, getting up to leave.

Batty had realised this would happen the minute he uttered those words. Frantically searching for something to say to diffuse the situation, he could only mumble, "I will drop you home." Just the worst thing to say.

"No need sir. I can get myself home and trust me, even though you may think I am dressed to get raped, I am very capable of defending myself," she fumed.

By the time the Captain returned to take the order for the main course, Batty was draining his glass and asking for the check. Robin had already left.

He gunned his Yamaha and headed home. On the way, he struggled with a strong urge to stop by at Robin's house and try and diffuse the situation. On second thoughts, he stopped himself. They were not lovers. They were work colleagues and friends at best. There was a common interest that brought them together and it was not romance. And most of all, after Shalini, he wasn't ready for another relationship. At least not yet.

He found Juggy going over some papers when he entered.

"So, how was it? Did you score today or not?" Juggy teased him guessing that he must have been out with Robin.

Batty sighed and didn't say anything. Better not to get into this discussion at this time.

"It has been quite a few days now - are you close to a breakthrough or not?" Juggy asked seeing that Batty had no desire to let him into his private world.

"I feel that somehow it is just around the corner but I have nothing concrete to base this on as yet," Batty said. "It is just a feeling of sensing it but yet not being able to prove anything."

"Guess what - I met your Doctor Manohar today in the Club. He was chatting with Mom there. It is amazing how Mom knows almost everyone. Looked a little under the weather, your Doctor Manohar I think," Juggy said.

Batty was still thinking of Robin and how to make amends when something made him look up sharply.

"*Masi* knows Doctor Manohar?" he asked.

"Oh yes, and she is quite fond of him as well. That Doctor has a way with women and knows how to make them feel special," replied Juggy.

Batty made a mental note to catch up with *Masi* soon.

The constant hum of his cellphone pulled him out of his meditative state in the morning. He was just lying in his bed ruminating over the investigation when the phone buzzed. It was Robin.

"Dude, I am heading out to the edit meeting and have a busy day. What is the agenda today? I should be free between 1 and 4 PM," she said without preamble.

She is also feeling that she over-reacted yesterday and this is her way of apologising for blowing up and ruining a promising evening, he thought.

"We should look for Devendra today. We should go and meet Shinde to call and find out who he is and fix up an interview with him. After that, I may want to spend some time at the Club," he said.

"And Robin, sorry about yesterday. Didn't mean to sound misogynistic. That was a joke that came out all wrong," he added.

"No issues Batty," she said, slipping into her usual half-teasing mode. "I fucked up too. Let's call it even ok?" she added.

Senior Inspector Ravi Lokhande was feeling refreshed and recharged after his four day break in Kolhapur. It was Rohini's nephew's wedding and her side of the family had taken special care of their Inspector son-in-law. The food at Kolhapur was to die for. He was still thinking about the mutton pandhra rasa this morning when was getting ready to go to work.

"Back to diet from today," said Rohini with barely concealed hostility, handing him his diet dabba. "Are you eating something on the sly every day? I am seeing no change in your weight. If anything, I think it has gone up. I am going to get a weighing scale and make you climb on it each morning," she said with an air of finality.

Lokhande's recharge evaporated. He could see his life in terms of interminable days of gulping down diet food and getting weighed each morning.

"Ok, ok we will do that baba, don't worry," he said putting on a brave face.

Deva, I wonder who put that idea in her head! Bye bye life, bye bye indulgence, hello emptiness he thought unhappily. This was certainly not a good omen to resume duty. His thoughts soon went to the pending investigation at hand. God knows what else that Latur boy Shinde and that army man had cooked up in his absence. Four days of absence was a long time for those two to get into some mischief.

"Ugach Kashala?" he bellowed at Shinde. Why did he have to unnecessarily ask the police team to go to Mumbai and dig up Rupali's past? "Are you going to find your murderer in Vasai or what?" he asked Shinde.

"Arre saheb, ACP Sir said that we should all fully co-operate with the Army fellow. He asked for it, how can I say no Sir?" asked Shinde innocently.

"And what did you find?" Lokhande asked.

Shinde informed him that the police team had just reached Mumbai the previous day and would be back a couple of days later with the findings.

"Get that husband of hers and let's do some proper enquiry with him," Lokhande said.

"Sir, Bartamanji has already made some progress I am told," Shinde replied.

"I am sure you know a lot more than I do

about this. In my absence, you two must have hatched many conspiracy theories I am sure," Lokhande said.

"Hello Lokhandeji, good to see you back," greeted Bartaman walking in and taking a seat opposite Lokhande. Robin was also all smiles and charm when she spoke to Lokhande. "How was the wedding? The food must have been great in Kolhapur, right?" she said, trying to put him at ease. Lokhande brightened considerably upon hearing food and Kolhapur. He was about to launch into a long winded description about the place, the people and the food but then the very next moment he checked himself. Putting on a serious face with no trace of warmth, he said, "I am sure you two are not here to enquire about my holiday. Tell me what you want and I am at your service as you know."

"We need Shinde to call Devendra and set up an interview with him," Robin said.

"Devendra? Never heard of him. And interview? Is he a movie star? Interrogation it is called madam, we are not reporters, we are the Police. We don't interview, we interrogate," he said crossly.

"That is why I said interview Lokhandeji. We will talk to him. If you guys talk, it will be intimidating. We would like to put him at ease and ask him questions," said Robin. Batty was just content observing this little pantomime.

"Arre Shinde, see what they want," he said loudly. He then turned his attention to a robbery that had been reported that morning at P C Jewellers on JM Road and directed a constable to do a panchnama of the crime scene, take stock of the situation and report back to him by afternoon.

"Bartamanji, Shinde will help you. I have to attend to the crimes that lowly people like us can solve, like robbery," Lokhande said with barely concealed bitterness.

"What's got into him today? He is generally not such a jerk," asked Robin under her breath.

Batty just shrugged and went over to Shinde.

Devendra turned out to be Devendra Jamdar, one of the public prosecutors for the state. Shinde briefed him about the matter at hand and he suggested that they meet him during the court recess around 1 PM at the District Court Building in Shivajinagar with their queries.

"Why would Rupali call the Public Prosecutor? Isn't that very strange and even more so since Prabhu More told us that there is an ongoing case against her in the criminal court for India Biofuels? Isn't this illegal?" asked Robin as they rode towards Shivajinagar on Batty's Yamaha.

"Indeed, very strange. There has never been a dull day in this investigation so far. Gets more and more interesting," Batty replied.

Devendra Jamdar turned out to be a 50ish,

balding, thin and slightly unkempt man with the demeanour of a court clerk. Devendra Jamdar had indeed been a court clerk who then passed his bar exam and became a lawyer. Practice was not easy and he barely could make ends meet. Faced with no other options, he decided to join the government as an additional public prosecutor. Initially starting out with petty criminal cases, with seniority, he had now become a senior additional public prosecutor, one among many, and handled criminal matters for the Public Prosecutor's Office. He was sitting in the court canteen and wearing his collar, a black striped trouser that made him look like a waiter and a crumpled white shirt. His junior was seated next to him holding his gown and his documents.

He greeted Batty and Robin perfunctorily and motioned his junior to take a seat at another table.

"I am not sure I understand your role in this matter," he said in a thin, almost feminine voice, coming straight to the point.

Robin noted with amusement that his voice must have been a big contributor in him not being a successful lawyer. No judge was going to pay serious attention to the voice that emanated from his throat. Must be a riot when pitted against a powerful defence lawyer with good court craft and face value, she thought.

"I am helping the police with this investigation under authority from ACP Jagdeep Kumar," Batty said.

"Do you have an authority letter? I cannot discuss things with you unless I see some document. I know ACP Jagdeep Kumar well but I need to see a paper," he said, digging in his heels.

"I can call him right now and have him speak to you. Rupali Jadhav made several phone calls to you during those few weeks. It is highly irregular for an accused to be in touch with the public prosecutor and I am sure the Chief Public Prosecutor will want to know more about this," said Batty quietly, deciding to call his bluff.

Devendra Jamdar seemed to shrink in his chair and he almost looked like half the man he used to be just a minute ago. Gone was the government babu demeanour. In its place, the court clerk surfaced.

"Sir, it is not what you think. That poor woman was innocent. I read about her gruesome murder - terrible. Prabhu More had recommended that I speak with her to help her as even his investigation had found her to be above suspicion in this matter. That Muslim guy was the mastermind. And it seems he may be absconding now. Poor woman was made a director and conned. I felt sorry for her. She used to cry and ask me to help her Sir. That's all." he pleaded.

"That still does not explain the many calls," Batty said.

"Sir, she was very nervous that she would get caught in this mess and hence she would phone me often to ask if she had anything to worry about. She was also going through a lot personally. I felt really sorry for her," he said and then went quiet.

Batty looked at him without saying anything. He kept staring at him wordlessly for what seemed like an eternity. Finally, Devendra Jamdar broke the uncomfortable silence.

"And I had also recommended a colleague of mine to help her defend herself Sir. He was handling her case from the defence side," he said trying to be helpful.

"There are no such numbers in her phone contacts Jamdar. Don't play games with me, I am not a patient man," Batty thundered.

Robin was now openly staring at Batty. She had seldom seen this side of Batty.

"No sir, I was only co-ordinating all her matters and I used to instruct the defence lawyer. I had taken upon myself to help her and she trusted me completely. She hardly knew her lawyer's name," he said.

"I am sure the rewards must have been handsome for you Jamdar," said Batty.

"No sir, I never asked for any money from her. She would only insist and pay me every time she met me for the case Sir. I had to pay the lawyer as well Sir," he said, trying to make Batty understand that even though he had been taken care of by Rupali, he still had expenses and thus had not kept all the money for himself.

"In fact sir, I handled her divorce case for free," he said, trying to be helpful.

"Rupali was married before? You also handled her divorce?" asked Robin incredulously.

"No, no Sir. *She wanted a divorce from Deep Kalra. I had drafted the divorce notice for her which she sent her husband. The matter was to come up for hearing at the family court next month,"* he said.

"When was this notice sent and can you get me a copy?" asked Batty.

"Around about a month ago," said Devendra. He looked at his assistant and nodded. The copy was handed over to Batty.

Both Batty and Robin looked at each other. *This meant that Deep knew that Rupali was going to leave him.*

Chapter 12

2003-2007

Rupali opened the French windows of her Lokhandwala Apartment to let in the sunlight and sipped on the masala tea that Sakhu, her maidservant, brought her. This had been her morning ritual ever since she had moved into this apartment a few months ago. Her dream of owning an apartment in Lokhandwala, a popular upmarket suburb of North Mumbai had come true. As locations go, Lokhandwala was a peculiar one. Having risen into a rag-tag collection of high rises and other buildings from a swamp in just two decades, the area was home to Bollywood directors, Producers, second rung actors, one or two yesteryear divas, music directors, singers and practically who's who of the film and television business. The area had a late start, started coming to life around 11 am and continued to buzz until well after midnight. Come evening, something curious happened in Lokhandwala. The area's many cafes and small restaurants were taken over by a species that were local to Lokhandwala and not found anywhere else. Hundreds of well-dressed and yet somehow rustic looking boys and girls dressed to show off their best assets packed the area's meeting places for no apparent purpose. The ordering was minimal as if trying not to add weight to their sculpted bodies or not to reduce further weight from their already depleted wallets. They just hung out for hours, exchanging stories and trying to land an opportunity. This was the world of Bollywood Strugglers - hundreds of whom arrived in Mumbai mostly from small town India with stars in their eyes which more often than not turned into smoke eventually. That smoke got into their eyes often but they put on a game face each day in search of their elusive destiny.

Thus, it went on, day after day, this odd collection of perfectly formed yet ill-starred humans living in the constant hope of bumping into someone who could give them a break. Some of them even rented an apartment between 4 or 5 of them just to be close to the action.

Model co-ordinators were the star attraction at these cafes and small restaurants. Offering the strugglers small modelling assignments and more often than not doubling as pimps, these model co-ordinators were the strugglers' lifeline. They kept the strugglers alive with the crumbs that their work generated for them which in turn allowed the strugglers to have at least one proper meal in a day and spend the rest on rent, clothing, gymming and grooming. Often, the less ambitious of the strugglers gave up their quest for stardom and got sucked into the false security of instant money. Prosperity beckoned them almost immediately. Suddenly, the world's goodies were within reach. Expensive branded clothing, accessories and shoes, the latest mobile phones and even an odd down payment for a car. From showing their pictures to film and television producers, they soon progressed to showing their pictures to businessmen, politicians, bureaucrats, cops and other inhabitants of the market that is the underbelly of every city in the world - the flesh market. And once again, the same model co-ordinators who got them bit roles also got them these lucrative contacts. Lokhandwala, by virtue of being a struggler market, was also the epicentre of the flesh market.

Rupali was at first elated at moving into her dream locality. She wasn't too sure but had some half-baked ideas about getting back into Bollywood on the production side now that she had the money and she was successful. She didn't have any contacts worth doing business with and despite her meeting people, nothing seemed to be promising. Sensing the need for family members to manage the household and to take care of the chores while she went about looking for opportunities, she had emotionally extorted Saraswati and Vitthal to move in with her and lock the Vasai house. Compared to her well appointed two bedroom Lokhandwala apartment, her old house in Vasai was more like servant quarters. She had furnished her apartment with everything that she had always wanted. She had spent more than half her earnings buying and doing up the house.

Vitthal and Saraswati were more than happy to stay with their earning daughter. Rupali had spent a small fortune on their clothing and provided them with all the creature comforts of life which they could not experience earlier. There was also Sakhu who looked after the house and lived with them. Saraswati maintained the house and kept all the finances and Vitthal helped with outside work. Rupali was relieved that she did not have to take any responsibility for the house and Saraswati and Vitthal generally left her alone.

The Indian family unit, the much storied keeper of middle-class morality and virtue, had actually long since morphed into a capitalist beast. Money, or lack of it, drove its actions, its behaviour and the standards of morality and virtue it was willing to impose upon itself in its quest for a better lifestyle. In an ideal world which was captured by Bollywood films from the era, Saraswati would have resorted to hard labour day and night to bring back food for the family in Vasai. Nirupa Roy would have been Saraswati in a film based on their circumstance. But something changed in the 1990s in India. Consumerism had arrived and had taken India by storm. Food was not the reason why people worked. Aspirations, consumer goods, standards of living, keeping up with the neighbours and the entire spectrum of advertising and globalisation driven desires and wants caught hold of the country's citizenry. Self denial was seen as idiocy and satellite television beamed images of *the bold and the beautiful* into the homes of middle class families. The family code of honour or ethics, at most times a thinly disguised excuse for lack of money, was finally buried. It was in this environment that Saraswati had found it an acceptable trade-off to opt for less laborious but clearly better paying activities to fulfil her family's daily needs as well as provide for some luxuries. After all, letting go of the old fashioned values of virtue and honour demanded adequate compensation.

By the time Saraswati moved to Lokhandwala with her daughter Rupali, money was the only thing that mattered. Matters had come to such a head that mothers happily planned the perfect manner in which to capitalise on a good-looking daughter and delivered their daughters' virtue to where they thought would yield the best payoff for the future of their family. Often, such earning daughters supported the entire family that fed on their income to further their own desires. Thus, fathers happily bought watches, shoes, clothes and made travel plans with their friends, brothers often tried to launch ill-conceived businesses and sisters funded their education - all on the back of the lone earning good-looking daughter who earned it all lying on her back most of the times. The mother often worried about the earning daughter's health, her well being and her activities keeping an eye out for unwanted boyfriends whose existence would only divert their precious daughter's income. The purpose was less motherly and more commercial - ensuring that the daughter was fit to go out and get in the money without distractions so that the family could prosper.

Both Saraswati and Vitthal were parents in this new Indian mould.

After moving into this house, Rupali had taken to drinking every evening and Vitthal would often join her. Saraswati would just sit alongside both of them and listen to their conversations. Most days, it centred around movies or TV Serials or some anecdotes from Rupali's Bollywood days or Banking days. There would be laughter and merriment on most days. Of late though, Rupali was growing more and more restless. She wasn't sure what she wanted to do and even though she went out to meet several people, the way forward remained as elusive as ever. Rupali was worried that the money was running out as there was no income. She obviously did not want to dance in a bar now that she had money and status.

Then one day she bumped into Sohail. Having known him as an assistant to the producers Munir-Rehan on the sets of Viraat, she had lost touch with him altogether since then. He called her from behind when she was talking to an acquaintance from her bollywood days.

"Hi Rupali, is that you? My God! Look at you? Doing really well haan?" he said.

Rupali took a minute to recognise him. Excusing herself from her friend, she went over to his table.

"Such a long time Sohail, how have you been?" she asked.

"Just in the middle of my first solo project. I am actually too excited. I will let you into a big bit of news that I haven't told anyone. Abhay Devdutt has agreed to do my film. It is a multi-starrer. The other cast is also super. It has Sanjay Khan's son, one more small hero, Hema's daughter and a couple of other girls. The director is the same one that had directed Gyarah - Abhinav Sinha. I am so excited," he said in one breath.

"That is great news Sohail! I didn't know you had done so well in the last few years since I saw you," Rupali said.

"Arre Rupali, even that hit Gyarah was my project. Once I set it up and got all the actors signed, some dirty politics started and I was replaced in my own film. Although I was there until the end of the shoot, my name was removed by this big hero who I cannot name...the one whose father is a legend in the film industry. It is now known as Nalin Manmohan's film but it was actually mine," he said bitterly.

"Abhay Devdutt knew about this and out of sympathy he offered to do a film with me if I came up with a good project. He has really helped me stand up again. The man is really great," he gushed.

Even though Rupali had been out of the film industry, she knew enough to know that Abhay

Devdutt was doing no favours to anyone, least of all to Sohail who was low life in the film business. No one really cared if he lived or died. That was the reality of the film business. Every man for himself. The smartest ones had the knack of screwing people with such finesse that the victim ended up thanking them. Abhay was certainly one of the smartest. Rupali could see that Abhay was looking to change his image from that of a serious, righteous hero to a more fun, with-it and cool hero. No one wanted to take the risk with Abhay in such a role so he had caught hold of Sohail and offered him a lifeline which would end up wonderfully for Abhay irrespective of how it ended for Sohail.

"When is the shoot starting?" asked Rupali

"We are doing pre-production work at the moment. I am in a bit of a jam. Abhay has asked for a large signing amount and I am running short. I don't want to go to Rajubhai who can finance me but then will take all the earnings away from the project. Abhay earlier said he did not need any signing amount but now because of the delay in locking the shooting dates, he needs the money as his wife Bhavna's birthday is approaching and he has promised her a bungalow in Alibaug. He needs the money for the down payment. I also need to sign up the rest of the main cast without which the financier will not come in," he said ruefully.

Rupali was very familiar with the manipulative ways of the top stars of the film industry but did not want to burst Sohail's bubble. The man clearly believed that Abhay Devdutt was his one true friend and benefactor.

"How much are you short by?" she asked.

"Eighty lakhs," Sohail said.

That was a lot more than what Rupali had left over from her Bank earnings. She contemplated investing the required amount. This would mean that she would have to mortgage her house and use up some of her surplus cash which would leave her with just 10-12 lakhs in her hand. This made her quite uncomfortable. But she was young and her entire life was in front of her. Plus, this was a chance to turn producer.

"Meet me tomorrow, same time same place. I may have a solution for you," she said.

Rupali thought about it for a long time that night. She sat in front of the TV in her living room watching some mindless soap but her mind was on Sohail. She could get to be a 50% partner in the film for that much money as Sohail must have put up hardly anything. Now he needed the money to sign up Abhay Devdutt and a couple of others and he didn't have it. Without Abhay and rest of the main cast, there was no project, no film. Yes, Rupali could extract her pound of flesh from him. She could see her name along with Sohail's in the film's credits - Produced by Sohail Mecklai and Rupali Jadhav. From a background dancer to a producer! All within 5-6 years!!!

Her decision was made. But once again, Rupali couldn't sleep.

In the film business, a project got locked once the basic script was ready and the main cast signed up. The rest was a cake walk after that. Finance was easily available and even though the rates were usurious, the producer was able to run his kitchen by siphoning off some money during production. That was the way the business worked. Everyone was happy. The Financier never lost money as his unrecovered debt was rolled on to the next film by the same producer in case the film didn't work and the producer got to produce movies and keep his banner alive. Once in a while, when the producer made a hit, the financier recouped handsomely and the producer also saw some surplus. If the film was a super hit, everyone got wealthy. This system balanced the uncertainties of the business. Since no one could predict which film would be a hit, the only way a financier could recoup was to keep funding more and more films by the same producer. And history had shown that every producer always produced hits sooner or later in his career. Some were better at it than the others.

But in 2006, Bollywood was dominated by the suits. For the first time since its 90 year plus existence, the financial analysts and corporate types had taken over the business of making films. Lured by that most misleading of all pieces of software, the spreadsheet, ex-bankers started heading studios set up by corporates and started commissioning films. The bankers decided, again guided by spreadsheets, that they were better off buying films outright on a cost-plus basis and on a project-to-project basis. This created massive incentives for producers to pad their project costs and sell it to the studios for a hefty mark-up. The spreadsheets showed returns that looked lucrative for the studios over the long term. What everyone forgot in their enthusiasm was that the film business was inherently risky and merely because a film was helmed by producers and directors with good past track records did not mean that it would be a hit. This business model came into a lot of grief later and most of the studios shut down in the next 7-8 years but at this time, this was the prevailing business model.

Rupali got to Cafe Coffee Day early and waited anxiously for Sohail. He was delayed and for a short while, Rupali worried that he might have got the financing and she would lose her opportunity. Sohail sauntered in 30 minutes later by which time Rupali had consumed two cups of coffee and was already feeling sick, having had the coffee on an empty stomach. Sohail didn't have much hopes from Rupali but he had learnt not to discount anyone in this business. Who knew who knew whom?

Rupali outlined her proposal to Sohail. She would fund all of 80 lakhs against a 50% stake in the film. Her name would be in the joint credits of the film as producer. She would be present in all the important meetings related to the film. Sohail could not believe his ears. Rupali had that kind of money? She was a background dancer just a few years ago. How did this happen? Sohail concluded that she must have someone backing her and not wanting to look a gift horse in the mouth, he decided to accept her proposal. In the next two days, he drew up a co-production agreement and once he and Rupali had signed it, he deposited Rupali's first cheque of 40 lakhs. The rest would follow in a few days she had said. Sohail was least concerned. Getting the first instalment of a film's financing is the most important thing. It is like shaving one side of your face. You have to complete the rest of the shave. Providing the balance then becomes the investor's problem. Films and Construction were the only two businesses where even a 90% finished product could not be monetised. It had to be 100% or else it was worthless. There was no salvage value. By investing 40 lakhs, Rupali was committed to the entire amount. That night, Sohail celebrated with his friends at a pub in Bandra. Unknown to Rupali, Sohail just needed 60 lakhs. *He had made the fastest 20 lakhs of his life.*

It took Rupali almost a month to get the mortgage of her house organised. She kept enquiring about the progress of the signing of the artists and the director and each time she asked Sohail simply reminded her that unless he had the entire amount, there was no point in signing up the small guys. The big whale would not come on board unless he was paid. At the end of the month, Rupali and Sohail met to take stock of the progress. Rupali handed over the cheque to Sohail for the balance 40 lakhs and asked to see the Abhay's confirmation letter at the earliest. Sohail delivered it to her in two days. Rupali was overjoyed. Their film was now a reality.

"I have some terrific news," said Sohail on the phone to Rupali. "Can we meet right away?"

"I have landed a different kind of financier. There is this company Definity Insurance. They have just set up shop with investors' money and are keen to start their business with a large project. They will help us sell the film to one of the corporate studios, get us an advance from the studio and also get the entire financing from the studio. They will underwrite any cost over-runs in return for a 10% profit share," he said breathlessly.

Rupali did not understand this too much but it sounded good. Where was the loss?

"I have told them that we need to make a table profit of at least 4 crores if we are selling to a studio," he said.

"What about our producer credit? " asked Rupali thereby revealing her one concern in this entire episode. She was really interested in being known as a Bollywood producer which would put her in an entirely different league.

"The studio only wants "presented by" in the beginning of the film. They will add their name to ours in the producer credit but we will certainly be there," said Sohail.

Rupali was beside herself with joy. Her luck was unbelievable. Her very first venture and so successful! She had made 2 crores on an 80 lakh investment. It was indeed a stroke of phenomenal good luck to have landed Sohail. She could see her own production banner clearly - "Roop Films Corporation" - her own name shortened to mean beauty which the film business was apparently about, at least on the surface. In her mind, she had indeed arrived.

Parmanand Deshbandhu took a deep drag on his cigarette. A handsome man of 48, Parmanand had seen early success as a television whiz kid. His television sitcoms had rocked the country with his innovative story telling, his keen sense of humour and his terrific craftsmanship during the Doordarshan days. He was superbly connected in the industry and several of the day's top actors had apprenticed under him when he was riding the crest of his popularity. Even if that was 20 years ago, his reputation was intact. The fact that he had not produced any work in the last 20 years did not seem to matter to him. He did not let anyone forget how he was the top draw in his heyday. Madanmohan Pujari was his friend for the last 20 years and although life had been partial to Madanmohan who had seen amazing success as a film processor, he never forgot the time when Deshbandhu had helped him buy his first processing machine by lending him the required money. Pujari dabbled in film production and though his company had been recently acquired by a star struck corporate, he was asked to head it and take the company forward. He had made an obscene amount of money from the sale of his company to the corporate and was the epitome of someone having the best of both worlds.

"Madan this is an amazing project," said Parmanand. "Abhay Devdutt, Zayan Khan, Sanjay Shetty, Rishabh Deshpande, Esha Malini, Diya Malik..." he trailed off.

"Directed by the new whiz kid Abhinav Sinha," he said in his best salesman imitation and laughed.

"Come on Madan, I don't need to sell you this one," he added.

"How much do you want for it?" Madanmohan asked.

"They are making it for 12.5 crores, I want 16.5 crores," he said.

"I will give you 15 crores," countered Madanmohan.

"You are a tough businessman Madan; I could push back but you are first a friend. I have no choice but to agree," conceded Parmanand.

The deal done, he whipped out his phone and called Sohail with the good news.

Rupali was unhappy at the prospect of

making just 1.25 crores. She felt like she had been cheated of 75 lakhs which was her rightful due. But even then, this was easy money.

As soon as the deal was signed and the advance received, Sohail got busy with the pre-production and the planning for the shoot. Bad news started almost immediately. Abhay refused to shoot in the location selected and wanted to shoot in South Africa. The budget was made with the majority of the shooting in Bangkok which was a much cheaper location and Sohail was in a jam. He called Rupali.

"We will need to raise atleast 2.5 crores more. The location change has cost us that much more. Madammohan is not going to budge from 15 crores. I have spoken to Definity and they are willing to fund it but will charge us 36% interest and they will recover first from what Madanmohan pays us when we complete the film," he said.

Rupali was crestfallen - her entire profit had vanished thanks to that scum Abhay.

"Don't worry, we have 50% of the profits of the film since Madanmohan is going to pass on half the profits once he recovers his cost," said Sohail.

Rupali felt slightly better hearing this. She stood to gain if the film became a hit and with the good star cast and the known director, the market was very positive for the film. *Whatever happens, happens for the best, she thought. Maybe we will make a lot more than what we lost.*

The film finally got completed at a cost of 19 crores. Sohail had run up the cost of the film in South Africa. Definity was alleging that he had siphoned off 2 crores in South Africa during the shooting. Sohail was sacked from yet another film and Definity took over the film to recover their investment. It then struck Rupali that this may have been the real reason why Sohail was thrown out of his earlier film. *He had swindled those guys as well.*

"I need to meet you urgently Madan," said Parmanand, his voice full of concern. Madanmohan agreed to meet him right away.

"I will be ruined Madan, the film has cost 19 crores and you have agreed to buy it for 15 crores. I am exposed for 4 crores and my company will go under if I don't recover this amount," Parmanand pleaded.

Madanmohan smiled gently at his friend.

"I know that the extra cost has gone into the location. As long as it is visible on the screen, I will cover it," he said.

Parmanand was relieved. He quickly arranged for Madanmohan to sign the revised papers for the film with the new price.

The good deed now done and Parmanand's company having now been assured of a return of their investment, the two friends sat down over a drink to discuss the future.

"Parmanand, the film is hot. I am getting offers from the trade far in excess of even my revised price and today, if I offload the entire film in the trade in various geographies and channels, I am looking at a 10-crore profit without even releasing it," Madanmohan confided in his friend.

"Why don't you do just that? In fact, I am going to insist that you do that and make the money," said Parmanand.

Madanmohan, known as Mr. Nice in the film business, was also a shrewd judge of people.

"What are you not telling me Parmanand? " he asked.

"I have seen the rushes Madan. The film is a disaster, it won't run even for a week," said Parmanand.

Madanmohan was stunned. He was now caught in a bind. If he let this be known to his people, the word would spread and his investment would come a cropper. On the other hand, if he did not sell it, he would still lose money if what Parmanand was saying turned out to be correct. He decided to ask his new Head of Motion Picture Business, a former banker by the name of Sunil Lakhanpal.

Having been a media investment banker at Fairgrowth Advisors, one of Mumbai's many investment banking boutiques that had suddenly developed specialisation in the media business due to the explosion in television and film business,

Sunil was considered very knowledgeable about the media business. He knew what made the business tick and this had helped him strike some landmark deals, one of which was the sale of Madanmohan's company to the star struck corporate. He had impressed the corporate's top management with his dealmaking and they offered him a chance to head the company's motion picture business, so named because the corporate was looking to replicate the American Studio model in India, under the watchful eye of Madanmohan. Sunil jumped at his chance to enter the real world of business. For him it was a leap from spreadsheets to operations - something that most bankers are least prepared for.

Madanmohan and Parmanand looked at Sunil as if he had lost it.

"Sir, I have seen 20-30 minutes of the film. It is brilliant Sir. The market is really hot for the film and I think if we don't sell any part of it, we will make 20 crores on top of the 19 crores it is costing us. I have done all the analysis sir. All factors have been modelled by me in a what-if analysis and my numbers are showing me that it will be one of the year's biggest money spinners Sir," Sunil was saying, puffing up his chest slightly.

Parmanand kept quiet and did not look at Madanmohan.

Madanmohan felt a slight headache developing which was threatening to escalate unless he made this idiot see the light of the day. It was a tough call. He had known Parmanand for more than 20 years and was highly respectful of his abilities as a director and a creative professional. Plus, he had volunteered his opinion of the film as a friendly gesture to try and ensure that Madanmohan did not make a loss on the film. The market was red hot and he could easily sell off and make a tidy profit but this idiot sitting in front of him was looking at his laptop and making decisions. If he shared his apprehension about the film not being up to the mark, Sunil would lose his nerve and the market would immediately sense it in his changed behaviour. If he did not tell him that, he would risk everything they had invested and they could end up losing a lot of money as there was another 5-6 crores of print and publicity money to be spent on the film before its release.

Parmanand came to the rescue. He looked at Sunil and said, "I am happy that this one is looking so good. My advice to you would be to cover your cost and then play with the upside once you have sold enough of the film to break-even. If what you are saying is true, I believe you will be able to cover your costs if you keep the top territories of Bombay, East Punjab, Delhi and Satellite rights for yourself and if by selling the rest of the pieces and territories you can cover your cost it might be a good strategy. That way you keep the biggest pieces for the maximum gain. The return on investment will be infinite as all costs would have been covered by the rest of the territories sold in advance."

Madanmohan flashed him a look of gratitude. He had provided Sunil with a solution that would appeal to him in his own lingo. Return on investment! The best thing to convince a banker.

Sunil grudgingly accepted Parmanand's idea. He didn't think much of him and considered him a dinosaur, but this infinite return on investment idea had legs. In his mind, he could picture the Power Point slide that he would present to the Board of the company on this project with the return on investment arrow shooting straight up! That would look awesome.

Rupali was trying to call Sohail without much luck. The disembodied voice kept telling her that his phone was out of coverage area. It was now three days after the release of the film and she was desperate to know how much money she had made. Not getting through to Sohail, she decided to land up at Parmanand's office.

"I have managed to avert a disaster. You have no idea what a mess Sohail had created. His irresponsible behaviour nearly sunk our company and almost broke my friendship with Madanmohan," Parmanand said embellishing the story a little more for extra effect since Rupali had no knowledge of what had actually transpired.

"I know Sir and I thank you for it. Just wanted to know how the film is doing and by when I will be able to recoup my investment of 80 lakhs and my share of profit," said Rupali.

"Haven't you heard? The film has bombed at the box office. The first day was packed but then the negative word of mouth killed the film. It is really a terrible film. I am surprised you haven't seen it," he said.

Rupali had gone with her parents first day first show. She loved the music and the action pieces but felt that the rest of the story was a little odd and didn't make much sense. Saraswati and Vitthal didn't say anything negative but being supportive, they assured her that the film was alright and such movies were becoming popular. Rupali was not convinced but seeing the packed movie hall, she stopped worrying about it.

"So sad. I would have been happy if it had turned out better. Anyway, since our investment is protected, we may not get much profit but our investment has been underwritten by Madanji's company so at least even if we don't make much money, we won't lose anything..." said Rupali.

Parmanand smiled.

Bringing out a sheet of paper from his desk drawer, he laid it in front of her.

"You know that our company had to pump in a lot of over-budget funding which Madanmohan has covered but only to the extent of the principal amount. Our over-budget funding is priced at penalty rates since producers are required to finish the film within the budget. We charge interest at 36% per annum which is also in the contract that we signed with Sohail and you. Calculating all that, you and Sohail jointly owe us around Rs. 55 lakhs," he said.

Rupali was thunderstruck. She had wagered everything on this movie. The deal was solid and Parmanand had covered all the costs. She had overlooked the interest element. She had assumed that it would be covered as well. It was an expensive oversight. That scum Sohail had made off with more than 2 crores without investing a penny and she had lost 80 lakhs and Parmanand was going to press for another 55 lakhs that he was claiming. Rupali knew that in the Indian legal system, it took several years for someone to recover their dues from a counter party but the fact that she had lost 80 lakhs was real. She had mortgaged her house and invested most of her extra cash as well. She had no income from which she could pay the Bank and keep the house.

The movie's title had turned out to be prescient. After much back and forth, Sohail's insistence had won the day and the movie was called "Crash". *It had certainly caused Rupali to crash. She had nothing left and she owed people on top of it. She had no option but to leave town.*

Chapter 13

"The first rule of investigation is to look for the person who benefits from the death," said Lokhande with the demeanour of someone making a profound statement.

"In your case, except for the servant, there are no beneficiaries at all," he said looking at Shinde.

"This matter has been needlessly complicated by all of you. Over thinking only makes matters worse. Sometimes, very brainy people fail to see simple truths clearly," he concluded.

It was 10 in the morning and Shinde was filling Lokhande in with all that had transpired in his absence in the Rupali murder case.

"So according to you Sir, who would have done it?" he asked.

Lokhande chose not to reply. He did not want to reveal that he himself was getting more and more confused with the emerging angles in this case.

"Best ask the person working on it. All I know is that if I was handling this properly and from the beginning, I would have solved it by now. But what to do? The Big Boss wants to indulge his cousin so here we are. Now that army fellow better solve this. If he makes a mess of it, I am going to refuse

ACP Sir if he asks me to bail him out at the last minute. By that time, too much mess would have happened even for me, Ravi Lokhande, to make a difference to the outcome," he said, completely oblivious to the fact that the last time he had got involved in a complex murder was probably while watching a movie.

Shinde's phone rang just as he was being lectured in effective investigation by Lokhande.

"I am coming over there in a few minutes to see the panchnama of Rupali's murder. I remember that there were some papers there as well," said Batty over the phone.

"Yes Sir, I will take out all the items and the list," he said.

"Take the name of the devil," Lokhande muttered in the background. Take the name of the Devil, indeed.

Batty got off his Yamaha and rapidly walked into the Police Station.

"Arre wah, new bike," beamed Lokhande.

"Not mine Lokhandeji, my nephew's," explained Batty.

Shinde had kept the panchnama ready. Batty went over it quickly.

List of cosmetics, books, strips of medicine... Crocin, Combiflam, Zolpidem, Sudin, Alka Seltzer, Aziwok, Allergan, Strepsils, Medicine Prescriptions from Dr. Manohar... Files...house papers, fixed deposit receipts, bank statements, loan agreements, mobile bills, credit card bills...

Batty flicked through the papers hurriedly. Rupali had not changed her name after marriage. All bank accounts, fixed deposits and her house, everything was in her maiden name. The house was mortgaged and bank statements showed fixed deposits being liquidated for paying instalments and meeting expenses. Mostly cash withdrawals and very little credit card spending. She was the sole account holder in all cases and the house was in her name alone. Looking at the last two months of bank transactions, Batty could see that Rupali's cash withdrawals were frequent and substantial. Rupali's cash was dwindling rapidly.

"At this rate, her money would not have lasted more than a couple of months," he said to Robin who had quietly appeared on his side while he was going through the papers.

Apparently, whatever was going on in Rupali's life was draining her financially. This also tied in with Dharam's description of Rupali having turned moody, depressed and unwell in the last few days of her life.

Deep was brought in for questioning soon after. Batty had informed Shinde the night before to call him over to the Police Station in the morning.

"I have no idea about this at all Sir, I never

received any notice of any kind," said a visibly shocked Deep upon being confronted about the divorce notice.

Batty thought that the shock was perhaps more at the discovery of the divorce notice which Deep had no doubt suppressed from them than for the fact of divorce.

"There is no reason why she would do that Sir," Deep said. "We were trying to have a family," he said.

Batty almost told him about the contraceptive pills but something made him hold back.

"Did you know that Rupali was almost bankrupt?" he asked instead.

"No Sir, I had no idea. Rupali was managing the house and all the legal matters Sir. That company cost me dear Sir. I was left with no work and a burnt reputation in this town. I often told Rupali to shift to Mumbai where we could start a new life but she would hear nothing of it," he said.

"Sir, please find the person who did this Sir. Please find my Rupali's murderer. The wait is driving me insane. I don't know what to do. I can't get any rest until you catch the culprit Sir," said Deep showing anger and frustration.

"Don't worry, it won't be much longer now," said Batty. *We are almost there. And don't fool me with the angry act, bugger. You are losing your mind out of anxiety.*

"Masi, *pairipauna*. How are you today," asked Batty settling into the wicker chair in the Club's large open verandah overlooking the garden. Juggy was also there sipping on his scotch. Batty was having a glass of fresh orange juice for a change.

"*Jeete raho puttar*. I am all good, not much worse for the wear, yes?" she answered with a twinkle in her eye. Shantadevi was a woman frail in person but formidable in spirit. She and Batty's mother were very similar in most ways. Having been an English lecturer much through her working life, her old fashioned English reminded Batty of a glorious bygone era when men were chivalrous and women were graceful. Batty would have much preferred that he be born in those times if he could have helped it.

"One more murder to solve?" she asked raising one eyebrow quizzically. "

Juggy never tells me anything," she lamented. "Ma, if you stay with me, I can tell you everything since I will then see you every day," complained Juggy. Despite her advancing years, Shantadevi had maintained her separate residence in Pune since her retirement. She wanted no part of Juggy's frequent transfers which would uproot her well-set life in Pune.

"*Masi,* Juggy has been kind enough to let me

look into one recent murder. You would have read all about it in the papers I am sure," Batty said.

"Oh yes that one...what was her name again... yes, Rupali. Such a gorgeous woman. What a pity. Poor Mukesh," she said.

"Mukesh?" both Batty and Juggy asked incredulously.

"Mukesh...Dr Manohar as you know him Juggy. Just the other day he was chatting with me. He was so disappointed poor chap. Sad that this happened to him," she said.

"*Masi* what are you saying? How does Rupali's murder affect Dr. Manohar?" asked Batty.

"They were to get married shortly. Mukesh used to bring that girl along quite often to the club. Juggy you may not have seen them since you haven't been around much in the last few months and even so, you may not have noticed them. They used to sit in that corner table over there with their backs to the world, lost in their own little space. What a lovely pair they made. Apparently, Mukesh had finally found true love for the first time in his life," she said.

"Wonder who could have killed such a lovely woman," she intoned.

Batty sat up ramrod straight. Now this all made sense.

Dr. Manohar and Rupali were a couple! No

wonder she had filed for a divorce from Deep.

The Good Doctor cursed inwardly. The odd couple was back in his office and waiting in the adjoining room.

Turning to his patient he said, "Mrs. Bakshi, there is no need to worry. It is only a cyst and can be easily removed surgically. Whenever convenient, we can schedule a surgery. It is a minor procedure and you will be home in a day after that. There is no need to worry at this stage but I believe you should get this done and not wait."

"But Doctor, we have a wedding in the family next month and I need to be able to attend all the functions in the wedding. I cannot schedule surgery for the next 45 days," the patient said.

These people were crazy. They were actually willing to sacrifice health for emotional reasons. When will Indians learn to take their health seriously? He thought ruefully. Time after time, he had seen patients whose attitude towards their health and self-preservation was so cavalier, it was shocking. Right from women who wanted to have children at the risk of their own lives to the present specimen who was more concerned about a wedding than getting a much needed surgical procedure done.

"No problem Mrs. Bakshi. But make sure it is 45 days and no later and if you notice any pain or bleeding, come to me immediately. I am not happy about this delay but you leave me with no choice," he said, trying to sound calm and unconcerned.

As soon as Mrs. Bakshi left, Batty and Robin sauntered in and took their places opposite the good doctor.

"What brings you here again? " he asked with thinly disguised irritation.

"Dealing with you, Doctor is becoming like pulling teeth. Do you realise that you not coming clean is hampering this investigation? I can have you arrested for obstruction," thundered Batty.

"Wait a minute! I have answered all your questions Mr. Bhowmick every time you have come to me. If there was a specific question that I have not answered or lied about, your irritation would be justified. Just because I am being polite with you, and I don't care who you know, I am not going to be accused of something that I have not done and definitely not when there is no reason. Please choose your next words very carefully as anything you say next will have implications Mr. Bhowmick," said Dr. Manohar, his temper now matching Batty's.

Robin kicked Batty just to ensure that he kept his temper in check.

"You and Rupali were planning on getting married and she had even sent Deep a divorce notice so that you two could start life as a couple," said Batty, his voice barely higher than a whisper.

"When your wife to be was murdered and you never came clean about your relationship with her, does this not make it look like you had reasons for hiding this?"

Dr. Mukesh Manohar slowly started to resemble a shrunken jellyfish that gets washed ashore sometimes in the rains on Mumbai's beaches. Gone was the irritation and in its place, an infinite sadness came over his visage.

"I loved her, really loved her. She was an amazing person. Deep had taken advantage of her and got her involved in a criminal enterprise. She was running around to defend herself and had lost everything. Remarkably, she still had her joie-de-vivre intact and would be scintillating company. It was almost as if the universe had sent her to me. Until I met her, I did not realise what I really wanted from a life partner. I had never felt this way about anyone else. True, she wasn't highly educated but she was street smart and she had class. I couldn't have asked for a better person. Unfortunately, fate had other plans and she paid the price. You have no idea what it is like to have loved and lost, Mr. Bhowmick," he said.

Batty's face twisted in a sardonic grin at the last line. His mind went to Shalini, now almost forgotten in the hustle and bustle of daily life. *Dear Doctor, I do know what it is to have loved and lost,* he said under his breath. It must have been audible as Robin stared at him with surprised eyes.

He immediately checked himself and brushed all thoughts of Shalini away. No matter how much time passed, all it took was a mention of love and the first thing that came to his mind was Shalini.

"You talk as if you are convinced that Deep is the one who has committed the murder. It could be something else entirely," said Batty.

"I knew her better than even Deep as she would confide in me. She told me the issues she was having with Deep and her ex-partner Abbas. Both these people had taken her to the cleaners for no fault of hers. Now that Deep discovered that she was planning on leaving her which would leave him with no place to go, he decided to do her in. What else can it be? It is certainly a crime of passion and not a robbery," he said.

"I know that. That is why we are investigating," said Batty with slight annoyance.

"In her divorce notice, Rupali has stated the ground for divorce as physical and sexual abuse and has claimed that she has medical evidence of the same. I am guessing that the source of that evidence is you and there was never any such thing," said Batty.

Doctor Mukesh Manohar nodded wordlessly.

"I wanted to help her and my being a gynaecologist with high credibility would have helped her case," he said.

"Whose idea was this?" asked Batty.

"Rupali suggested it to me one day when we were discussing the way out of her predicament," he said.

Robin ordered an uncharacteristic black coffee. Batty was sipping on a lemon tea.

"I am getting more and more convinced that Deep is our man," Robin said. "He had the motive, now that we know about the divorce, and he certainly had the passion ignited by the receipt of the divorce notice. Even the doctor seems to think so," she added.

"Robin, you underestimate the role of one person in this entire episode - Rupali herself. I don't much care for the Doctor's views except for the fact that he admitted to his true feelings about Rupali. Isn't it amazing that everyone believes that Rupali was framed and innocent in the entire India Biofuels affair? And all of these happen to be seasoned men who have seen enough of this world. First Prabhu More, a hardened cop in the EOW section that deals with financial crimes, then Devendra Jamdar, a public prosecutor and finally Doctor Manohar who is a man of this world. All three of them believed that Rupali was a victim," Batty said.

"So if such seasoned men believed it to be true, doesn't it stand to logic that it must be true. Moreover, since none of them had any vested interest in Rupali," Robin said.

Batty looked at Robin with some degree of

concern.

"What has happened to your journalistic instincts?" he asked.

"You don't see the problem in this situation at all? It is very clear to me what has happened here," he said.

"All three were made to believe that Rupali was innocent and a victim. All of them believed her, all of them had sympathy for her. One was madly in love with her. The other two were totally sympathetic towards her despite the requirement of their professions to be analytical, impartial and to some extent, distrustful. Rupali was no ordinary human being. She was a master manipulator." Batty said.

Robin looked up with a start. Batty was right. She kicked herself for being blindsided. *Rupali had managed to get to her. Even after her death! Master manipulator indeed!*

Chapter 14

2008-2009

Pune reminded Rupali of an overgrown Vasai. There was actually very little comparison between the two places except that Vasai felt like a small town. Pune was clearly much prettier and the climate was a lot more salubrious. However, there was a world of difference between the people in Vasai and Pune. While the denizens of Vasai were street smart and had gotten their smarts from the giant Metropolis where most of them worked, Puneites had no such training. Laid back and slow to the point of being frustrating, Puneites were a different breed altogether. Not entirely country bumpkins and not fully city dwellers, Puneites were a half house somewhere in between. Parts of Pune behaved like they lived in a very affluent part of a large city while other parts behaved like they were in the boondocks. Today's Pune is far more vibrant but a decade ago, Pune had just begun its journey into vibrancy but wasn't quite there yet.

Rupali had decided to shift to Pune as it provided proximity to Mumbai and yet the distance that she needed. She had sold her Mumbai property to settle the bank's mortgage and had landed around 35 lakhs after paying off the bank. She had no intention of paying Definity anything on the film. There was no way they were pursuing her legally for the 55 lakhs that Parmanand claimed that she and Sohail owed her jointly. Any fool knew that in the absence of a personal guarantee to repay someone or mortgage of tangible assets, Indian courts took anywhere between 20 to 30 years to process a law suit for such recoveries. She intuitively knew that if Definity sued her, she would be able to counter-sue and claim that Definity's interest and penalties were usurious. In any case, Parmanand never pursued any legal remedies against them since he had come to the same conclusion.

Rupali had kept her Honda CRV and had rented a two bedroom apartment in the upmarket Koregaon Park area of Pune. She knew that appearances mattered everywhere and in smaller towns, these mattered even more.

Clover Park View was a recently constructed 7 storey apartment in Koregaon Park which was perfect for Rupali. The rent was not cheap and at Rs. 17,500 a month, the instalment of another Rs. 20,000 on her car and living expenses of herself and her parents at another Rs. 70,000-75,000 a month, she was looking at a monthly outgo of over a lakh. With no income in sight, this was a big worry for Rupali. Her remaining capital would be gone in a couple of years unless she could do something that made her some more money. She had already spent 15 lakhs furnishing the house with all the required amenities that she was now very much used to.

She scanned the daily newspapers carefully for business ideas and opportunities. She was tempted to dabble in the stock markets but thought better of it which was prescient as the Crash of 2008 also went on to decimate all gains for Indian investors in the following months. She would make it a point to go out every day and sit in various cafes of Koregaon Park. She sat there alone apparently browsing her phone but her ears were tuned to people's chatter on the tables around her to pick up gossip and interesting tit-bits about things that she could perhaps use.

It was a typical Pune evening with a slight nip in the air. Rupali was sipping her cappuccino at German Bakery trying to listen in on a conversation that was going on behind her about raising money from investors. The main speaker, a gentleman who was addressed as Sudeshji by his guest, was saying, "Something about this project doesn't come across well. I can easily raise 200 crores for you but I am not convinced that this is a viable project. I know your father well and hence I agreed to meet you outside my office but this needs a lot more work, son."

Rupali was getting intrigued by the discussion and was listening intently with her back towards the two men.

Just then, she saw another face which brought back memories from her past. *It can't be. Oh God, it is!*

"Faheem! My God, it has been such a long time and look at you! You look so different! I wouldn't have even recognised you if I had passed you by on the streets," she exclaimed with a sharp intake of her breath.

Putting a finger on his lips, Faheem said, "Abbas. Abbas Kadri. Scientist and Research Fellow. ICRISAT, Hyderabad."

"What? How?!!" asked an incredulous Rupali.

"Not here, I know a quiet place where we can sit and talk," said Abbas.

Before they left German Bakery, she noticed that Sudeshji had left. She summoned one of the captains of the restaurant she knew well.

"Rajesh, I need your help. I was sitting checking my phone when I overheard a very interesting conversation on that table behind me. I found Sudeshji very interesting and his ideas very practical. You know me, I have been coming here regularly. I would like to meet him someday. How do I get in touch with him?" she asked innocently.

"Arre Madam, he is Sudesh Mittal, the boss of Morningstar. He is Pune's biggest stock broker and stays not very far from here. This is his favourite spot. The next time he comes here, I will pass on your message to him," the captain said, happily pocketing the 500 rupee note that Rupali had slipped him.

"Not yet, I will let you know when," she told Rajesh with a conspiratorial smile.

They were sitting in the almost empty restaurant of Ashirwad Hotel, one of the many slightly seedy hotels that dot the landscape of Indian cities. Not part of any large chain and made for budget travellers, such stand-alone hotels are found all over India in all its cities and towns, big and small. During the day, these are love nests for amorous couples where rooms are rented by the hour to make up for lack of occupancy. The restaurant of Ashirwad Hotel was called Annapurna named after the Goddess of food in Indian mythology. At this time of the day, it was almost empty with a couple of stragglers hanging around having tea and pakodas. Faheem, now Abbas, chose a corner table which was out of earshot. As soon as they were seated, Rupali burst out with excitement.

"You are now Abbas? Where did you vanish all these years? And what is this scientist thing? What is going on?"

Abbas smiled and said quietly, "All in good time Rupali. But first tell me what are you doing in Pune?"

She told him all that had transpired since they last met. The version that Abbas heard was slightly modified from the original. As Rupali told it, it was all about her getting suckered by Sohail; her trusting the wrong person and despite her better judgement; she feeling sorry for an old friend, made the blunder of lending him money. Her own greed and the desire to become a producer in the film business was conveniently left out of the narration.

Abbas clucked ruefully.

"Rupali, you are too trusting. Business is not for you. You and I are a winning team. Let me tell you something - I have a scheme for you which will work even better than our Metro Bank job," he said. He then proceeded to tell her all about Jatropha cultivation and how this was a gold mine for investors but more importantly, a chance to make serious moncy for thc two of them.

Rupali listened to him intently. It was indeed interesting and even though she knew nothing of this plant thing, it sounded very good.

Abbas then told her how he had created an identity for himself based on his father who had retired from ICRISAT and had passed away some time ago. He had all the research papers lined up and complete proof of the concept. He had also identified land that could be ideal for cultivation of Jatropha.

"All we need to do is to find investors," he said.

"How much to we need? And where will we

find investors from?" asked Rupali.

"You just gave me the break I was hoping for when I met you at the German Bakery. Sudesh Mittal is the ideal candidate for this. We need to raise around 100 crores and Mittal's firm will do it for us," he replied.

"Arre, I just casually asked about him but I don't know him!" she exclaimed.

"Rupali, has anyone ever been able to say no to you?" he said suggestively.

"Look, you and I will be partners in this and if you bring Sudesh on board, we could create a 500-crore company in no time. This thing is red hot. Everyone is talking about this today. We are the only game in town as there is no one even thinking about doing something on this scale," he said.

"Dear Rupali, I am deeply concerned that you lost all your money in the film business. That business is not for outsiders like us. These film fellows only work well with their own kind since they need each other. Everyone else is cannon fodder for them...open to be exploited! I promise you, you and I will make at least 10-crores each out of this venture even before the company starts producing anything. And the rest will be bonus," he added.

Rupali reflected on this. She realised that Abbas had figured out how to make money even before this company took off. Which clearly meant that they were scamming investors, making their money and then leaving matters to fate. If it worked, the investors made money. If it didn't, it was a business loss and like many start-ups, this would go bust. Having once tasted blood in the Metro Bank case, she also was now more confident that she could figure out a way of getting out of tricky situations intact. No one really suspected a beautiful woman in financial crimes unless her fingerprints were all over it. She will have to be careful about that. Abbas was a criminal anyway and he would once again disappear if matters got heated up. Abbas also sounded a lot like Sohail. That one had cleaned her out. She would have to be careful, that this time, the same thing didn't happen.

Also, no one could possibly accuse her of anything if she could play the victim card once again like she had successfully done earlier. Only this time she would have to be far more careful. She was no longer an employee. She was going to be a co-owner. This was clearly different. But she just might be able to come up with a survival plan!

Abbas was also convinced that she had no head for business. This was exactly as she intended. Most people think of beautiful people as those living off their looks and not their brains; particularly when it comes to women. What they do not realise is that most beautiful women are some of the smartest people on the planet. They know how to get what they want and they openly use their sexuality to get what a normal person cannot even dream of. They become aware of their power over people in their young age and as they enter their youth, they realise what a winning hand fate has dealt them. You will never find a beautiful woman that is poor or down and out. The beautiful have won life's lottery at birth. For them, it only gets better and better from there.

To Rupali, 10 crores sounded like retirement money. Obviously, worth a shot. She was bored and worried at the same time as it is. Her money would run out sooner rather than later and this looked like something that made sense and was worth the payoff. There was nothing else happening in her life anyway.

"Lucky that you bumped into me then," she said brightly. "God wants us to work together again Abbas. I trust you completely but I don't understand much of business as you know. I will do what you guide me to do," she said trying her best to appear sincere and gullible.

"I did not bump into you dear Rupali, I found you," said Abbas looking at her directly. "It took a while to locate you. Once I realised that my scheme could work, I needed a partner who can convince people to put in the money for reasons more than the merit of the project. And you can mesmerise anyone," he added.

"People don't know you or me. Even if I can

talk people into things, we have no track record of having made money for people. We have no references in this city and our backgrounds are weak. This is not going to work," said Rupali.

"I am aware of that. While my meeting you was not luck, what was real luck was you finding out about Sudesh Mittal. This is a sign from the heavens. He has people's trust. All you need to do is convert him. He will bring in the rest. And that, my dear Rupali, you can do with your eyes closed. I have seen what you did to a room full of people at Daawat Bar. Sudesh should be a cake walk for you my dear," he said.

"I will need time though. This can't be done quickly," she countered.

"We have all the time in the world. Would three months be sufficient?" he asked.

"That should do," she said.

The stage was now set for their act to begin.

Colonel Shyam Punjwani opened the door to find Rupali standing there with a container of his favourite sabudana wada. Even though Rupali had become his neighbour recently, Colonel Punjwani was quite fond of the Jadhavs. Being a widower with only one daughter who was married and lived in Canada, Punjwani had no other family in close vicinity. Saraswati being a terrific cook and Punjwani being a foodie, it was common to see food being delivered to Punjwani several times in a month. Punjwani was not nosy and did not ask questions about their background and the Jadhavs did not volunteer much. He was also fond of Rupali as his own daughter was about the same age.

"Wah! Sabudana Wada - my favourite!" said Punjwani with barely concealed glee.

"Do tell your mother that she is beyond compare in the food department. Even my late wife, god bless her soul, was a good cook, but your mother is something else altogether," he said.

"Uncle, don't be funny. Mother is a good cook. You unnecessarily praise her and then we can't even say anything. If we find flaws in her cooking, she instantly calls us ingrates and lets us know how much you appreciate her food. You are making things tough for us Uncle," Rupali said with a large smile on her face.

"By the way Uncle, you are a member of Poona Club, aren't you? Can I become a member too?" she asked.

Punjwani explained to her that Poona Club had stopped accepting new membership applications for the last 10 years and even now, there was a long waiting list that had not moved much in the last two years as the Club only admitted new members when someone died.

"But you can always come with me in the evenings when I go to the Club. I see that you are sometimes at home in the evenings. I am going there shortly - do you want to accompany me?" he asked.

Rupali had browsed the website and ran a google search on Morningstar over the previous week with the help of another neighbour's daughter who had a computer at home. She had found that last month, Morningstar had hosted their "employee of the year" function at the Poona Club. She deduced that being an owner driven company, it must be Sudesh whose membership of the Club would have made it possible for the company to host this event. It was an educated guess for an uneducated Rupali but it turned out to be correct.

Rupali made it a point of going to the Club two or three times a week with Punjwani. They would sit in the verandah of the Club and while Punjwani would nurture his scotch, she would either have a cappuccino or coconut water. They would talk about the goings-on in the world and Punjwani, after his two drinks, would warm up to his army and war stories. Having seen action in both the 1971 as well as the 1965 wars, both of which India had won decisively, he had a lot of stories to tell Rupali. To Rupali's delight, she often spotted Sudesh at the Club. Whenever she would see him leave for the rest room, she would also make it a point to excuse herself and go to the ladies' toilet. She would actually keep a watch to see when Sudesh emerged from the toilet and would then deliberately cross his path such that he had no choice but to notice her. This she was careful not to do too often but after the first couple of times, they started nodding at each other first and then smiling and then even exchanged a hello. In a month, they had started exchanging greetings and made some small talk. Sudesh would often stop by their table and make small talk with her. Then one fine day Rupali threw the bait.

"Sudeshji I wanted your opinion on some investment that I am planning to make. You know I am not really a financial or a business person but someone I know recommended my name to a scientist who has worked on some breakthrough that I don't understand," she said looking at him with a mixture of expectation and hesitation.

"I am sorry if I am such a bother to you. Maybe this is not an appropriate topic for this place," she said hurriedly.

Sudesh was overjoyed. He had been toying with finding a reason to spend more time with Rupali. In his business, he did not come across many women as it is and the one or two he had come across looked like dud small cap stocks - very little to recommend, no future, no scope and a dead-beat investment. This one was a true blue chip though. Being a leading stock broker, the city's creme de la creme was his clientele including top industrialists, senior government officials, cops and some ministers. By no stretch of imagination good looking, Sudesh more than made up for his lack of good looks with an aura of power and authority and like several men with power and authority, his appetite for women was insatiable. He normally used the city's top madams for escort services but the thrill of a conquest was something else altogether. Like finding a multi-bagger stock that not all could find and benefit from.

"Not at all Rupali. You are welcome at my office anytime that you wish to come over. We can discuss your investment proposal at length over a cup of coffee," he offered trying to conceal his delight.

"They are constantly following up with me but even though I know this is genuine thing, I am totally lost in this," she said.

"Would tomorrow 4 PM be convenient to you, madam?" he asked solicitously.

Morningstar was spread over 10,000 sq ft on Fergusson College Road in the heart of the city on an entire floor in a recently constructed building. The place exuded wealth and power. Rupali was directly shown to Sudesh's cabin. He occupied a corner office of around 600 sq ft with an anteroom, a private pantry and a shower-cum-toilet all included in its confines. Tastefully done up with walnut wood and brown leather, the centre of the room had a large glass topped L-shaped table which had a row of computer monitors on one side which showed the bid-offer positions and transactions as well as price movements of key stocks and bonds.

Except for a pen stand and a silver Ganesha, the table was bare. Sudesh had dressed carefully that day and he was wearing a crisp white linen shirt pressed to perfection stitched to be worn untucked over grey slacks. His shirt was open at the collar and the top button was also undone. He wore a thick gold chain with an OM diamond pendant that touched his hairy chest. On his feet were Bally loafers.

Rupali had also dressed carefully. She wore a deep necked top over blue jeans and she was fully aware of what she was displaying. The two gladiators were circling each other. *Each thought the other was a sacrificial lamb.*

Sudesh was bowled over when he saw Rupali. The swell of her breasts beneath the fitted top and the exposed cleavage drove him crazy. He used all his willpower to prevent his hands from trying to touch them. He solicitously asked Rupali if she would like tea or coffee. Rupali settled for a cappuccino.

"Yes madam, please tell me. How can I help?" he asked her.

"I know this scientist Abbas. He is like a genius at ICRISAT and he has developed some incredible technology that allows higher extraction of something called bio-diesel from some plant starting with J. I am so bad with names," Rupali said.

"He trusts me but doesn't know many people and wants to commercialise his discovery. He asked me to put some money. I have some that I have inherited from my grandfather by way of property in Mumbai that I can sell and some idle fixed deposits but I would feel better if someone with your financial acumen could guide me and help me structure this investment. It is a top-secret idea with huge returns and Abbas is worried that if the idea leaks, more people will get in with more money than us so I would ideally not like to share it with outsiders. But somehow, even though we don't know each other well, I felt like I could trust you," she said.

Sudesh was suddenly interested. A beautiful, desirable and available moneyed lady with a money spinning idea. And willing to put in her own money as well. It couldn't get better than this!

"No worries on that account Madam. We are used to handling very sensitive things. You have no idea what kind of clients I have. They would not even like me to reveal their identities to anyone," he said.

"That makes me feel so much better," said Rupali. "I can definitely relax around you then."

Rupali explained the entire project to him. Sudesh, like everyone else, had been reading a lot about the potential of the Jatropha plant to meet India's energy requirements and this seemed like the area of the future. He was always looking for the next big thing. Before the Y2K boom which was followed by the dot com boom, he had got his clients to invest in a little-known company called Infosys which had skyrocketed in value since then and had made instant millionaires of so many of his clients. He had also bought some and profited handsomely from it as well. He had seldom lost money for his clients and hence had their implicit trust. Such investment ideas came once in a decade. Who knew - maybe this one was the next Infosys.

Sudesh did not want the meeting to end so soon. He said, "I have a few more meetings today. Would it be okay if we continued our discussions over a drink at the Club? I don't think it is the day your uncle comes to the Club. So we will have unrestricted time to discuss our project."

Rupali agreed. Sudesh wanted to spend more time with her. An evening invitation was a half-way mark to the bedroom. This is generally how men indicated which direction they wanted this to go. A proposal for a drink or dinner or both meant that the man intended to woo the woman and eventually convince her to sleep with him. There is usually no other play than that in a man's mind. None of them were looking for soulmates, companions or any such romantic rubbish. Even though they made all those noises and tried to say the right things, in the end, they were just looking to get laid. Rupali, of all people, knew this extremely well.

"You must try the Mai-Tai here, it's very good," said Sudesh as they settled into one of the wicker chairs in the Club's lawns. "There is a nip in the air and a Mai-Tai will keep you warm," he added. Rupali had no idea what Mai-Tai was but she understood that it was alcoholic and that was what she wanted.

"Sudeshji, before we get on to business, I would like to know more about you. You are a very interesting personality and I would very much like to know more about you," she said.

Sudesh could not have been happier. He promptly launched into a long-winded tale of his childhood, how he made his first trade, how he started Morningstar, how he made his first million before Morningstar, how he had delivered several multi-baggers for his clients, who his clients were and where he saw himself in the next five years. Nothing like a beautiful woman wanting to know more about you! Rupali was listening with rapt attention and what looked like wide-eyed admiration to Sudesh. In reality, she had to keep her eyes wide open to avoid falling asleep. She was also four Mai-Tais down. Sudesh had finished almost six or seven scotches in the same time. He had started to slur slightly and Rupali, though totally sober, also added a little heaviness to her speech to match Sudesh's slurring.

"Rupali, tell me truthfully - do you have a boyfriend or are you engaged?" Sudesh suddenly asked veering away from his bragging session.

Rupali allowed some colour to come to her cheeks. She shook her head in response.

"How is that possible Rupali? Such a gorgeous woman is single?" he asked, slurring on gorgeous.

"Sudeshji, I am still looking for someone who I can look up to as a companion. Most men are too immature. I want someone who is accomplished, a man of the world and who can teach me things I don't know. I am not hung up on a formal relationship or marriage. I will know when someone like that presents himself in front of me," she said with a mysterious smile.

Sudesh's animal brain was now on total alert. Rupali had just told him that she wouldn't mind a relationship with him. Today was certainly his lucky day. He frantically tried to think of how to take her to bed at that very moment. The opportunity then presented itself. The Club steward walked up to their table and said, "Sir, we are closing the bar. Please place your order as we need to close the billing."

Sudesh made a face at the steward.

"We have just started my friend. How can we finish so soon?" he protested.

"We have had quite a bit Sudeshji, lets continue another day," Rupali said, fully expecting Sudesh to vehemently protest.

"No, no. We still have a lot to discuss. May I suggest that we go to our company guesthouse which is fully staffed and not far from here? No one will disturb us there and I will drop you home once we are done," Sudesh said making a desperate attempt to extend the evening.

"It is already quite late Sudeshji. We should be going. You have been a most gracious host so I don't want to refuse you so maybe for just one quick drink at the guest house and we can be on our way then," she offered.

Morningstar's guest house was in Kalyani Nagar which was not far from Koregaon Park. Tastefully done up and spread over 2,500 sq ft, the guesthouse had two sitting areas, two bedrooms, a servant's room, a large home theatre setup with cinema chairs for 10 people in a corner, a dining area and a kitchen. Narayan, the cook and Krishna, the caretaker were in attendance. Sudesh guided her to an intimate sitting area adjoining the master bedroom and ordered their drinks. The caretaker fixed her a near perfect Mai-Tai and Rupali could see that Sudesh was a man of style and liked to live well. Half-way through their drinks, Sudesh offered to show her around the guesthouse. He started with the farthest parts of the apartments and finally came to the master bedroom. Rupali was admiring the art on the wall of the master bedroom when Sudesh leaned against the door to shut it without locking it. Rupali noticed it from the corner of her eye and asked to use the bathroom attached to the bedroom. Sudesh was suddenly unsure of what to do next. The liquor in his brain was egging him on and his instinct was to lock the door and embrace Rupali when she came out of the bathroom. His rational brain was telling him not to be an idiot and to not rush matters. Rupali could get offended and then he would lose her permanently. A beautiful moneyed woman could find many advisors. The best course was to let it be. She had already come to his guesthouse. The next time would be easier since the stage had already been set. Yet his animal brain told him that the time was now and they were both drunk. He could get away by apologising if things didn't go his way. While he stood there debating with himself, the bathroom door opened and the decision was taken out of his hands.

Rupali was standing there draped only in a towel.

Sudesh felt the next few days go by in a blur. His days were busy going over Rupali's business plan and getting into the details of Abbas's achievements and his scientific data and research. His nights were full of ecstasy and he was always looking to rush through the day so that he could reach his guesthouse and meet Rupali. Sudesh took an instant liking to Abbas and he found him capable and sincere. Rupali had already told him a lot about Abbas and he was all that Rupali had said he would be. The project looked really good, the numbers seemed to indicate very good returns with a potential bumper prize if the company did well and they could go public. Sudesh had spent quite a bit of time with Abbas and convinced him to allow Morningstar to privately raise 100 crores from their investors. Sudesh had also involved his head of client relationship, a handsome Punjabi by the name of Deep Kalra who shared his boss's views completely. Abbas was not keen as both Rupali and Abbas felt that since Abbas's research was a breakthrough that was not known to the outside world, they were worried about exposing their business secret to Sudesh's investors, many of whom were leading businessmen and could be a potential competition to Abbas and Rupali.

Showing masterful strategy, Abbas and Rupali planted the germ of the idea in Sudesh's head, blindsided him with Rupali's beauty and his own lust, resisted him which made him more aggressive to push for a more ambitious target and finally delivered the knock-out punch. By now Sudesh was totally convinced of Abbas's project and was willing to raise money from his investors. Deep had also assured him that this would be a cake walk. But this was not enough. Abbas and Rupali knew that many of his investors were shrewd businessmen and they were worried that one or more of them may decide to do a little background-check on Abbas and Rupali and their skeletons would come tumbling out which could mean the end of everything that they had worked for. That was a chance they simple could not take.

One evening, in the middle of all this, after

Sudesh and Rupali had had what Sudesh thought of as wild passionate sex, a description Rupali did not really endorse having seen and had better, Rupali seemed upset. She usually put up a son-et-lumiere show for him each evening when they had sex and Sudesh was convinced that Rupali had never had such wonderful sex before. Rupali herself had admitted as much to Sudesh once or twice coyly after sex taking care not to say it too often. She had also wondered once or twice loudly to him during times of passion as to how she got along without him all these years. Done right and with the right amount of sincerity, such praise has an electrifying effect on men. After all nothing boosts a man's ego more than having a woman tell him on his face that he is great in bed. Their vanity does not let them suspect anything otherwise and they get more addicted to their sexual partner. In Rupali's case, she was not asking for anything from Sudesh. At least not anything that Sudesh could obviously realise.

"What is the matter sweetheart? Why so serious?" asked Sudesh doing his best imitation of the Joker.

"I am in a fix. The property in Mumbai that I was going to sell to invest 40 crores in Abbas's project has developed some issues. I am unable to sell it. The lawyers are saying my grandfather's will has to be probated. I had no idea. This will take months. How will I be able to invest in Abbas's project now? You will find investors I am sure but

I will lose all the upside and opportunity. After all it is my project and I should make good money from this. I am really upset. I wish I had met you sooner - you would have advised me correctly I am sure and resolved this issue much earlier," she said breathlessly on the verge of breaking into tears.

"Is that all? What am I there for sweetheart? I will invest in your name. You pay me back when you make money. No interest, only principal. The least I can do for you dear Rupali. Don't worry at all," Sudesh said.

"No, that is not fair. You are too generous. I have no right to take advantage of you. Only if you agree to a 50:50 split I can consider your offer. You invest in my name and we split the profits 50:50 after repayment of your investment," she said.

"I would not take your money Rupali but since you are insisting, I agree. Now let me show you some magic. The project needs a total of 100 crores. You were planning on investing 40 crores. Abbas was getting sweat equity against his scientific discovery. The outside investors were putting in 60 crores for around 30 percent of the company. What if we restructure this one? Let's say both you and Abbas get 25% each and I get 10% as sweat equity and I get my investors to put in 100 crores for 40%? That way the company is worth 250 crores on day one and your stake is worth 62.5 crores and mine 25 crores. No investment required," Sudesh crowed.

"Can it be done? Sounds too good to be true,"

said Rupali now smiling.

"I will put in 25 crores for my 10 percent and take it out by way of land purchase when investors put their money. That way I will establish the valuation and since I have invested, my investors will ask very few questions and we will close the subscription at 100 crores," said Sudesh.

"Oh Sudesh, you have solved one of my life's biggest hurdles. I don't know how I can thank you. No, actually I do know how I can thank you," she said yanking at Sudesh's bathrobe.

"This is the smartest guy in the whole of Morningstar," said Sudesh introducing Deep Kalra to Rupali. "He has a magical hold over all our top clients and if he says something, they cannot refuse," he added.

"Sudeshji you are too kind. These are all his clients but they are good to me. They know I represent Sudeshji and treat me as his alter ego. They also know that every recommendation that I make is blessed by Sudeshji," Deep said.

"I am sure that is not the entire story and you are too modest Deepji. All real achievers are modest and believe in spreading the credit around. I am sure you are as good as Sudeshji is saying if not better," said Rupali.

Deep was pleased. A beautiful lady with impeccable manners. Also moneyed. Some people did have everything.

"I have spoken to some of our clients and they seem to be interested. Since you are also investing your money at the same price as them, they are happy to tag along. They just want to meet Rupali and Abbas once to understand. I am thinking I will gauge their reactions and then arrange one town hall meeting for all of those who are interested. Abbas can make the presentation and Sudeshji you can answer all the queries," said Deep.

Rupali was beginning to appreciate Deep's expertise in financial selling. This was a different business altogether and the crux of selling financial instruments was to create greed. If investors got a sense that they would be left out of a lucrative deal, they would clamour to get in. If, on the other hand, they got a sense that the fund raising was not going well, even if they liked it, then they would hem and haw, waste time and ultimately say no. The first rule of this world - people want what they can't get. If it is available, it is suspect. There was also another angle to Rupali's respect for Deep. Sooner or later, they would need an insider friend who was skilled and a professional. Sudesh, for all his wealth and power, was not a professional. He had his uses but once the money was raised, she would need Deep to keep a check on Abbas. She didn't trust Abbas at all and if Deep could be made to weigh in from her side and not Sudesh's, she would have an effective counterweight in the company. But the time for that was a little further down the line.

"The Lehman Brothers' collapse is not a lone incident. I can see that it will hurt us really bad," Deep was saying to Sudesh when Rupali entered his office.

"This is India, what have we got to do with Lehman?" Sudesh asked incredulously.

Deep explained how it was now apparent that the instruments that the players in the US financial system used to gamble, the CDOs, were a huge risk to the entire world and India was not insulated.

"Matter of time," he said.

"From our immediate perspective, we should close the fund raising on the Jatropha project quickly otherwise the interest could vaporize," cautioned Deep.

"You may be right. I am seeing a little slackening of interest among some of the people who were very keen on investing. I have had no calls this week since Monday which is not a good sign," said Sudesh.

"Here's what I suggest. You call Neterwala and tell him that you regret how he missed out on the subscription which was so oversubscribed that we had to turn down some people," Sudesh continued.

Deep understood immediately what Sudesh was trying to do. Kill the supply so that the demand can emerge. They had let the deal remain open a little too long and the financial news from the US was starting to give people in India some jitters already. Closing subscription would mean that the fence sitters would jump in and while they may not get all the money that they were looking to raise, they may end up with most of it anyway. Neterwala was a medium size investor who was very well networked and though this deal was not what he would normally invest in, the fact that it had closed and he had not responded on time so had been left out would be conveyed by him to the entire investor community. Hopefully, some of them would then call Deep wanting in.

"Sudeshji I am getting angry calls from our clients asking to be let into the deal. I have taken a rough total of the interest and it is around 50 crores so far. May not go much higher," said Deep.

"Great! Now get back to each one of them and tell them to keep this absolutely confidential. Accept their money and inform them that they are always to claim that they were a part of the original allotment," said Sudesh. "Just ensure that they believe that they are the only one. Put one or two through to me so that I can personally get them the allotment and it looks like I intervened to make it happen," said Sudesh with a twinkle in his eye.

And, in the next two weeks, they had their 50 crores. Very soon after that, the Indian stock markets tanked and remained that way until the end of 2009. They had managed to raise money in the nick of time.

Chapter 15

Vinay Shahastrabuddhe wasn't feeling very well that morning. Uncharacteristically, he had eaten a large breakfast having slept early the night before without eating. His faithful retainer, Madhav, had made a three-egg masala omlette and he had devoured it with three slices of toast with heaps of butter. To top it, he had two glasses of fresh orange juice and two cups of coffee. By the end of it all, he was regretting it and feeling quite sick. The fact that he had to deal with dead bodies after such a large meal did not help.

It had been quite a few days since he had worked on Rupali's autopsy and even though he had more or less concluded, something had made him set it aside for a later date. He was hoping to spend more time on the autopsy and clear a couple of niggling doubts that were on his mind. This morning, he had finally found a time block of 2-3 hours where he could get into this subject. It had been more than a week since he had told Major Bhowmick that he would revert in a couple of days. Since Bhowmick had not called to remind him, he surmised that either the case had been closed or he was still wound up in the investigation. Having known Bhowmick earlier, he believed it was more of the latter than the former. The Major would not be expected to close the case without getting his final verdict.

What he now saw puzzled him a bit. Since there were 16 stab wounds, these were a mixture of ante-mortem, peri-mortem and post-mortem wounds. When a victim is being stabbed, the first one or two stabs, if rendered in such a manner as to cause death, would be ante-mortem or prior to death, wounds. These usually show signs of inflammation which post-mortem, or subsequent to death, wounds seldom do. Ante-mortem wounds also show a lot more blood around the wound since the heart is beating and pumping when the wound was inflicted. Peri-mortem wounds, in contrast, are those made when the death has occurred just before the wound and shock and haemorrhage resulting in death have taken place. There is minimal, if any, haemorrhage in the wound because of the very low blood pressure due to shock and the dying process.

What Vinay saw today on closer examination was a mixture of all three but with one or two curious characteristics. Usually, ante-mortem wounds have irregular contours as the victim is usually moving while peri-mortem and post-mortem wounds are cleaner since the body by then has become still. In Rupali's case, all wounds were clean and there was no irregularity in their contours at all. Vinay then remembered that she was reported as lying down on the bed and had been perhaps stabbed in her sleep since there did not appear to be any resistance at all from the shape of the wounds. Like knifing a cold slab of meat, he thought.

There was also a lot of post-mortem bruising since blood had pooled under gravity as it does not clot after death and caused bruising of lower limbs, arms, hands and feet. Some of the smaller blood vessels had also haemorrhaged under the pressure of the pooled blood. Vinay made a mental note to check for LTB4, short for Leukotriene B4, in all the wounds, a chemical that is found only in ante-mortem injuries that is involved in inflammation. Post-mortem and peri-mortem injuries generally do not have LTB4. This would help Vinay confirm the nature of each injury.

Vinay also made a mental note to additionally check for Mast cells in each wound. These cells contain chemicals that start the healing process and help control the flow of blood. Degranulation of Mast cells would mean that the wound was ante-mortem. Both LTB4 and Mast cell exploration would need more time, quite a bit of it under a microscope. Vinay's thoroughness was his hallmark and his dogged pursuit of even the tiniest doubt had provided several investigators and Batty with many an insight in the past.

Vinay now stepped back and looked at the dead body again. He tried to enact how someone could have stabbed Rupali. He was sure that death had occurred swiftly or perhaps while Rupali was asleep and she had had no chance of a resistance. The face had also not registered surprise or shock which was unusual. The wounds were also a little odd. They had the same angle of entry on both sides of the body which indicated that the murderer was ambidextrous. Suddenly, Vinay's head cleared and he looked up in shock. There was another possibility.

There were two people involved in the stabbing. One on each side of the body.

Batty was listening intently as Vinay first explained to him and then finished explaining his theory. While Vinay hedged his bets by saying that he still had to examine the LTB4 chemical and the mast cells for degranulation of each wound, his conclusion had been reached that there were two people involved in the murder. Batty immediately gunned his Yamaha and reached the police station in record time.

"Aga Hil, Hil pori hilla, tujha kapadila tilla. Tujha kapadila tilla ke Lokhande ni pakadle tula," Lokhande composed a ditty on-the-spot by inserting his own lyrics to a marathi folk song, delighted on being presented with an open-and-shut case. The suspect, a woman in her late thirties, was staring at him clearly doubting his sanity. A woman constable accompanied her.

"See this is how cases are solved. Reported yesterday, solved today. The famous PC Jewellers case," he bragged to Shinde.

Shinde badly wanted to tell Lokhande that everyone knew it was the CCTV footage from the jewellery shop that had helped nab the culprit. This was no investigation; it was just looking for suspects. Hardly exemplary police detective work.

Instead, he simply nodded and said, "Sir, promotion pukka" which pleased Lokhande immensely. Throwing caution to the winds and putting the weighing scale out of his mind, Lokhande was contemplating ordering a vada pav when Batty made a dramatic entry. On the way, he had called Robin and asked her to drop everything and rush to the police station. She was just entering when Batty rushed in.

"We now have clear evidence. Please arrest Deep and Abbas. They have together killed Rupali," he said breathlessly.

Lokhande looked up in shock. *Two murderers for one murder? This time the army guy had certainly lost it.*

Batty explained to him and Shinde his conversation with Vinay and a police party left to take custody of Deep. Lokhande got busy in sending an urgent look out notice for Abbas with his photographs to all police stations in Maharashtra and neighbouring states.

"You killed her didn't you?" said Batty with barely hidden contempt.

"She wanted a divorce from you and wanted to marry Doctor Manohar. You couldn't take it. This would have ruined you and made you homeless since you had no money of your own.

Doctor Manohar has told us all about your issues with Rupali. Out of anger, you sought out Abbas who I believe had a grudge from the India Biofuels time since Rupali had gotten away scot free and you channelled his anger into a convenient revenge for you," said Batty.

Deep didn't react at first. He weighed the consequences of a response but his mind was rushing in different directions. One part of him told him to ignore this and until Batty could prove it, there was no harm that could come to him. The other part of him was just too tired of everything. Rupali gone, his future looking bleak and now he had to contend with the slow but sure progress of this investigation that would ultimately wear him down. He made his decision, finally deciding not to defend himself. When he looked up to face Batty, his face looked like death.

"Yes, I killed her. She was always a gold digger. Money was everything to her. She first used Sudesh by getting him into a honey trap and got him to raise the money. She then made sure that she took more than her share of the spoils as she was very much in the know of what Abbas was up to. Once she saw how good I was with investors and impressed with my business and corporate knowledge, she then dropped Sudesh and shacked up with me. I was led to believe I was the real deal for her and she wanted to settle down. She used me to frame Abbas first and then when the money ran out, she conveniently switched to Doctor

Manohar. Both Abbas and I were her victims," he said, suddenly feeling very relieved and very tired at the same time.

"Where did you hide the weapon?" asked Batty.

Deep looked at him wearily.

"I had taken one of Doctor Manohar's trophy knives that he kept in his clinic. We used it to stab her and left it on the body. I don't know how it disappeared," he said.

"That I can tell you my friend. You texted Doctor Manohar from Rupali's phone to come quickly. You expected Doctor Manohar to arrive, find the dead body, lose his wits, call the police and get arrested as by that time he would have handled his own knife and his prints would have been all over it. In your mind, it would have been just deserts. Two birds with one stone. Stupid idea, not very well thought through. Doctor Manohar turned out to be smarter than both of you. He came, he pocketed the knife, thoroughly cleaned it and put it back in his collection since I did not see any gap in his array of tools when we first visited him," said Batty.

Deep looked on wordlessly.

Shinde stepped up and asked for Lokhande's permission to speak.

"Sir, the police party returned from Mumbai last night. Their findings indicate a certain amount of truth in Deep's statements about Rupali. This is their entire report," he said, handing over a search report to Batty.

"Why wasn't I informed?" asked Lokhande with annoyance demanding to know what he wasn't told of the search party's findings.

"Sir, I was trying to discuss this with you in the morning but you were busy with the arrangements for the CM's visit tomorrow," he said.

Having remanded Deep into custody, Batty went through the search report. The real Rupali was revealed to him right from her Vasai days: her movie industry dabbling, the Bank job, her film production misadventure, it was all there. Batty learnt that Rupali's parents had died in Pune within a gap of one year soon after the India Biofuels deal soured. Vitthal of a heart attack and Saraswati, of multiple organ failure following severe pancreatitis. Rupali had informed some of her Vasai neighbours upon Saraswati's death for the prayer ceremony and the police party had found Saroj and some other neighbours who were aware of the entire sequence of Rupali's life since Saraswati confided in them. The Police party had also brought pictures of Faheem, Rupali and Arvind from Mumbai. Batty wasn't too surprised to see that Faheem and Abbas were one and the same person with some cosmetic differences.

"My guess is you will not find Abbas. He had

a knack for vanishing like he did during the Bank job. He will surface after a few years with another identity and an altered appearance. If you trace all his close and distant relatives, you may be able to get close to him. The Mumbai Police do not seem to have done a particularly diligent job in the Bank case," Batty observed.

Just then his phone rang. Lokhande had reported to Juggy about the closure of the case and he was calling to congratulate.

"Very good Bartaman, super job. You came through for me, like always. I have the CM's visit tomorrow to take care of in the morning. Will be working late into the night today. See you at home later tonight. Tomorrow we celebrate," said an overjoyed Juggy.

"Not a big deal Juggy. The case sort of solved itself it seems," said Batty joylessly.

"It was nothing I could not have done. I had said from the very beginning that the husband must have done it. The saheb did not listen to me and instead he got the army fellow involved. Now after wasting a couple of weeks, he is saying the same thing," Lokhande let out some steam lying beside Rohini.

Rohini propped herself up on one elbow and looked at him with irritation.

"How come you never get your due? This is not the first time I am hearing of this. Why don't you make a proper case for yourself with your higher officers? I am getting tired of your cribbing all the time. Either leave this job - we have enough anyway - or do something about it. Stop playing victim all the time," she said without much emotion.

"Arre, you don't know politics in the force. Best to let sleeping dogs lie. How does it matter to us who solves it? One headache less for me. We get good money from the builders to ignore complaints from the flat buyers and other financial cheats. Why create unnecessary headaches. Go to sleep baba, you have an early morning tomorrow. I was just letting you know that your husband is no less brilliant when it comes to solving crimes," said Lokhande, clearly avoiding a confrontation with her on this subject.

Rohini turned her back towards him and reflected on his words. She realised that her husband was under-appreciated and knowing him probably for good reason and needed some reinforcement to his confidence. She privately didn't think much of his intellectual abilities but aloud she said, "It is the Force's loss. They don't know how to recognise good officers and they don't value them. Don't worry. You have done well despite not being recognised. The kids and I are very happy with your progress."

Lokhande smiled with satisfaction in the darkness. He was certainly blessed to have Rohini.

Batty could not get rid of a niggling finger of suspicion in his head. Something was still not sitting right. Later, while gulping down half a pint of beer with Robin, he voiced his concerns with Robin.

"I am still not convinced that this is over. It somehow feels wrong. I am not saying that Deep did not have the motive or he didn't do it. He certainly did and for God's sake, he has confessed already. Abbas and he had the motive and executed the plan. The building's half-finished status helped them evade detection and there were no witnesses. If Deep had not confessed, we would not have even been able to convict him since there is literally no murder weapon, no prints, nothing. Merely circumstantial evidence. The court would have thrown out this case in the first hearing. There has to be more to it somehow." he fretted.

Robin reached out and touched his forearm.

"Stop being hard on yourself. Merely because your previous cases were the equivalent of a jigsaw puzzle does not mean that this one was a lesser accomplishment. Were it not for you, Lokhande would have beaten a confession out of poor Dharam and locked him up for good. Perhaps even hanged him. Sit back and reflect on a job well done. It was after all your digging that brought out the hypothesis and revealed so much more about the case which led to Deep's confession," she said.

"Rupali turned out to be real character, huh? What a wily woman. For somebody who did not even complete her graduation, she pulled off a perfect scam. Without getting caught at any time. She had remarkable talent," added Robin.

"Not to forget the willingness to use her sex appeal liberally," said Batty. "I am convinced that Prabu More, Devendra Jamdar and even the Mumbai Police investigating officer for the Bank scam were lured by her sob story liberally sprinkled with her willingness to please them in whichever way they wanted."

"I wonder why she was depressed and unwell in her last days though? Does not come across as someone prone to those feelings from whatever we have come to know about her so far," mused Robin.

A flicker of something flashed in Batty's mind but before he could grasp it, it was gone leaving him with a distinctly uneasy feeling.

Juggy came home around 11 pm. Sushma had retired and instructed their domestic help to serve dinner to Juggy when he came home. Batty was up trying to occupy his mind with television and failing miserably at it. He looked up when Juggy walked in.

"I have some rum that I brought along with me from the camp. Forgot to give it to you. How about it?" Batty asked Juggy.

Looking at his watch, Juggy's first inclination was to say no but he sensed that Batty wanted to talk and something was eating him up from inside. He knew him well enough to know that he really didn't have a choice. Batty wanted to drink rum and so they had to drink rum!

It was almost 1.00 am when they got rid of the empty bottle of rum. Juggy had barely managed three drinks but Batty had polished off the rest of the bottle. Juggy had a quick dinner and went off to bed. Batty's head was swimming. He hadn't eaten for hours and the liquor had hit him on an empty stomach. He did not even want to eat. Instead, he lay down in his room. Liquor had quietened his anxious mind to a large extent. In his drunken stupor, he was trying to recall that fleeting sensation he had felt when Robin was talking. What was she talking about? Oh yes, she was talking about how Rupali was depressed and unhappy and unwell in her last days. No! She was talking about why Rupali was depressed, unhappy and unwell. There was no apparent reason for it. She had her life all figured out and was looking forward to settling down with Dr. Manohar. Then why the sadness? He couldn't quite place that. His thoughts went to Dr. Manohar. The crafty bugger hadn't told them about the murder weapon. But then again why will he volunteer? The last thing he would want to is to get accused of a murder he had nothing to do with. He had already lost the love of his life. Ah, losing the one you love. He knew that feeling. Shalini. His one true love. What plans they had made for the future. He clearly recalled the slight quickening of his pulse every time he saw her. No one had been able to do that to him since then. She was literally tailor-made for him. Despite being so close, she hid her condition from him for such a long time.

If only he had known, she would be with him today. He had had absolutely no idea about Shalini's clinical depression. She had never told him. But then she was so full of life. He could not have suspected it anyway. He had been very serious about her. Perhaps, no, not perhaps. He was sure that he would have married her. If only she had not overdosed on her pills and ended her life. Shalini. What a tragedy! The memory of Shalini brought tears to his eyes. He was all alone so it was okay to cry. If only Shalini had not overdosed and if only somehow he had known. He would have certainly prevented it. His life would have been so different if she had been alive today. He could still recall with great clarity her beaming face, the perfume of her hair, the feel of her touch on his skin, her eager expression when he talked to her about his military life....

Batty suddenly sat bolt upright. An image flashed before his eyes. He had overlooked something; an image of something that did not belong in that setting. Something out of character that he should have caught but hadn't. Now it all made sense. He had the missing piece of information that solved the jigsaw puzzle. The funny thing was, all along, he was unhappy about the outcome today since it did not look like a jigsaw puzzle. Apparently this was one but was concealed. All murders were jigsaw puzzles and this one had finally emerged. He had also just chanced upon the missing piece.

Chapter 16

2009-PRESENT DAY

India Biofuels collected 50 crores and Rupali had been leaning on Deep more and more to understand the paperwork, how the company functioned, the powers, roles and responsibilities of the directors and the signatories, among other things. Sudesh was on the Board and he was also a shareholder. Deep was a director. It was Deep who had advised Rupali and got passed a resolution of the Board resting all powers with Abbas and also designating him as CEO and Managing Director. The same resolution named both Sudesh and him as investor nominees and non-executive directors. Only Rupali and Abbas were whole time executive directors. This ensured that when the shit hit the fan, it would be mostly Abbas who would be deep in it. But it also meant that Abbas would have no oversight on almost anything. He could easily swindle all of them.

Once the funds were banked, Sudesh had called an emergency meeting of the four partners. Deep was also very much a part of the group on Rupali's insistence and Sudesh had noticed Rupali's increasing fondness for Deep. While she still kept Sudesh happy and satiated, the frequency of their meetings had come down a notch and she chose to spend more time with Deep particularly during office hours taking his advice on the company and its various issues. Surprisingly, Abbas was not much involved in all this, and hardly consulted. Sudesh suspected that in Rupali's world-view, people were good only to the point of their usefulness. Sudesh was now aware that Rupali was almost entirely transactional. If you were the person of the moment, Rupali's attention was on you 100%. She would make you feel like you were the most important person in the world for her. She would listen with rapt attention to everything you had to say, laugh at all your jokes, compliment you on everything from your appearance to your dress sense to your smallest of qualities whether present or not and would also sleep with you if she thought it made sense to cement the relationship further. During sex, her entire focus was on pleasing you and giving you a great time. It was as if she could will herself to be your girl friend who hero-worshipped you. The combination of attention, admiration and great sex from a beautiful, desirable woman was something most people never get in their lives. It was impossible to resist. The nearest most people came to this was in the dance bars where if you were a big spender, the best-looking girls and dancers had eyes only for you and made you feel special by openly flirting with you to the exclusion of the rest of the crowd. Rupali had cut her teeth in that business and took this several notches higher in real life.

Sudesh understood that having collected 50 crores, his utility would be limited for Rupali from here onwards. Sure enough, once the funds were banked, Deep became the centre of attraction for Rupali. She still kept Sudesh humoured as he was a part of the Board of the company and she wanted a 3-to-1 dominance on the Board. Deep, however got most of her time and attention outside Sudesh's knowledge. Sudesh, the canny Marwari, suspected this anyway. If Rupali was transactional, he was fine with it. Who knew when the need would arise again. He could be as transactional as the other person if needed.

Addressing the partners, Sudesh said, "We have achieved nothing short of a miracle. In this market to raise 50 crores is not a joke. I would say we were very lucky. Now this creates a different problem. Abbas, your project was for 100 crores which involved putting up an extraction plant as well but obviously we haven't raised that kind of money. We still need to deliver returns to our investors who have invested based on my reputation and the fact that I have skin in the game as far as they are concerned. I want to hear from you: how do we proceed? Because, if there is no certainty of making money, I would rather return the funds than ruin my reputation."

Sudesh had absolutely no intention of returning the money. But he still wanted to turn the screws on Abbas and the others and ensure that a plan B was in place.

"Sudeshji, we have enough money for the investors to make money. Not to the extent we were promised, but we can take extraction facilities on lease since my process involves catalysts and reagents that are in proportions known only to me, I do not see this as a challenge. In fact, this money will be used more efficiently. We will just use this for buying land and cultivating Jatropha," said Abbas.

Rupali was impressed. Abbas was doing a hell of a job. His answers were extremely convincing. She had not told Sudesh or Deep about Abbas's real intent since that would have meant shooting themselves in the foot and would have put an end to the project itself. She had already cornered Abbas by shifting loyalties of both Sudesh and Deep towards her as an insulation from Abbas in the future but to Abbas she had maintained that she was doing her part of the job which was to keep Sudesh and Deep under her control so that Abbas can have the field to himself. All three men believed her. Abbas didn't care either way. She had told Abbas in no unclear terms that he was expected to share all the spoils of the excess land purchase 50:50 with her. Abbas had said 10 crores each for the two of them. Well, the amount was now half of that. But, that was still 5 crores each. Not a small sum in Pune in 2009.

The process of land identifying and buying went on for almost a year. Rupali had made

Sudesh depute Deep to supervise Abbas's land buying. She had told Sudesh that he must have his most trusted man as supervisor so that all three of them can be sure that the investors' money was put to good use. Whenever occasion arose to double check Abbas's dealings by being physically present for negotiations for land purchase, she would masterfully keep Deep occupied with her since she knew in advance when the dealing was going to take place. Abbas would call once he knew that Deep was in the middle of a session with Rupali in some Pune hotel. There was clearly no way Deep was going to abandon that for a business negotiation session. His guilt though would get to him sometimes and he would ask Rupali if he could trust Abbas with business dealings. Rupali would innocently tell him that since Abbas was also a partner, why could they not trust him? Deep, however, always maintained with Sudesh that he had vetted every transaction that Abbas was making. He could hardly tell Sudesh why he was not able to make these meetings. Abbas had the field to himself all the time.

"What do you mean the crop failed?" bellowed Sudesh, the veins on the side of his temples looking for an exit through his skin. It had been one and a half years since land had been bought and the reports of the crop were just coming in.

"How can the crop fail in all the land parcels. You had claimed that Jatropha needs mostly wasteland and we bought land that was better than wasteland just to cover that risk. Now, how can the crop fail?" asked Sudesh incredulously.

"I have sent the seed samples to ICRISAT for analysis. We have only bought the recommended seeds. We also tended the crop diligently, ask Deep," Abbas said in an even voice.

Deep had no clue what that meant. He had never been on a single site and he had no idea of what Abbas had done. He was immersed literally, figuratively and physically in Rupali. He could not get her out of his mind from morning to the time he fell into exhausted sleep in the night. Presently, he was forced to concur.

"Yes Sudeshji. I believe Abbas has done what he had promised. We must investigate this thoroughly. Abbas - could this be foul play by competitors? It looks to me like that for sure," said Deep.

Sudesh was not buying any of this. He was already smarting as Rupali's interest in him had waned considerably in the last one and half years and the previous month, she had shocked him by informing everyone that she and Deep had got married in front of a court registrar. It had been months since he had met Rupali. And now this.

Looking back on the entire episode late in the evening while sipping on his scotch and smoking a rare cigar at the Poona Club, Sudesh realised with a jolt that the sequence of events coincided perfectly as if in a prepared script.

It was as if someone had set out to con him. Not someone, Abbas. And maybe Rupali but he couldn't be sure about her. She had no head for business or did she? He was getting more and more certain that his clients had lost their money. He had taken out his investment in the first land purchase which was inflated in the company's books. The rest of the land in all probability was worthless, the technology bogus and the money gone. He blamed himself for showing Abbas the way in the first place due to his own greed. He decided to investigate a little just to confirm his suspicions.

What he found out was worse than what he had suspected. The land was not even worth 20% of the amount paid by the company. The company had spent almost 40 crores on land and with the balance kept for working capital which had been used on seeds, water, site preparation, fencing, security, office expenses, salaries and other cultivation expenses. The actual cost of the land was not even 8 crores and it was completely worthless. Abbas had returned his 12.5 crores by way of inflated land purchase but in the process, skimmed almost another 20 crores for himself. His money was back safe but his reputation would be ruined. There was no way to prevent that. Unless someone made a police complaint for cheating against Abbas. That someone would have to be taken into confidence by him.

And that was how India Biofuels hit the headlines in Pune's newspapers and even made it to the inside pages of Mumbai newspapers, although in much less detail. The Police investigation and the court case took a toll on Rupali and Deep. They had bought a lovely flat at Vinayak Apartments assuming that Rupali would get her promised rewards and had started living there soon after. Deep was keen on starting a family. Rupali did not want to get tied down with Deep since the rest of her money was still not forthcoming from Abbas. There was no regular income after this mess and for the second time in her life, she had to take out a mortgage on her flat just to meet day-to-day expenses. She intended to pay off the mortgage with the balance money she expected to receive from Abbas but as time passed by, she was growing apprehensive since she knew how the mortgage had gone the last time around. She did not know that Abbas had made three times the money he had given her from the land deals. She had an inkling that since Abbas was left to his own devices, he may have taken out a larger share but did not know the extent of the scam. She had now begun to suspect that Abbas was not going to come through with any more money for her and this unsettled her and set her on edge.

Meanwhile, Deep's continuous badgering for an addition to the family had begun to irritate Rupali. To get rid of him, she told him that she had some gynaecological issue which was creating problems for her in conceiving. She was also getting tired of joyless sex with Deep every day. After all, in Rupali's book, Deep was no longer useful so everything about him started to irritate her. Deep promptly suggested they take an expert opinion and treatment. He suggested that they go to the city's top gynaecologist - Dr. Mukesh Manohar.

On the way to the clinic, Deep gave Rupali a complete background on Dr. Manohar - his family wealth, his single status and his great reputation as a doctor and a gentleman. By the time they reached at the clinic for the appointment, Rupali had already made up her mind about what to do next. Her plan was ready and the target was Dr. Manohar. If this worked well, Rupali would be rid of the vicious circle of crime, struggle, apprehension and loss. But she would have to play this one very carefully.

Rupali had no idea that Doctor Manohar was such a good looking person with amazing manners and attitude. The Doctor couldn't help but notice that his patient was extraordinarily attractive and desirable. When he examined her, it was not merely clinical, he would later recall. He even thought he ought to check her mammary glands for any lump but he banished that thought just in case it came across as too much in the first visit. Gynaecologists are generally thought to be clinical and uninterested in the anatomy of their patients since they are required to deal with the female anatomy day in and day out but anecdotal evidence seems to suggest otherwise. Gynaecologists end up having more affairs with their patients than other doctors and patients feel a greater sense of closeness to their gynaecologists than other doctors. Dr. Manohar was known to keep his personal and professional life completely segregated and there had never been any slightest hint of any impropriety on that front. Until he met Rupali, of course.

Rupali had also employed her best seductive skills, subtly, in the examination room. Without making it obvious at all, she hinted in a conspiratorial tone that she did not want to have her husband's baby even though he was insisting on it since everything was not as it should be in their marriage. She asked him to insist on another visit and say that the initial examination needed to be backed up with several blood and urine tests. She silently thanked him when he did that and took his cell number to take another appointment once her test reports were ready. Deep thought Rupali seemed happy and ascribed it to having found an expert that would treat her problem. Rupali was happy since the first salvo had been fired and the Doctor had chosen to maintain her privacy and accede to her request. This meant that his curiosity had peaked. She had also noticed the slight flush on the fair Doctor's face when he was examining her.

The Good Doctor's phone pinged. It as a WhatsApp message, most probably a forward. He saw the name of the sender, smiled and started to read the message.

A lady was due later in the week for an appointment with the gynaecologist. Early one morning she received a call from the doctor's office to tell her that she had been rescheduled for early that morning at 9.30am and it was already around 8.45am. Since the Doctor's office was almost 40 minutes away, she had no time to spare. She rushed upstairs, threw off her dressing gown, wet the washcloth that was sitting next to the sink, and gave herself a quick wash in "that area" to make sure it was at least presentable. She reached the Doctor's office, stepped up on the table and got ready for the examination. She was a little surprised when the doctor said, "My, we have made an extra effort this morning, haven't we? Thank you for the presentation" but she didn't respond, not sure what it meant. After school, her six-year-old daughter came home and asked for the washcloth. When told to get another one, she replied, "No, I need the one that was here by the sink -- It had all my glitter and sparkles in it."

Doctor Manohar laughed out loud at Rupali's joke on WhatsApp. He wrote back asking her when he should be ready for her presentation.

Rupali wrote back saying that she was out of glitter but she hoped that he would still like her presentation.

Doctor Manohar was hooked. Never before in his life had he met someone like Rupali. What a woman and what zest for life. Full of energy and mischief, Rupali had started dominating Doctor Manohar's thoughts during the day and his dreams at night.

After the first day when she had come in with her husband, she had sought him out directly and asked to meet at his clinic alone. He had asked her to come in after his usual appointments around 7.00 PM one evening. She had confided in him about how she was stuck in an unhappy marriage and how she had been duped by Deep of all her money that she had inherited and how even her flat was mortgaged to pay for Deep's misdeeds. She told him a bit about the India Biofuels saga which the Doctor was anyway aware of having read about it in the newspapers a few months ago. She told him that this was Deep's project which he had conceived with his friend Abbas and she had been talked into investing her inheritance as well as take out a mortgage on her house to support his venture which turned out to be a con job, something that she realised much later. She wanted out but he was after her family heirlooms which were priceless and was trying to get her to start a family so that she would be even more committed to him.

Doctor Manohar was livid at Deep. As far as he could see, here was a beautiful blameless woman whom Deep had exploited for his own ends and was intent on exploiting still further. She was fed up enough to contemplate a divorce from him. He paused briefly before making up his mind. What he was about to do was not ethical and it would entail him using his professional credibility in making a false statement just to help Rupali. For a brief moment, Doctor Manohar wondered if he was letting his lower body lead his head in this matter. He shook all negative thoughts out of his head and assured a visibly upset Rupali, "Don't worry, if you want a divorce, I will help you get one. You will have to allege physical abuse and unnatural sex. As your gynaecologist, I will support your statements with my affidavit. The court will have no option but to give you a divorce."

"Oh Doctor! I don't know how to thank you. You are most kind. I don't know how I can ever repay you," Rupali said.

"Maybe by having dinner with me tonight at the Club?" Doctor Manohar asked her with a smile.

Rupali looked up from her bank statement. Deep was saying something constantly in that annoying mosquito buzz voice of his.

"How will we manage such high legal expenses? All the money we made from the project is already being sucked out slowly for these lawyers and cops," he was saying.

Rupali shot him an irritated glance.

"My money Deep, not ours. I made it, not us. Since you had nothing to do with it, why don't you just give me a little break here and let me figure out what's best for us," she said with barely concealed contempt.

Deep was taken aback at the savage volley. Rupali hadn't been herself ever since she had lost both Vitthal and Saraswati in the span of one year. Of late, she seemed irritated when she was not preoccupied which was all the time. She was drinking a lot, almost every evening. She was also not keeping well and was looking sick.

What looked like irritability and preoccupation to Deep was actually Rupali internalising her grief and the shock of having lost the only family she ever had. She had, for some reason, never thought about her parents' mortality and when it happened without warning, it took her completely unawares. She was finding it hard to deal with. The comfort of being able to confide everything in Saraswati and Vitthal's silent but supportive presence was now gone forever. The incident was also making Rupali re-evaluate her life's journey so far.

No doubt she had come a long way from the Vasai days. No doubt she had learnt life's lessons along the way and tried not to repeat her mistakes. No doubt she had also grown in shrewdness, had sharpened her manipulative skills and developed a mercenary attitude towards achieving her goals, with whatever means necessary. She smiled ruefully thinking of the time when she was scared to act in front of the camera. If only those guys could see her now. She had morphed into a natural actress capable of emoting, on demand, whatever was needed to suit the purpose. But she was also getting tired of it all. Maybe it was the death of her parents. Maybe it was just fatigue. In the good Doctor, she had finally found what she was looking for. Here was a man who had not stripped her naked with his eyes the first time he saw her. He had taken his time and they were getting comfortable with each other as time went by. She felt she should finally consider genuinely getting involved with Doctor. It was easy to fall in love with him. This time, she was going to let herself go.

Rupali fell in love with Doctor Manohar over several evenings at the Poona Club. Initially, she could not tell if it was love but subsequently, she figured it must be since she felt very differently around Doctor Manohar. Thus far, her encounters with men had been purely transactional. She wanted something from them so she had offered herself in return. Or she had used her charms to manipulate them. In the present case, even though it had started that way, she was also getting involved with Doctor Manohar now that she had come to know the man that he was. She had started to look forward to their meetings. Always at the Club and seated at the verandah or the lawns in the evenings, Rupali enjoyed these evenings. Doctor Manohar was a great conversationalist and his knowledge of most subjects was astounding. He was very well read and was adept at talking about things that interested his guests. No wonder people said that he had great bedside manners. He knew what to say to whom.

With Rupali, he spoke mostly about the

society, his own background and funny instances from his own past, some amusing anecdotes with his patients and about things going on in the world around them. Rupali restricted herself to jokes about her own made-up life and included some Bollywood titbits attributing these to some of her friends from school who worked on the creative side. She portrayed a picture of herself and her parents as coming from a higher middle class family settled in Vasai in Mumbai but with ancestral land and assets in Mumbai that she had liquidated to fund Deep's venture after her parents' death. She gave the reason for her shift to Pune as her father's ill-health and their Doctor's advice to take him to a less humid place.

This was also the first time she was being wooed by someone whom she herself desired. The perfect gentleman, Doctor Manohar had not made a single pass at her. At the same time, he was not shy of responding to a sexy text. It was almost as if Doctor Manohar had an in-built control valve which made him react in exact proportion to the stimulus. Rupali wondered if this meant that if she took off her top will Doctor Manohar follow suit and then wait for her next move? She smiled at that thought. Doctor was looking at her over his Beefeater and tonic and caught her smile.

"I am sure I did something to deserve that smile," he said.

"Just thinking of something," she said.

"A penny for your thoughts Rupali," said Doctor Manohar.

Rupali simply shook her head and smiled. It had now been several weeks and there had been no move by Doctor Manohar to add any physicality to their relationship. She had read somewhere that the only men who did not straight away want to jump into bed with a woman were those who were considerably less endowed. She hoped that was not the case with Doctor Manohar.

Today though, the Doctor was more drunk than usual.

"Ok, never mind that. Let me tell you what I was thinking. I was thinking this evening how big an idiot this Deep is to not appreciate someone like you," he said clearly wanting to continue in the same vein.

"Rupali, I have to confess something. I know it looks very wrong, you being married and all that and I swear this is something I have never done. Since you are convinced about divorcing Deep, I wanted to throw my hat in the ring. Will you marry me?" he said in one breath, not trusting himself to breathe in between lest he lose his nerve.

Rupali was delighted. She had never imagined that her game plan would play out so soon, so well and with such mutually felt emotions. She did not reply immediately but chose to let a smile play on her lips for the longest time. After letting Doctor Manohar's words hang in the air for what seemed like an eternity, she said, "Yes Doctor, I will marry you. Just help me get rid of that pest."

Doctor Manohar was overjoyed. Rupali was everything that he wanted from a life partner. He simply couldn't wait for her divorce to happen.

"You seem to have had more than your usual quota Doctor," she said. "Let me drop you home and settle you."

"Not Doctor, Mukesh please," he said happily.

Rupali opened Doctor Manohar's apartment with his key. He was too inebriated and unsteady to attempt it. It was late in the night and his retainer Madhav had retired to his servant room. They tried to make no noise and more or less succeeded in their endeavours. She laid him down on the bed and started to undress him to put him to bed.

"You first," said Doctor Manohar, resisting her hands trying to unbutton his shirt. Rupali smiled at him and teased, "Are you sure Doctor? It might just make you tipsier. Then don't say I didn't warn you."

That night was like a feast for the famished for Doctor Manohar. He had never been happier in his life. Rupali snuggled up to him after they were done and once she heard him snoring gently, dressed up and left for home.

She soon discovered what an asset Doctor Manohar was. Once he knew Rupali was being prosecuted in the India Biofuels case, his used his massive social standing and connectivity to ensure that Prabhu More, the investigating officer in the EOW was convinced of Rupali's innocence and Devendra Jamdar, the public prosecutor also did not press for charges against Rupali. He also asked Rupali to request Jamdar's help in her divorce matter against Deep. Doctor Manohar's high connections had indicated to Jamdar that he should go all out to help this woman who had a genuine case and needed to be taken out of the clutches of Deep. Rupali was delighted with all the support. Doctor Manohar was a one-stop shop for all her life's problems. She was falling more and more in love with this amazing and kind man. It helped that he too was madly in love with her, was very wealthy and wanted to marry her. Finally, her struggle for financial security and a wonderful life was nearing the finish line.

The phone rang just as she was stepping out to meet Doctor Manohar at the Club. Since she was still with Deep at Vinayak Apartments, he did not pick her up but instead met her directly at the Club. It was Sudesh.

"Madamji, how are you?" asked Sudesh. Rupali could hear the leer in his voice.

"Good, good Sudeshji and what about you?" she asked.

"Madamji, I have something that I need to discuss with you. It's all business I assure you. Can we meet at the Club this evening?" he asked.

"Not today Sudeshji, let's keep it for tomorrow at your office?" she countered, not wanting to run into him at the Club with Doctor Manohar.

Sudesh indicated that his office would not be ideal for the meeting and instead suggested lunch at the Club. Knowing that Doctor Manohar would be busy at the Clinic at that time, Rupali agreed to meet him.

"Where are you going?" Deep asked just as Rupali hung up on Sudesh.

"I am trying to set up something new with some people I know so that I don't run out of money in the near future. It would be good if you also did the same. At least bear your own burden for a change," Rupali shot back, her explanation not entirely untruthful.

"I know I am a burden on you but what do I do Rupali? My reputation has been finished because of India Biofuels and no one will touch me in this city. I have told you so many times that we should go to Mumbai. I know some people there who may be able to get me some work in the financial services business. You know Mumbai is a massive market and I have good people management skills. But somehow you don't seem to be interested at all," Deep said.

"Your two-bit job isn't going to pay my bills. I need a big hit to pull out of this hole. At this rate, I will end up losing this house also," said Rupali.

"This house also? How many houses have you lost in the past? Is there something I don't know about you? Don't I know your true nature? First Sudesh, then me. I am noticing that since some time now, you talk of "I" instead of "We" every time. Is there an issue here? Is there now another one in your life already?" asked Deep.

"It was always "I" Deep since you have never lifted a finger - first to pay for this house, then to meet expenses, then to tackle with my legal issues that have cost me an arm and a leg. All along, your contribution has been zero. You nicely excluded yourself from the Company's management so nothing came on you. You could have also saved me. Instead, you married me thinking all this money would be great for your future. You did not fall in love with me Deep. You used me for your future. I was your retirement plan and financial security rolled in one," said Rupali raising her voice.

"Can you keep it down? Or do you want Dharam to also know everything about us? Why don't you also shout about how you have been denying me in bed these days? Just so that the servants get an idea about what is going on. You only sleep with people if you have something to gain from them, right? Once a whore, always a whore," thundered Deep.

Rupali wanted to punch him but instead ignored him, picked up her handbag and banged the door behind her. Deep's words were ringing in her mind and suddenly, with a jolt, she realised that these were the exact words her father had used for her mother a lifetime ago.

This relationship was truly over and if ever she thought that she should have any misgivings about doing this to Deep, his words put an end to her remorse. The bastard deserved whatever was coming to him. She made a mental note of pushing Jamdar for the divorce notice.

That evening, Doctor Manohar was in a sombre mood. He had received news that one of his patients, whom he also knew socially, had lost her husband. Apparently, the guy was suffering from diabetes. He must have also had low blood pressure but apparently that went undiagnosed. The wife, who was his patient, was suffering from high blood pressure. The diabetes medication and the blood pressure medication were stored in the same medicine cabinet and one morning, not having his glasses on, the husband popped the blood pressure pill instead of his diabetes pill since both looked similar. The guy's blood pressure plunged, he fainted in the bathroom and hit his head on the sink and died. Doctor Manohar had just attended his funeral before coming to the Club.

"People in this country are so casual about their medication and so careless. Once small mistake can be fatal these days as the medicines of today are very potent. This guy was not very old.

So much unfulfilled potential lost," he was saying to Rupali.

"I am sorry for your loss Doctor but what about my loss? We are meeting after three days and I am feeling very unfulfilled already," said Rupali seductively.

Doctor Manohar visibly brightened. There was no grief in the world that great sex could not cure; at least temporarily. Tomorrow was always another day.

"Madamji, you have forgotten me," Sudesh started as soon as the bearer had taken their lunch order. Rupali had ordered a soup and a salad while Sudesh had ordered a club sandwich and a glass of orange juice to wash it down with.

"No Sudeshji, I have been toiling to make ends meet. You know that after that fiasco, I have been hit financially so badly. Just toiling and trying to make ends meet," said Rupali wondering what Sudesh had cooked up now.

"That's what I am saying Madamji. You have forgotten me. There was a time when our ends used to meet and you used to toil above me," he said, smiling with his pan masala stained teeth.

Rupali wanted to slap him. Keeping her composure with some effort, she sidestepped his lewd comment and said, "Sudeshji, we both know how much we have lost in that deal. Why bring up old matters that can only make us sad. It was a moment of indiscretion for both of us at that time and we got carried away. I am a happily married woman now and this talk is not appropriate even if my husband may suspect my past relationship with you."

"Madamji, you did not understand me. I am missing you. I miss all the wonderful evenings we used to have together. I think I may have fallen in love with you even though at my age such a thing is not taken at face value. I only discovered when you went out of my life and to my surprise, you shacked up with my employee. I have never come across a case where someone has the Boss and yet settles for the employee. I think even you realise your mistake Madamji. I would like us to be together Madamji. Let's rekindle our spark," said Sudesh.

Rupali kept quiet. Her mind was working furiously trying to figure out how to neutralise Sudesh. She could straightaway say no to his face and walk away from there. But she knew Sudesh. He definitely had something up his sleeve for him to be so audacious. She decided to wait for it to emerge.

"As you know my business has gone bust. My wife has also left me but she left me since she realised that I am pining for you. I no longer have the guest house but now I live all alone. There is no one at my place. We can rekindle our past together Madamji at my humble abode. I have enough money to take care of you for life. That Deep can't even pay for your cosmetics even if he tried his best. Come back to me Rupali, I want you," he said, making it look more and more serious.

"How do you know that even I want to same thing Sudeshji? As I see it, it was something that was there in my life at one time. I have since moved on. I have a lovely married life with Deep now and we are looking to add to the family. This is highly inappropriate Sudeshji. We should not be talking about these things. Let's leave it as a wonderful memory. *Who afsana jise anjaam tak laana na ho mumkin, use ek khubsoorat mod dekar chhod na achcha,"* she said quoting from an old Hindi film song which essentially said that if an affair can't be taken to its conclusion, it is better to give it a beautiful turn and let it go.

"Kya baat hai Madamji, isi ada par to hum jaan dete hain," said Sudesh, admiring her panache.

"Lekin hum bhi kya karein Madamji. Sau baar janam lenge, sau baar fana honge, ai jaanewafa phir bhi hum tum na juda honge," he added quoting another line from yet another old Hindi film song that talked about how he and Rupali would be lovers even if they were reborn a 100 times and perished a 100 times.

He slid a slim folder towards her wordlessly.

Rupali opened the folder and the bottom fell out of her world.

Compiled by one Anant Narvekar, a private detective in Pune, the folder had a few neatly typed sheets and some photographs. In it were details of her entire life including her Vasai childhood, her Bollywood days, her bar dancing days, her Metro Bank scandal, her film financing days, some pictures of her with Sudesh that left nothing to the imagination and some recent photos of her with Doctor Manohar.

Rupali understood Sudesh's message loud and clear.

"But why this Sudeshji, what have I done to you," asked Rupali in a small, helpless voice hoping to appeal to Sudesh's better side.

"I was missing you, Yaar! But seriously Rupali, you and I are tied at the hip. We cannot separate. You are the reason why I have suffered so much and lost my entire business and reputation. I know you have benefitted immensely from this deal since I can see it but can't prove it but there is justice in this world. I know that your legal and financial troubles will consume all the money that you made from me. With Doctor Manohar, you may have yet pulled off your masterstroke. I have no problem with you shifting from Deep to him and I don't want to come in your way but Madamji after today *jo waada kiya who nibhana padega, roke zamaana chahe roke khudaai tum ko aana padega,"* said Sudesh deadpanning the entire time and quoting another old Hindi film song meaning whatever promises you made, you will have to keep and even if the universe is trying to prevent you, you will have to come to me.

"What if I do not heed?" asked Rupali, now trying to see how far Sudesh would go.

"Madamji, why do you want me to destroy everything that you have worked for? It is simple matter for me to send a copy of this file to Doctor Manohar. That will be the end for you. Of course I will also lose you but I have already lost you anyway. This way, it will be win-win for both of us. You keep what you desire and I get what I desire," he said smoothly.

Rupali thought it over quickly. There was really no way out. For now, she had no choice but to humour Sudesh and give him what he wanted. Her mind made, in front of Sudesh' eyes, Rupali transformed from a helpless woman to a woman who knows the effect she has on men and knows how to manipulate them. She allowed a slow, wicked smile to surface before saying,

"Are you still as good as you used to be?"

"Try me out Madamji. I assure you I will not disappoint you in any manner. Tomorrow 8.00 PM at my residence. I will text you the address," said Sudesh, getting up to leave.

Rupali was back in her old dog-eat-dog world. For now, she would have to inhabit two worlds simultaneously and hope that her luck held until she found a solution to Sudesh. She recalled someone once saying to her that every problem came with a solution. *You just had to find it.*

For the first time in her life, Rupali felt repulsed giving in to Sudesh' demands. She hated every minute of it. So this is how being in love felt, she thought. A stranger's touch suddenly felt unwanted. Sex was torture. After a couple of sessions with Sudesh, Rupali was feeling more and more desolate and morose. There seemed to be no redemption for her. It did not help that Sudesh was like a man possessed, hell bent on taking revenge and enjoying every minute of it. He did not care that Rupali did not show the same level of participation as earlier and was merely going through the motions obviously looking forward to going home every time they met. For Rupali, it was a double whammy. Sometimes, she ended up meeting Doctor Manohar after meeting Sudesh and it tore her apart that she was living a double life which Doctor Manohar had no idea about. Rupali felt unclean and guilty when she was with Doctor Manohar. If Doctor Manohar felt something amiss, he never mentioned it. Rupali, in the meanwhile, was slipping into a deep depression with every passing day.

She decided to talk to Doctor Manohar about her mental state and visited his clinic unannounced one day. While she was waiting to be shown into his chamber, she noticed a distinguished looking man of medium height, salt and pepper hair and a trim moustache waiting to see the Doctor as well. Mrs. Bharucha came in and said, "Mr. Anant, the

Doctor will see you now."

Something about the man rang a warning bell in Rupali's head but she couldn't place it. It was also a fairly common name. She had never seen him before but his presence filled her with a vague sense of foreboding. She quickly brushed aside her sense of dread and smiled when at long last, Doctor Manohar saw her after what felt like almost an hour. She tried to lighten up the conversation at first but then eventually told him about her feelings of depression and her increased drinking as a consequence. Apparently Doctor Manohar wasn't listening. Instead, she was surprised to see him staring away from her into space with sadness in his eyes. She had never seen him like that before. He turned to look at her and said, "Sorry dear, something has come up... a terrible thing with a dear friend. He has just lost the love of his life so I have to rush to console him. Can we meet tomorrow?"

Rupali nodded with understanding and left his chamber.

Doctor Manohar lowered his head in his hands after she left.

"What medicines are these?" she asked Sudesh just as he rolled over after their session. Rupali had seen, on the bedside in Sudesh's bedroom, a very attractive metal pillbox with the day of the week on each small pill holder to help compliance. She had opened it to see what was inside.

"Oh, just my blood pressure medicines. I take two of these every day. I had a bit of an issue with that earlier but now since we have met and have started meeting again, my blood pressure seems to be under control. My doctor says I should check for a month and then stop it altogether. Otherwise my blood pressure will fall too low. I have you to thank for this. Sex with you has helped me overcome my stress. It is helping, after all," he said laughing, heading to the bathroom.

Rupali quickly looked into the waste bin by the side of the bed and found an empty strip of the drug Amlodipin. She noticed it was 2.5 mg and quickly slid it into her handbag.

She waited to be shown in to Doctor Manohar's chamber for almost an hour. Mrs. Bharucha was appropriately apologetic and had told her at the outset that Doctor had said not to be disturbed as he was busy with a personal matter with his lawyer. Rupali was getting bored and had asked for a doodle pad. Mrs. Bharucha had given her the clinic's old writing pad with the old letterhead which was being used as rough paper as the Doctor had made some new, more attractive, stationery. Rupali doodled for a bit and then quietly folded a few blank sheets and shoved these into her handbag.

Apparently, whatever was bothering Doctor Manohar had not gone completely. He still seemed a bit off. His eyes had a strange shine, almost like a man possessed by some obsession. He smiled a wan smile at Rupali and waved her to a chair in front of his desk.

"Yes, my dear, what can I do for you?" he asked with a slight hint of sarcasm. Rupali caught it but ascribed it to his personal anguish over his friend's situation.

"How is your friend now?" she asked.

Doctor Manohar looked at her without comprehension. Suddenly he blinked and registered her question.

"Oh, he is fine, he is fine. I think I have found a way to console him. I think I have found a way," he mumbled.

"Ah yes, my dear. You said you were feeling depressed. I can't imagine why. Must be something temporary. After all, your divorce is about to come through and then you and I will soon be together, isn't it?" he continued.

"Why don't I give you a little something to ease your way? Take these, twice a day for two weeks. And you will be right as rain" he said, picking up his pad and writing a prescription for her.

"Anything to avoid Doctor?" she asked playfully.

"Nothing really. This may make you a little drowsy but anyway you don't drive so should not be an issue," he said.

"And when are we meeting Manohar? It has been a couple of days now," she asked.

"Very soon, my dear. Very soon," he said.

Rupali was a little disturbed by Doctor Manohar's lack of interest the entire time. It was almost as if he wasn't there at all. The image of the man with salt-and-pepper hair and trim moustache flashed before her eyes for a second for some reason. She was again filled with a sense of foreboding. She brushed aside these thoughts and concentrated on the task at hand.

"Please show me all the brands for Amlodipin 10mg please," she said to the Chemist in Shivajinagar.

"Do you have a prescription Madam?" asked the Chemist.

Rupali produced a prescription signed by Doctor Manohar for Amlodipin 10mg, 2 tablets a day for 30 days.

"For you Madam? This is a heavy dose," said the Chemist.

"No, my mother. She has very high blood pressure which is not coming under control due to her urinary tract infection," she said.

Rupali had deliberately chosen a Chemist not too near and not too far from the Doctor's clinic. Since the dosage was heavy, some Chemists would check to see if everything was alright. If too near, the Chemist knew the prescription style of the

Doctor and could easily call to check. If too far, the Doctor would not be known and the Chemist could call to verify. Someone not too far would have heard of the Doctor but would not really have had much of his prescription pattern and when presented with an acceptable explanation, was least likely to check.

The Chemist brought out six different brands of Amlodipin 10mg. He explained that while lower doses of the drug were made by over 50 companies, the high dosage had only six manufacturers. Rupali selected the brand where the tablet was visible and despite being a higher dosage, was about the same size as what she had seen in Sudesh' pill box. She bought six strips and left.

That evening, she emptied Sudesh' pill box of all the 30 pills and substituted the higher dosage when Sudesh was in the bathroom. Sudesh never suspected a thing. It took him 11 days to die of a sudden cardiac collapse, his blood pressure having reached fatally low levels.

Chapter 17

Batty could barely wait until dawn. He had kept pacing all night waiting for daylight to break. He had a lot of work to do. As soon as it was 7 AM, he placed his first call. The person at the other end of the call appeared surprised and confirmed the two details that Batty had asked him for. Batty already knew the answer but he had to confirm his hypothesis for sure. He then called Shinde and asked him to rush to the Police Station. Shinde dutifully called Inspector Lokhande to inform him of Batty's call.

Lokhande was on the pot browsing through his Facebook timeline. He was going through the birthday pictures of his niece in Yavatmal. Looked like a nice party. He had missed going there. The entire family was present except for him and his family. They had even posted pictures of the food at the party. To Lokhande's perpetually food deprived mind, these pictures looked amazing. He should have been there. This cursed job. No time for anything. Like those who smoked heavily swore that unless they smoked at least one cigarette, they could not clear their bowels, Lokhande swore by Facebook. Nothing like 15 minutes of browsing to clear his bowels. What a feeling that was. Suddenly the phone rang loudly and stopped Lokhande mid-dump. He cursed loudly. That monkey from Latur. Over-smart and over-intelligent. Never calls for good news. For this call alone, he would demote him. Didn't he know that this was Lokhande's most important task of the day? Without clearing his bowels, his weight would not budge and he would be forced to take another dabba of diet food and then check weight again the next day. Aargh! Rohini had made his life miserable. And now this moron had called just when he was clearing himself. Loudly and with great annoyance, he bellowed, "Tell me Mr. Shinde, who has died so early in the morning?"

"Sir, Bartamanji had called. He is coming to the Police Station to gather some material from Rupali's panchnama. I thought I should inform you Sir. I think you should be here Sir," said Shinde, slightly crestfallen at Lokhande's tone.

Lokhande cursed again. Now what? These guys won't even let me shit in peace, he thought unhappily wondering what had happened that he had to stop mid-dump and rush.

"Did he tell you anything else?" he asked Shinde, still unhappy and irritated.

"No sir, he just said to rush to the station," answered Shinde.

Batty and Robin were waiting outside when Shinde got down from his bike. Lokhande was nowhere in sight but Shinde knew, he would be hotfooting it to the station as soon as he could manage. His usual time was 10:30 am but today he would have to make it in record time. Shinde smirked inwardly at the thought. God knows how Lokhande had become a senior inspector of police. He deserved to be no more than a beat constable.

Before Shinde got there, Robin tried talking to Batty about what had happened overnight. The last thing she remembered was that they had solved the case and the matter was over. What had happened since then? Had Juggy said anything to Batty? Batty simply declined to answer any of her questions and assured her that he would reveal all in good time. Robin knew better than to press further.

Shinde brought out the items that were taken from Rupali's home and were kept in a container. Batty hurriedly went through these and picked up a piece of paper, compared it with a medicine strip, noted the details and made a quick call after going outside to speak in privacy. The receiver of the call told Batty what he had wanted to hear. Having finished the call, Batty came inside and looked at Robin. His eyes were shining with excitement. Just then Lokhande entered, his shirt unbuttoned near his belt, clearly a consequence of haste, resulting in a peek of pale skin from underneath. Robin smiled at the vision.

"Lokhandeji, we have finally solved the case," said Batty with great satisfaction.

"Solved the case? Yes, I know, that was yesterday. You have come here at this hour just to say that to me?" Lokhande asked incredulously, his mind on his unfinished morning business.

"No Lokhandeji. We have just solved the case. Yesterday was probably an error but we can only say for sure once forensics returns with a definite answer in a couple of hours. I have already spoken with Vinay and he has confirmed my suspicions. He is preparing his final report as we speak," said Batty.

"Is there a twist again?" asked Shinde and immediately regretted it when Lokhande glared at him.

"Yes there is. I should have seen it earlier but I did not. Now I am sure. Lokhandeji, please arrest Doctor Manohar for the murder of Rupali Jadhav," said Batty quietly.

Lokhande and Shinde simply gaped at him.

Lokhande was the first to recover his composure.

"Do you know who he is? I am not arresting him until I have seen proof of why he is being accused. It is alright for you to have your flight of fancy. If it turns out unfounded, I will lose my job," said Lokhande, the distress evident in his voice.

"Lokhandeji you know me. Have I ever made you arrest an innocent man?" asked Batty.

They had all gathered at ACP Jagdeep Kumar's office. Doctor Manohar had been taken into custody. Livid at first, he had then demanded to know the charges and demanded to see his lawyer. Batty had gone inside the cell and had a quiet word with him after which Doctor Manohar had sunk to the ground, all the fight gone out of him. Batty had then asked Dr. Manohar a few questions and the replies he got were to his satisfaction and had proved his hypothesis even further. Juggy was keen to know all the details as were Robin and Shinde. Lokhande had begged off as he had an upset stomach and had to rush home to take rest. Juggy was irritated but there was nothing much he could do about it since the man had reported sick.

Batty started to lay down the entire case.

"This is an extraordinary case born out of the self-limiting attitude of our people. The people of this state have a phrase "Ugach Kashala?" Meaning "why bother". The mental block of getting into what people consider unnecessary detail, or extra work, has led to an attitude where if at first they find something incriminating, they stop looking for more. Sorry to say this, but this has been evident from day one to me in everyone involved in investigating the case. Not only the police officers at Deccan Gymkhana police station, but also in the case of Prabhu More of the EOW and the Mumbai Police investigative officer before that, in the Metro Bank case."

"Let's start at the beginning. In the Metro Bank scam, if the Mumbai Police had been more diligent, Rupali would not have gotten away scot free. No doubt she used her charms but a healthy dose of scepticism would have nabbed her sooner or later. They also never found Faheem who returned as Abbas to unfurl a much larger con. For them, since Arvind Nair was caught, it seemed enough. Getting away with a crime emboldened Rupali to commit another one. I don't have all the details of her life between the scams but we know that she tried her hand at film financing and got conned herself. She had to move to Pune where she was trying to figure out how to survive. Abbas sought her out and detailed the scheme to her. He needed her to get Sudesh to buy into their scheme. Again, Prabhu More did not exercise diligence. The minute he found Abbas, he stopped inquiring as to how the others could have been complicit. It does not seem to have occurred to him that with three other directors who may also have been beneficiaries, there could be other angles apart from Abbas," Batty explained.

"Prabhu More also never sought to enquire how Rupali and Deep were subsequently married and how they came into such an expensive apartment on their own when both had apparently not benefited from the crime."

"Rupali was clearly a smart operator. She dumped Sudesh for Deep since she needed him to protect her from the repercussions of what

Abbas was doing. She struck a side deal and left Abbas to face all the music. Abbas was arrested and then released on bail. He was seething with anger and seeking revenge. Rupali dumped Deep for Doctor Manohar since the money had run out and she needed to go to the next level. This was her final play and she came very close to getting what she wanted. Doctor Manohar fell for her and was looking to get married to her. He was openly introducing her to his social circle as his fiancee. Rupali had almost reached her goal. She took Doctor Manohar's help and connectivity in convincing Prabhu More of her innocence and again with the Doctor's contacts, got the public prosecutor Devendra Jamdar to dilute the case against her. She also used Jamdar to send a divorce notice to Deep alleging physical abuse which the Doctor wilfully agreed to substantiate. Deep was shocked and on the verge of losing everything. He was penniless and had banked on Rupali all along for his survival. He was hurt and angry. He got in touch with Abbas and the two compared notes. I am guessing that Deep would have told Abbas all about how Rupali had conspired from the beginning to ensure that Abbas gets the rap for the scam. Out of options and staring at a life in jail for Abbas and a life on the streets for Deep, they started planning Rupali's murder."

"Rupali's luck finally ran out. Sudesh had also realised that he had been conned. He could see that both Rupali and Abbas had gained at his expense.

He had lost his business, his reputation and even his marriage. Since Abbas was already facing charges and was being tried by the Pune District Court, he decided to find out all about Rupali. He approached a private detective, Anant Narvekar, to dig up everything about Rupali. Unknown to Rupali, Sudesh had clandestinely clicked pictures of him and Rupali in several compromising positions using concealed cameras initially for his own voyeuristic pleasure but these later became a potent weapon to bring Rupali down. It is my belief that Sudesh started blackmailing Rupali to once again have a physical relationship with him since he had discovered her entire background and her closeness to Doctor Manohar which both she and the Doctor did not bother to hide."

"Meanwhile Narvekar, after having compiled his findings and reporting those to Sudesh, decided to spill the beans on Rupali to Doctor Manohar. When he found out, Doctor Manohar was devastated. He was also very angry at having been conned by Rupali. Seeing her pictures with Sudesh that left nothing to the imagination, Doctor Manohar was left with a few choices. One was to accept the reality and carry on with Rupali as if nothing had happened which was now impossible as the real Rupali would have never been worthy of sharing Doctor Manohar's life if her past had been known. The second one was to break off the relationship which was not simple as Rupali would want to know why and too many people in the society of which he was a leading member knew about his impending marriage plans. This meant a serious loss of face for him. The third option was that Rupali could disappear. That led him to his only other choice which was to make her disappear or rather eliminate Rupali. This must not have come naturally to him I am sure but here again the deep dark depths of the human mind have always confounded and surprised those who make it their life's work to study it. Again here Rupali's luck running out comes into play.

Unwittingly, Rupali gave him the tools to execute his plan. She went to him complaining of depression and resultant excessive drinking. Doctor Manohar prescribed a high dose of anti-depressant Zolpidem. Despite the limit of dosage for women being 5 mg, he prescribed Rupali 10mg and asked her to take it twice a day. I believe Doctor Manohar would have been equally happy with Rupali being extremely sick and slowly withering away but ten days of overdosing coupled with Rupali's alcohol intake eventually resulted in severe central nervous system depression, loss of consciousness and eventually death. *Rupali had actually died just before Deep and Abbas stabbed her, maybe an hour or so before."*

"Deep stole a surgical knife from Doctor Manohar's collection of old surgical tools and used it to kill Rupali with Abbas's help. They then left the knife on the body and sent a text message from Rupali's phone to Doctor Manohar calling him to the murder location. Deep wanted to frame Manohar to complete his revenge. Doctor Manohar came after receiving the message, saw the dead body, took the knife, cleaned it and put it back in his collection secretly delighted that with Rupali now stabbed, he was off the hook completely and there was now not even a remote chance of him being a suspect. He was sure that "ugach kashala" would come to his rescue as once Police saw the stabbed body, all efforts would be made to nab the murderer and his drug overdose would go unnoticed."

"I called Vinay Shahastrabuddhe and he confirmed that there was no LBT4 in Rupali's wounds and there was no degranulation of the mast cells which clearly indicates that all of Rupali's wounds were post mortem. So while Deep and Abbas did stab her, it was Doctor Manohar who killed her."

There was complete silence in the room as the occupants digested what was presented before them. Juggy let out a low whistle.

"No wonder you had a bee up your bonnet last night Bartaman, great work buddy!" said Juggy.

"This Narvekar fellow I know. Seems very odd that he would betray client confidentiality, which is a cornerstone of their profession. That part does not seem to sit well I would think," he added.

"Unless we factor in family ties and gratitude," said Batty.

"Narvekar, as Doctor Manohar admitted to me a while back, is his third cousin. Doctor's father had played a crucial role in supporting Narvekar's mother when his father died early leaving her penniless. Narvekar was only paying back his debts," said Batty.

"What about Sudesh, isn't it strange that he died around the same time as Rupali?" asked Robin.

Batty smiled and said, "I am willing to bet that Sudesh was killed by Rupali in the exact manner in which she was killed by Doctor Manohar. I believe that she found out about Sudesh's medicines and somehow forged a prescription, most probably Doctor Manohar's prescription, to switch him to a higher dose."

"This has turned out to be such a theatrical tragedy. Rupali got rid of Sudesh so she could spend the rest of her life peacefully with Doctor Manohar. The Doctor, meanwhile, had already decided to get rid of her. Even if he hadn't, Deep and Abbas would have killed her that night anyway. So irrespective of who finally ended killing her, Rupali would not have escaped death," said Robin.

"Yes, her death was certain," echoed Batty.

Chapter 18

Later that evening, Robin and Batty were seated in their old favourite Classic Rock Cafe and sipping on their beers. Neither of them was in a mood to celebrate. The night was early, the place was quiet and the karaoke regulars were still to arrive.

"Strange how in this case medication, something we hardly notice, played such an important part. Doctor Manohar killed Rupali and Rupali killed Sudesh with medicine overdose. So strange and so creepy. Whatever happened to good, old fashioned murder with guns, poisons, stabbing, strangulation, pushing off a cliff and several other usual modus operandi?" asked Robin.

"There was a knife involved, Robin for sure. But yes, the overwhelming use was of medications. In fact, modern medicine has become so potent and these so closely resemble narcotics that overdosing is almost always fatal. On the one hand, modern medicine has prolonged man's lifespan and while on the other, their abuse has become a life-shortening tool as well. On the one hand they giveth and on the other, they taketh away..." trailed off Batty.

"Most advanced countries restrict the prescription and dispensation of dangerous medicines but even there, rampant overdosing is common with compliant doctors. In India, the problem gets compounded as medical records are not centralised and not known. The patient keeps all the medical records and that can be easily manipulated. There are enough doctors that write prescriptions for banned substances for money. I used to know a friend in college who was addicted to codeine and always got his doctor to prescribe him Grillingctus CD, which was a popular cough syrup with codeine that was sold only under prescription. My friend claimed he could sleep better with codeine and he was more effective the next day, after consumption. Rupali took this several notches higher. She forged the prescription. But I doubt that she would have ever done that without having come into intimate contact with Doctor Manohar. I am quite sure that the original idea must have come to her from one of Doctor's chats or patient situations. She had the idea and the opportunity both. She merely took advantage of the situation to solve a problem," completed Batty.

"Rupali was anyway not a procrastinator. She believed in doing something about a situation. Not to sit and fret about it. Always practical, always transactional... Except that one time that she fell in love with the Doctor. Her love for him did not alert her to the change that must have come over Doctor Manohar once he discovered the truth about her. Sad that an otherwise sharp person with superb survival instincts was let down the one time she needed her instinct the most. Blame it all on love, I guess," said Robin.

"People believe what they want to believe anyway," Batty remarked.

"Rupali was so sure of her relationship with Manohar that she never critically evaluated his responses to her. But then Manohar was also skilful in hiding things as we have seen. He is a very good liar. But it was nothing to do with love. Human beings do fall in love despite themselves," concluded Batty.

"So do I conclude from all this that Major Bartaman Bhowmick believes in love? What am I supposed to surmise from this sudden turn? Any message for mere mortals like me?" teased Robin.

Just then, the karaoke operator walked up to Batty and asked him, "Sir, seeing you after a long time. A Billy Joel song tonight?"

Batty looked at Robin and said, "Yes, let's do *'keeping the faith'*."